T0123275

Highest Praise for
Leo J. Maloney and His Thrillers

For Duty and Honor

"Leo Maloney has a real winner with *For Duty and Honor*. Gritty and intense, it draws you immediately into the action and doesn't let go."
—Marc Cameron

Arch Enemy

"Utterly compelling! This novel will grab you from the beginning and simply not let go. And Dan Morgan is one of the best heroes to come along in ages."
—Jeffery Deaver

Twelve Hours

"Fine writing and real insider knowledge make this a must."
—Lee Child

Black Skies

"Smart, savvy, and told with the pace and nuance that only a former spook could bring to the page, *Black Skies* is a tour de force novel of twenty-first-century espionage and a great geopolitical thriller. Maloney is the new master of the modern spy game, and this is first-rate storytelling."
—Mark Sullivan

"*Black Skies* is rough, tough, and entertaining. Leo J. Maloney has written a ripping story."
—Meg Gardiner

Silent Assassin

"Leo Maloney has done it again. Real life often overshadows fiction and *Silent Assassin* is both: a terrifyingly thrilling story of a man on a clandestine mission to save us all from a madman hell bent on murder, written by a man who knows that world all too well."
—Michele McPhee

"From the bloody, ripped-from-the-headlines opening sequence, *Silent Assassin* grabs you and doesn't let go. *Silent Assassin* has everything a thriller reader wants— nasty villains, twists and turns, and a hero—Cobra— who just plain kicks ass."
—Ben Coes

"Dan Morgan, a former Black Ops agent, is called out of retirement and back into a secretive world of politics and deceit to stop a madman."
—*The Stoneham Independent*

Termination Orders

"Leo J. Maloney is the new voice to be reckoned with. *Termination Orders* rings with the authenticity that can only come from an insider. This is one outstanding thriller!"
—John Gilstrap

"Taut, tense, and terrifying! You'll cross your fingers it's fiction—in this high-powered, action-packed thriller, Leo Maloney proves he clearly knows his stuff."
—**Hank Phillippi Ryan**

"A new must-read action thriller that features a double-crossing CIA and Congress, vengeful foreign agents, a corporate drug ring, the Taliban, and narco-terrorists . . . a you-are-there account of torture, assassination, and double-agents, where 'nothing is as it seems.'"
—**Jon Renaud**

"Leo J. Maloney is a real-life Jason Bourne."
—**Josh Zwylen**, *Wicked Local Stoneham*

"A masterly blend of Black Ops intrigue, cleverly interwoven with imaginative sequences of fiction. The reader must guess which accounts are real and which are merely storytelling."
—**Chris Treece**, *The Chris Treece Show*

"A deep-ops story presented in an epic style that takes fact mixed with a bit of fiction to create a spy thriller that takes the reader deep into secret spy missions."
—**Cy Hilterman**, *Best Sellers World*

"For fans of spy thrillers seeking a bit of realism mixed into their novels, *Termination Orders* will prove to be an excellent and recommended pick."
—*Midwest Book Reviews*

The Morgan Files

Twelve Hours

For Duty and Honor

Leo J. Maloney

KENSINGTON PUBLISHING CORP.
www.kensingtonbooks.com

LYRICAL UNDERGROUND BOOKS are published by

Kensington Publishing Corp.
119 West 40th Street
New York, NY 10018

Twelve Hours
Copyright © 2015 Leo J. Maloney

For Duty and Honor
Copyright © 2016 Leo J. Maloney

All rights reserved. No part of this book may be reproduced in any form or by any means without the prior written consent of the publisher, excepting brief quotes used in reviews.

All Kensington titles, imprints, and distributed lines are available at special quantity discounts for bulk purchases for sales promotions, premiums, fund-raising, educational, or institutional use. Special book excerpts or customized printings can also be created to fit specific needs. For details, write or phone the office of the Kensington sales manager: Kensington Publishing Corp., 119 West 40th Street, New York, NY 10018, attn: Sales Department; phone 1-800-221-2647.

PUBLISHER'S NOTE
This book is a work of fiction. Names, characters, businesses, organizations, places, events, and incidents either are the product of the author's imagination or are used fictitiously. Any resemblance to actual persons, living or dead, events, or locales is entirely coincidental.

LYRICAL PRESS, LYRICAL UNDERGROUND, and the Lyrical Underground logo are Reg. U.S. Pat. & TM Off.

First electronic edition: June 2020

ISBN-13: 978-1-5161-1090-2
ISBN-10: 1-5161-1090-0

First print edition: June 2020
ISBN-13: 978-1-5161-1091-9
ISBN-10: 1-5161-1091-9

While writing this book I spent time in New York City and spoke to many police officers and firefighters there. I dedicate this novel to all the innocent victims of 9/11 and to all the courageous men and women who were the first responders to that horrific terrorist attack. Thank you to all military personnel and first responders for your service to our country. God Bless America.

Thanksgiving Day, 11:00 A.M.

The Bahrainis walked into the Park Avenue lobby of the Waldorf Astoria precisely at the appointed time, Acosta noted, looking down at his watch. Four of them, each in a sharp dark gray suit, tieless, all sporting facial hair in various styles. They walked with deliberate strides in a loose V formation, one man taking the lead. He had a trim black moustache on an angular face of light olive skin. His eyes were hidden behind dark gold-framed aviator sunglasses, but as he drew closer, Acosta saw an impassive expression—the face of a man who would be hard to please. Acosta adjusted his tie.

"That them?" asked Shane Rosso.

"I would believe so, Mr. Rosso."

Rosso grunted in response. He was a simple man, an aging ex-cop of few words and, Acosta suspected, just as many thoughts. He was no good with guests, lacking the fine-tuned sense of politeness and propriety needed to work luxury hospitality. He was a fine head of security, though, and Acosta preferred him behind the scenes where he belonged. But the newcomers had asked for him to be present at their arrival, so here he was.

Acosta drew a handkerchief from his pocket and dabbed at the sweat on his brow. Then he slipped on a solicitous smile and walked a few paces to meet the new arrivals, hand extended for a shake.

"Welcome, gentlemen," he said.

"I am Makram Safar," said the man, offering no sign that he'd seen Acosta's hand. His accent was mostly BBC, with only a hint of the hardness of the Middle Eastern speech. "Head of security for Mr. Rasif Maloof."

"Welcome to the Waldorf Astoria, Mr. Safar," Acosta said, drawing back his hand, and, not knowing what else to do, bowing. "My name is Angelo Acosta, assistant manager. I'm here to help you with anything you might need in preparation for Mr. Maloof's visit."

Safar met Acosta's gaze for the first time through dark lenses. "I was told that the general manager would be here." He looked at Mr. Rosso, the fish-eyed, thin-haired grunt in the rumpled suit. "I take it this is not him."

"I'm afraid Mr. Floyd will not be here today, sir," said Acosta. "I guarantee that he will be here tomorrow for Mr. Maloof's arrival. This is Mr. Rosso, our head of security."

Safar raised an eyebrow. "But he is not here today?"

"My apologies, sir. I could certainly call him for you, sir, if you—"

"There will be no need," said Safar, waving his hand. "You will do. We will need access to your security station— exclusive access—for the duration of Mr. Maloof's stay."

"Yes, that had been discussed," said Acosta. This was completely against protocol, and exposed them to significant liability. But Maloof was paying them a not-so-small fortune to rent the Presidential Suite, and their general manager, Jerry Floyd, would brook no argument on this guest doing exactly as he pleased.

"Is there a problem?"

"No problem at all, sir," Acosta reassured him. "You'll have full access to our security capabilities. Mr. Rosso here will make sure that you have everything you need."

"Good," said Safar. "We require three members of the cleaning staff on call at all times, but no one is to come into Mr. Maloof's suite without being sent for. I cannot emphasize this point enough. Do you understand?"

"Of course, sir, we—"

"We will also need access to a secure and exclusive Internet connection, and you are to have a personal halal chef and laundry service on short order. Is that clear?"

"Perfectly, sir. All that has already been arranged, as per your advance instructions."

"Good," said Safar. "We have more men who will arrive with Mr. Maloof's luggage shortly."

"I'll have the porters waiting for them."

"Nobody is to handle Mr. Maloof's luggage but us," said Safar with unexpected sharpness. "Just have the keys to the suite prepared and we will take care of the rest."

"Certainly, sir. Now, while your key cards are prepared, I can personally take you on a guided tour of our amenities. We boast a twenty-four-hour fitness center conveniently adjacent to our—"

"We have read the website," said Safar. "That won't be necessary."

"Very well," said Acosta, masking his chagrin as he gestured toward the chairs in the lobby. "If you gentlemen would like to take a seat as we get your key cards squared away."

Rosso followed as Acosta made his way to the reception desk.

"I do not get paid enough for this shit," Rosso grumbled. "Babysitting a bunch of . . ." his voice trailed off into a mumble.

"Screw this up and neither of us is going to be paid at all," said Acosta. "Because we're going to be out on our asses."

"You know they're going to wreck that room, don't you?" said Rosso. "It's always the same with these guys."

"They are paying us enough to do whatever they want," said Acosta. Then he turned to the girl at reception. "You, uh . . ."

"Debra," she offered.

"Debra," he said, "is the suite ready for our special guests?"

"Housekeeping is just about done, Mr. Acosta." He looked down at his watch and considered that he might just get off work on time. Things seemed to be running smoothly, and suddenly Thanksgiving at home seemed like a real possibility. All he had to do was to get organized and keep everything humming.

Acosta took the express elevator upstairs and did a quick check of the multiroom suite—he had gone through it much more thoroughly earlier—and then returned to the lobby, where Safar and the others sat in stiff silence.

"Gentlemen, please follow me."

It was a silent ride up. Upon arriving at the floor, Acosta opened the door marked THE PRESIDENTIAL SUITE. He gestured at the sprawling three-bedroom, 2,245-square-foot apartment appointed with Georgian furniture. "Would you like me to give you a tour? We have some exclusive items donated by past US presidents, which are themselves—"

"We will manage from here," Safar cut him off. "My men will be coming down to confer with Mr. Rosso on security. Please tell your staff to stay clear from this floor unless summoned. Is that clear?"

"Of course," said Acosta. He stood, expecting further directions. Instead, Safar just said, "Go."

Acosta bowed and took his leave. *Just three days,* he told himself as he got into the elevator and hit the button for the lobby. And just another ninety minutes before he could leave, if all went well.

Acosta emerged into the lobby, walking as if he had purpose, but his step lost its spring when he reached the front desk. He was not actually needed anywhere at the moment, but he was still running on the nervous energy of attending to their exacting guest. He thought of calling the chef to confirm once more, but he had already done that not two hours before. Out of the corner of his eye, he saw two of the Bahrainis emerge from the elevator and started toward them before he noticed that they were moving toward Rosso, who escorted them into the back rooms. Acosta sighed and threw up his hands, then walked back to the front desk and called over a guest who was in line for checkout.

Before long, a town car arrived with the remaining two members of Mr. Maloof's security team and the luggage. As instructed, Acosta directed them to the elevator and left them there to go up on their own to the correct floor. He glanced at his watch. Quarter of an hour to the end of his shift. Bob would be arriving to relieve him within minutes if he wasn't late, and Bob was never late. He shifted his weight on his aching feet.

There was a lull in checkout, and it looked as though Acosta might actually be getting out of there when a man in a cheap black suit, clearly a livery driver, walked into the lobby. He looked around and identified Acosta as the one in charge, going straight for him.

"Hey, you know where those Arab dudes went?"

"Do you mean the Bahraini gentlemen?" asked Acosta.

"Arab, Bahraini, I don't care," said the driver, agitated. "I brought them all the way in from the airport, and I still haven't been paid."

"I'm sure it was just a misunderstanding," said Acosta. He picked up the hotel intercom and dialed their room. "We'll get this sorted out in a minute." The phone returned a busy signal. He pressed down the hook and redialed. Busy again. "I'm sorry," he told the driver. "I can't get through."

The driver leaned on the counter. "Listen, man, I gotta get

going. If I don't make it home in the next hour, the wife's gonna have my head. Can't you take care of it? Charge it to their room or something?"

"It's against policy," said Acosta. "I really can't."

"Hey, man, I gotta get out of here," said the driver. "But I ain't leaving until I get paid."

Acosta cast a sidelong glance at the clock. If he didn't make it out within the next ten minutes, he'd hit horrendous traffic.

"Let me see what I can do," he said. He walked to the elevator with slight trepidation, reassuring himself with each step. Maloof wasn't there yet. What harm could there be? They would appreciate the service he was providing in letting them know personally.

Acosta got into the elevator and hit the button for their floor. He planned out what he was going to say. The right level of deference and solicitousness would disarm their complaints, he was sure. It was just a matter of taking it *far enough.*

The elevator doors parted open and he walked to the Presidential Suite. The door was ajar and he heard talking inside. He approached the threshold.

"Gentlemen, pardon me for interrupting," he said, knocking lightly and pushing the door open. "I'm afraid there is a situation—"

Acosta caught sight out of the corner of his eye of something black and heavy on the dining room table, which he could just see from the door. A second look told him it was several heavy black objects, and a third confirmed the suspicion that hovered at the edge of his consciousness.

Guns. Not just handguns, but those—what were those called? Submachine guns. Like Uzis, but not quite. Certainly something way beyond what this kind of security team would need—and wouldn't they need permits for this kind of thing? What could be their—

His thoughts were interrupted as he saw that Safar was

standing across the entry foyer, looking right at him. Acosta backed away as Safar moved forward.

"I truly, deeply apologize, sir," began Acosta.

"Not at all," said Safar with a vicious grin and a solicitude built on the most menacing undertones. "Please, Mr. Acosta, come in."

He drew closer. Acosta could not hope to evade him without turning around. But he clung to the hope that, if he made no explicit sign of what he had seen, Safar would not stop him. "There really is no need," he said. *How far was the elevator?* He didn't dare look back. He took tiny backward steps, the logic of cornered prey taking over his mind. "I'll come back at a more opportune time."

In three more strides, Safar reached him. Acosta froze. "Please," he said, his face inches from Acosta's, his breath hot like a lion's. "Stay."

Acosta turned to run away, but as his finger pressed the elevator button, he saw a flash of black cross in front of his eyes and felt a tug at his neck, so tight. He couldn't breathe. He was pulled back and his legs gave out. He fell on the carpeted floor, the wire tight around his neck—surely it would be cutting into his skin by now—as his lungs burned for air. He heard a *ding,* and the last thing he saw before the world faded to black were the art deco doors sliding open to reveal an empty elevator paneled with rich mahogany.

Black Friday, 6:13 A.M.

The tablet shook in Alex Morgan's hand as the train rocked side to side. She set it down on her lap in frustration. Reading was going to be impossible. She shut her eyes and tried to lean her head back but soon realized that the noise in the car was going to make sleep impossible, too. She opened her eyes and saw that Clark had his phone raised up to take a picture.

"Smile," he said.

Clark Duffy, tall and gangly in a hoodie with red earbuds popped into his ear. Clark Duffy, who smoked clove cigarettes and played a badly tuned guitar on which he knew four chords. Clark Duffy, who'd been her friend for years, but had lately been making awkward passes at her, and had not taken her polite ignoring of those passes as the rejection that it was. This was building toward an unpleasant confrontation that she didn't like to think about. It had gotten to the point that she was actually a little put off at making the trip down to New York with him.

"Wanna see?" he said, turning the phone's screen toward her. She leaned forward. Normally she wouldn't care how she turned out in other people's pictures, but she was still getting used to her new pixie haircut, and the unfamiliarity of her own visage got the better of her. She was pleased to see that the short brown hair framed her face quite nicely, bringing out her brown eyes.

"Cool," she said, leaning back and turning on her tablet again.

"You should have smiled," he said. "You've got a really captivating smile. Your teeth are, like, super white and straight. Too bad you're so short."

She stuck her tongue out at him. "I'm five seven."

"Oh, I get it, you're a giant," he said. "What're you reading?"

"Just the news," she said, hoping to avoid conversation.

"What's so interesting in there anyway?" he asked, pulling out his earbuds and fiddling with his phone. "I don't really follow that stuff." He put the phone and earphones into the pouch in his hoodie.

"Something about Ramadani's visit," she said.

"I've heard that name before." He frowned.

"The president of Iran," she said. "Navid Ramadani? Ring a bell?"

"Ah," he said, nodding. "I remember seeing that on the

news. I mostly read *Pitchfork*." He laughed. "How about giving me the highlights?"

"Well, he's here for a state visit," she said. "To discuss nuclear power, nuclear weapons, and conflict in the Middle East. Hold on," she said, and searched for a picture on her tablet. She picked the first hit on the search, a portrait that showed his serious and vaguely handsome face head-on, with its well-defined jawline, thick eyebrows, and neatly trimmed beard. "Here," she said, handing it to him.

Clark took it in his hands. "Looks young," he said.

"He is, for a President," said Alex.

"He's one of the bad guys, right?" He handed her back the tablet.

Alex grimaced. "He's actually hoping to put all that stuff behind us," she said. "Everyone knows that he's coming to the US to make a kind of peace offering."

"*Everyone* knows?" He grinned.

"Well, everyone who reads about this kind of thing. He's all about bringing the US and Iran closer together, putting the bad blood behind us. "

"So he's pretty different from the last one, right?"

"Yes. But not everyone in Iran is happy about it," she said. "Especially the Ayatollah."

Clark raised an eyebrow. "Now, I know I've heard that word before. I'm getting some vague association with the seventies."

"The Supreme Leader of Iran," she explained helpfully. "The first one came to power after the Iranian Revolution of 1979. This new guy, Nasr, who rose to power after the death of the old Ayatollah just last year. He's—let's say, *critical* of the US and the West in general, and would sooner see us as opponents."

"Kind of an asshole, then?" he said with a puckish smile.

"Kind of an asshole," Alex conceded. "And he *really* doesn't see eye-to-eye with Ramadani."

"That's the current President, right?"

"Right," said Alex.

"And he's a good guy?"

"It's not about good and bad guys, Clark. Everything in foreign policy is a mix of interests and agendas. Just like every other politician, he has complex ideas and interests and is under various pressures that often conflict with each other, and he's doing his best to negotiate between them. At the moment, it looks like his stance and policies align well enough with our own interests as a country that we might come to call him an ally."

Clark frowned, trying to sort this out. "But is this Ramadani guy a good guy or not?"

It was hopeless. "Let's say he's a pretty good guy."

"All right. See? That's all you needed to say. Nice and simple."

Alex slumped in frustration. "So you're meeting up with your dad in New York?" she asked, changing the subject.

"Yeah," he said. "Mom didn't invite him to Thanksgiving, so he really wanted me to spend the day with him today."

"Well, that should be fun," she said, not knowing quite what to say.

"You're meeting your dad, too, right?" he asked. "But your parents aren't divorced, are they?"

"Oh, no, my parents are super in love," she said, and cringed at her own words. Clark's parents' divorce was always an awkward subject, and Alex never quite knew how to talk about it. He never seemed bothered by it, but she couldn't imagine not having both her mother and father under the same roof. "Anyway," she added, trying to forget her comment, "he had an early Thanksgiving dinner with us, and then went to the city. Business."

"I wish we didn't have all this dad stuff to deal with," he said. "Maybe then we could've spent the day together instead."

Alex pretended to be watching the scenery. "I guess."

"Hey, isn't your dad a classic car dealer?" Clark asked.

"Yeah, he is," she said, affecting innocence. She was getting practiced at keeping up the lie about her father's double life. "Why do you ask?"

"What kind of business does a classic car broker have on Thanksgiving anyway?"

Alex grinned in her mind at the secret she shared with her father. "Beats me."

6:55 a.m.

Dan Morgan walked on a patterned carpet past ornate furniture and knocked on the door to room 2722 of the Waldorf. He saw the pinpoint of light in the peephole disappear, then the deadbolt being undone. The door opened and was left ajar. Morgan took the cue to push it open and saw the back of a black silk nightgown and a long shock of blond hair. The acrid smell of smoke hit his nostrils as the figure turned around and leaned against a heavy carved wooden table, posing seductively and taking a long drag from her cigarette with full, ruby-red lips.

"I don't think they allow smoking in here," he said as he let himself into the foyer of the suite and scanned the room for potential threats. His trained eyes could assess a situation in seconds. Over the years, he, like many other covert operatives, had developed a sixth sense for danger. Nothing struck him as a potential threat, except the cream-skinned, hazel-eyed beauty in front of him.

Adele Sauvage, she called herself.

"But it's *so early,*" she said, pouting, in a light French accent. "Can't I have just one? Please?"

Her bathrobe was just loose enough to show a hint of a white lacy bra underneath. Her makeup was gently smudged, but Morgan could tell it had been freshly applied. Her feet arched up in black stiletto heels. Her hair was messy—not like the hair a woman who had really just woken up, but lightly tousled, as women do to give the faintest hint that they have just been having sex. The whole setup was too casual not to have been meticulously arranged. Most men wouldn't notice, but for a woman like Adele, sex was a deadly weapon. In Morgan's line of work, it paid to know all about deadly weapons.

"Smoke, or don't," he said, closing the door behind him. "I don't care. We have business to do here."

"Oh, but business is so boring."

"Do you need time to make yourself decent?"

"Oh, I'm *never* decent," she said with a girlish giggle, sitting down on an overstuffed loveseat. "Why don't we do something *fun*? Let's have a drink."

"I don't drink. And it's seven in the morning."

"You're no *fun*," she pouted. "I think I like your friend Peter better."

"Peter Conley is an idiot for a skirt," said Morgan. "But I have trouble believing even he would fall for this whole routine." He wondered if anyone did as he caught sight of himself in the mirror. With short-cropped dark brown hair and strong, masculine features, he was tall and had a powerful body. And yet, he didn't flatter himself to think that Adele's behavior had anything to do with his looks.

"Routine?"

"This whole . . . Adele Sauvage persona."

"I don't know what you are talking about." She lifted a well-toned leg onto the sofa. "I *am* Adele Sauvage."

"*You* are Marjorie Francis from Akron, Ohio," said Morgan, closing the curtains in the foyer. "Your hair comes from a bottle and your accent comes from Brigitte Bardot movies."

Adele smiled. "You've got the tongue of a viper."

"I'm just not the kind of sap who makes up your clientele."

"People fall for what they want to fall for," said Adele, her voice now adult and self-assured. Morgan turned around to look at her. She had risen, her coquettish pose replaced by

a disdainful hand on her hip. "You learn that when you trade
in fantasy. But I don't think I have to tell *you* that, do I, Mr.
Secret Agent Man?"

"Morgan will do fine," he said. "Now, I understand you
have something for me?"

"I do," she said, with a sly grin. "And you have something
for me?"

"It's on its way," said Morgan. "As a matter of fact, your
dear friend Peter Conley is bringing it to us."

"Please tell me he's not bringing *cash,*" she said. "I
specifically asked no cash."

"No, no money," said Morgan. "We're bringing a very expensive gift from an anonymous admirer. A valuable antique
that we guarantee can be sold at auction for at least two hundred thousand."

"Ooh, is it shiny?"

"*Very* shiny," said Morgan. "That would be us holding up
our end of the bargain. Now, where's yours?"

"My end of the bargain is right here," she said, reaching
into her robe. Morgan's hand went for his gun, which wasn't
there—it wouldn't have made it past the hotel's metal detec-
tors. But there was no danger. She merely pulled out the
stamp-sized memory card that Conley had given her two
nights before and held it between her thumb and index finger. "The contents of the smart phone of Jasper Elliott."

Morgan reached for it, but she slipped it back into her
robe. "No, no, no, *monsieur* Morgan. Not until my payment
arrives."

Morgan threw up his hands. "Fair enough. Conley should
be on his way."

"I suppose we'll have to stand each other's company for a
few more minutes, then." Adele circled the table.

"Nice digs we've set you up with," he said, looking around
the suite. The carpet and upholstery were sky blue, offset by
an off-white armchair and beige wallpaper. Altogether, the
seats, the wrought iron coffee table, the Tiffany fireplace

screen, the end table, and the desk gave the suite a feeling of clutter. Morgan's wife, Jenny, the interior decorator, would have loved it. Morgan liked his spaces to be spare.

"Oh, please," she said. "At my rates, this is on the low end for my clients. Plus, when you have lived in the palace of the Sultan of Brunei, there is little in the way of luxury that can impress you."

Morgan raised his eyebrows in interest. "You'll have to tell me all about that someday."

"I really don't," she said.

Morgan sat back in the armchair, which was stiff and uncomfortable for all its fanciness. "I guess discretion is a big deal in your line of work."

"Frankly, it's more for what they say than what they do," she said. "It's the dirty little secret of my profession, Mr. Morgan. We spend quite a bit more time having conversations than on our backs. There's a premium on a girl who can talk about everything from Shakespeare to Derrida to the Red Sox."

"What's a girl who can talk Shakespeare and Derrida doing being an escort?"

"To make the kind of money I make at my age," she said, "the only other way is to be a different kind of whore on Wall Street." She leaned in and whispered, "I think my kind is much more dignified."

Morgan flashed a grin at her, and she returned it until something seemed to catch her eye though the narrow opening between the curtains. Morgan followed her gaze to see a procession of police cars.

"What the hell?" He stood up to get a clearer view. He tried to get his face flat against the window in order to see as far up Park Avenue as possible. He made out a couple of town cars bearing flags with green and red details.

He heard the beeping of his radio communicator in his ear. Conley was hailing him. "Morgan here. What's happening? Thanksgiving Day parade come a day late?"

"It's Ramadani," said Conley. "The President of Iran. I just got off the phone with Bloch."

"He was supposed to—"

"Stay at the Plaza, I know," cut in Conley. "Change of plans, evidently. I got the package, but I'm not getting inside until this dies down."

"All right," said Morgan. "Keep me posted. Out." He cut the mic and turned to Adele. "Is there any chance I could get that little piece of plastic off of you on an IOU?"

"Oh, baby, sorry, but I don't work on credit," she said. "Rule number one." She sat back on the white armchair, extending her legs on an ottoman and letting her high heels dangle off her toes. "You want it, you've got to pay for it."

He looked through the half-drawn curtain at the loose police cordon that was forming around the hotel entrance. A crowd was gathering, and he saw no sign of Conley. "Looks like it's going to be awhile." He thought about Alex. She'd be arriving at Grand Central Terminal pretty soon, and it was getting increasingly unlikely that he'd be able to meet her there.

"Honey, I've got all day," she said. "It's not like I was going outside on Black Friday, anyway. _I_ beat the crowds by staying in."

"Well, it looks like the crowds came to us," he said.

"I can think of worse places to be stuck," said Adele, and picked up the receiver on her hotel phone. "Breakfast? You're buying."

_7:18 a.m._

Shir Soroush stood at the window overlooking Park Avenue, arms crossed, the entire city at his feet. In his mind, the various strands of the plan were converging. Months of planning led up to this moment. Righteous energy surged through his body. _Soon,_ he thought. _So soon._

He turned at the sound of footsteps approaching, wooden

heels padding on the carpeted floor. It was a man with a large hooked nose and a thick beard despite his relative youth. Zubin.

"I have made contact with Razi, Salm, and Sharzeh," he said. "They are in position."

"Good," said Soroush. "What of the Secret Service?"

"They have two men here already, but they are scrambling. They were caught completely off guard."

"And Ramadani?"

"The President is on his way up with Asadi and Taleb."

"I'll be ready to welcome him," said Soroush. He walked to the foyer and waited, hands clasped at the small of his back, until the elevator arrived at the floor and Ramadani emerged accompanied by his secretary and chief of staff.

"Sir," Soroush said, offering his hand for a shake. "Welcome to your accommodations in New York City."

"Shir, it is good to see you," said Ramadani. "You've done a good job here." He gestured to their surroundings. "Beautiful. Classic."

"Thank you, sir," said Soroush, hiding his contempt. Ramadani's fine features, a straight nose and strong chin, more suitable for a movie star than a statesman, concealed a weakling and a traitor to his people.

"Professional as always," said Ramadani, making his way from the foyer to the living room. Soroush followed. Its light-colored walls, floor, and upholstery gave it an airy and light feeling. "Have you had a chance to see the city?" Ramadani asked, admiring the furniture. "You should find time to relax. Enjoy yourself. Take time to do a little shopping tomorrow."

"It is profane," said Soroush. "And it would take me away from my duties."

Ramadani chuckled. "You are too grave, Soroush. You will have your time off here. I suggest you take it."

"I am here to serve the Islamic Republic and no less," he retorted.

"As you will," said Ramadani. "I need to go over some things with Taleb before the meeting with the American president. We'd like something to eat as we do." He motioned toward the dining room.

"I will ring the chef," said Soroush.

Ramadani's nose crinkled as they passed a closed door. "There is a strange smell coming from in there," he said.

"It is a bathroom," said Soroush. "I recommend that you stay clear of it, sir. The smell is due to a plumbing issue that the hotel has already assured me they will fix posthaste."

"Make sure that they do," said Ramadani.

Soroush's mind went to the body of the hotel manager, so fat he hardly fit into the bathtub. The ice was not preventing his decomposition well enough. But it did not matter. They were so close now. By the time he was found, his death would hardly register as significant next to the events of the hours to come.

7:42 a.m.

Lisa Frieze adjusted a loose lock into the tight bun that held her auburn hair as the steel double doors of the elevator opened onto the twenty-third floor of 26 Federal Plaza. She checked her makeup in the metal's reflective surface, rubbing out a smudge underneath her hazel eyes. Then she stepped out in strides that were bolder than she actually felt. She'd driven down IED-riddled streets and been under fire more times than she could count, but walking into the New York City FBI field office for the first time was giving her the jitters.

She walked past a deserted reception area and let herself in through the door to a wide-open office. A single row of fluorescent lights illuminated the long computer-lined desks that populated the room. The sky outside, through the window, was the grayish blue that always awaited the sunrise. In one corner was a figure hunched over the desk, his short brown hair and brown face lit by his computer monitor. He had a breakfast sandwich in one hand, from which he took a full-mouthed bite.

"Excuse me, I—" she began, but stopped when she noticed her voice had come out too softly. "Excuse me," she said, more boldly. "My name is Lisa Frieze—Special Agent Lisa Frieze. I'm here to see Clement Chambers."

The man swiveled his chair to look at her and held up his hand as he chewed. "Down that hall, first door on your right," he said, with his mouth half-full. He swallowed hard and added, "You the rookie?"

"That's me," she said, coming closer. He wiped his free hand on his pants and extended it to her. "Nolan," he said. "Good to meet you."

"Likewise," she said, gripping his greasy hand with practiced firmness. Little things like a handshake mattered—it was too easy not to be taken seriously. The last thing she wanted in the new job was to be pegged as a *girl*. "Anything I should know before going in there?"

"Oh, you haven't met the boss yet?" said Nolan, teeth flashing white in the twilight. "Let's see . . . you get used to him?"

"Encouraging," she said with a light chuckle.

"But seriously," said Nolan. "He'll be sizing you up. Be straight and don't be spooked. You'll do fine."

She made her way down the darkened hallway, then knocked on the door marked CLEMENT CHAMBERS—AGENT-IN-CHARGE, COUNTERTERRORISM with three measured raps.

"Come in!"

She opened the door to a well-lit office cluttered with boxes of files. Behind the desk, framed by alternating bands of gray venetian blinds and the lightening sky, was Chambers, a ruddy man of medium build with blond hair and a blond moustache, familiar to her from pictures alone.

"Ms. Frieze, I presume," he said, shuffling papers before

standing and extending his hand in greeting. He appraised her as they shook.

"Mr. Chambers," she said. "It's a pleasure to meet you."

"It's good to have you in the ranks," he said, without sounding convinced. He sat down and laid an open file in front of him, on which Frieze saw her head shot. "Take a seat." He clicked a pen in his right hand as he leafed through the file.

"I've got my letters of recommendation from Agent Training and Linguistics," she said, reaching into her briefcase.

"That won't be necessary," he said as he looked through the file. "I have everything I need here." He leaned back in his chair, holding the file up like a book. "BA in Middle Eastern Studies, graduating with honors from the University of Chicago. Fluent in Arabic."

"And Farsi, sir."

He looked up at her, and continued. "Two years in Afghanistan and eighteen months in Iraq as a contractor for the US Army, working as a translator. I understand your service there was . . . not without incident."

She squirmed in her chair. "I've been—"

"Declared fit for duty by a psychiatrist, I know." He clicked the pen again. "I don't take issue with that. But I know what PTSD can do to an agent. And I don't like trouble, Ms. Frieze."

"You won't have any from me," she said, locking eyes with him.

He looked down and closed the file. "You were a translator," he said. "Making good money. In fact, I know you'd be making more today if you'd continued as a translator than now that you've undergone special agent training."

"Is there something wrong with that?" she asked.

He rested his elbows on the table and steepled his fingers. "Greater risk, less reward. Which leads me to ask you— what does bring you to our doorstep, Ms. Frieze?"

She stared at him just long enough to convey that she didn't need to answer his question. Then she said, "To better serve my country and the Bureau, sir."

Chambers grinned. "Yes, I'm sure." He picked up the pen again and sat back. His chair squeaked against his weight. "You came in on a rather unusual day," he said. "The arrival of the Iranian president means most of our team is scattered around the city. This has been weeks in preparation. There's not much we can use you for today. I can have you shadow one of our agents coordinating with the Diplomatic Security Service." He stood up, and Frieze followed suit. "Let me get you acquainted with your desk."

As she turned to walk out, the door opened and Nolan leaned into the office. "Ramadani's switching hotels."

"What the hell do you mean, he's switching hotels?" demanded Chambers.

"He's not going to the Plaza," said Nolan. "Apparently his motorcade is on its way to the Waldorf right now."

"You have got to be kidding me," he said. "Why the hell am I only hearing about this now?"

"They sprung this on everyone. I only just got the call from the NYPD. They're calling it a security measure against possible planned attacks on the Plaza."

"Damn it," said Chambers. "Was *anyone* on our side privy to this?"

"Doesn't look like it," said Nolan. "Information's still sketchy. We're scrambling to get up to speed."

"Christ," said Chambers. "Unbelievable. Get everyone up to speed, then find out whatever you can. What a goddamn nightmare. Rookie!"

It took Frieze a moment to realize he was talking to her. "Yes, sir?"

"Get up there."

"Up there, sir?"

"To the Waldorf. I want a full roster of hotel staff and

their work schedules within the hour. Do you think you can manage that?"

"Yes," she said. "Yes, of course."

"I meant *now*," he said. *"Go! Get moving!"*

She walked down the short hallway ahead of Nolan.

"Getting pushed out of the nest already, huh?"

"Oh, please," she said. "Asking a couple of questions of a hotel clerk. How hard could it be?"

8:26 a.m.

Tracie Flowers, ten years old, sat next to her mother as the train clattered along the Long Island Rail Road. The train had pulled out from Pinelawn at 7:39 A.M., a full three minutes late, she had noted with some dissatisfaction. But she had been pleased that the train had reached the other stations with no additional delays, and they were on schedule to pull into Penn Station at precisely 8:37, with a journey lasting exactly the projected fifty-eight minutes. Tracie found this pleasing.

Being content at having fit the train's progress into a neat pattern in her mind, Tracie counted the seats, the windows, and the slats on the luggage racks. She counted the passengers all along the way, keeping track of those who entered, those who left, and the luggage that each had stowed up on the racks. She counted the number of people wearing hats, those using headphones, and the number of people with each hair color. (She was distressed that she couldn't quite classify one man's hair as either red or blond. Her mother cast the deciding vote for blond, and all was well again.) She took each of the numbers and factored it, then figured out if it could be expressed as a sum of primes, and then found complex mathematical relationships among them, as well as between each one and the current day, month, and year.

This occupied her mind for most of the forty-five minutes of the ride so far. At 8:32, right on schedule, the train's brakes began to whine as it pulled into Woodside. She heard the familiar hiss and opening of doors, and Tracie mouthed the announcement of the station along with the recording. Things became disordered as people got up and others came in, and it took a moment for everything to settle down and Tracie not to become overwhelmed. The train started moving again, and she got busy with the task of mentally recording those who had gotten off the train and those who had gotten on. The person wearing a patterned knitted cap was gone, as was the one with short-cropped black curly hair and the one with the red-and-white striped beanie. Among the newcomers were a bald man and a younger guy whose hair was long and greasy.

Tracie counted them up and tried to work out what, from her previous counts and calculations, had changed. Except that when she tried, not everything added up. Something was off about the new numbers, about the scene in that train car. Sometimes she just had the *feeling* that something was wrong, and it took a lot of thinking to figure out what it was. Anxiety welled up in her. They were nearing Penn Station. She only had six minutes, by her calculations, to figure out the puzzle, or else, in her mind, something very bad would happen. Her mom would say that it was only her OCD, that nothing really was going to happen. But to Tracie, it was real. If she didn't find out what was wrong, she had the inescapable feeling that someone was going to die.

She closed her eyes and went through the numbers in her head, number of passengers and hats and hair color, until she noticed that it was something about the baggage. She looked at each luggage item stowed on the rack above the seats, straining to see each piece, making a mental connection between each piece of luggage and its owner.

There was one piece of luggage that didn't belong to anyone on the train. It was a blue backpack that had belonged to the man with curly hair—the one who had gotten off at Pinelawn. *He had forgotten it!* The thought was distressing to Tracie, but she knew how to fix it. She pictured a line, like the ones she imagined connecting each piece of luggage to each passenger, stretching from the backpack, through a tiny crack in the doors, and all the way back to Pinelawn, to a faceless, curly-haired figure standing on the platform. The backpack now was connected to its rightful owner in her mind, and everything seemed fine again. Nobody was going to die because of her carelessness.

She could feel the pull of the train's deceleration, and then she heard the announcement over the PA—which she again mouthed as the conductor spoke—that they were pulling into Penn Station. The train came to a stop, and people gathered their things. A few of the more hurried ones lined up at the train door. Her mother tugged at her sleeve and stood up. The doors opened and they moved forward with tiny steps, Tracie counting each one. They walked a few feet, and Tracie looked up to see that they were right next to the blue backpack on its rack. She once more imagined it to be connected to its distant owner.

Tracie Flowers never made it out of the train. Her mind cut to black before she could even feel the blast that killed her.

8:48 a.m.

Alex put her tablet into her black Targus backpack to the familiar whine of the brakes as the train rolled into Grand Central Terminal. Passengers around her shuffled, at least three quarters of them getting to their feet before the train came to a complete halt. This wasn't the normal commuter crowd, but rather the Black Friday shoppers whose moods ranged from antsy to bloodthirsty.

The doors slid open and cool air streamed in. Alex waited while people elbowed each other to get off. Clark hung back, waiting for her to make the first move. Once the aisle had cleared, they followed the slow-moving crowd onto the platform, walking a few paces behind the crowd to avoid the tumult. It also gave her room to look around as she emerged into the elegant marble concourse. No matter how many times she walked into it, Alex always had to stop and wonder at its beauty. The sun's rays filtered in from the stories-high east windows, casting pools of light that reached the information booth with its four-faced brass clock.

"It's really something, isn't it?" she said, turning to Clark to see that his attention was immersed in his cell phone. She scoffed under her breath and surveyed the crowd, opting to take the main exit and leading her distracted friend across the concourse.

Alex's instincts told her that something was wrong before she was aware of it. At first, it was an unconscious uptick in the number of ringing cell phones, and then in the buzzing of several people in the crowd. Something about it was disconcerting, even if she couldn't put her finger on what. And then, as they were passing the clock in the center of the concourse, Clark spoke, playing out a conversation that was happening in minor variations throughout Grand Central terminal.

"Alex," he said. "There's been an attack."

"Where?" she asked. Clark had his eyes glued to his smartphone.

"It's all over Twitter," he said, holding up his phone so she could see the screen. The same message appeared in the familiar telegraphic style, shared by several people, celebrities alongside Clark's personal friends. *Bombs in Penn Station.* She pulled out her own phone and checked the news, but only one of the news outlets had reported on it, and all it did was refer to the now-viral tweet.

"We need to find my dad," she said. Policemen, she now saw, were fanning out, and she saw two K9 units walking out onto the concourse.

"Was he staying near there?" Clark asked.

"No, he—"

She was cut off by a man's voice on the PA. "This is an emergency. We are beginning immediate evacuation. Please remain calm and make your way to the exits in an orderly fashion."

Jesus, Alex thought as people began swarming to the exits. A terrorist looking for maximum damage couldn't hope for a better situation than this funneling of the crowds. Alex pulled Clark by the arm. "Come on!"

People were streaming out of the heavy wooden doors, so many that the sidewalks couldn't hold them all and they were spilling into Forty-second Street under the Park Avenue overpass. Alex was knocked side to side by the crowd and lost touch with Clark. The heat and crush of the mass of people knocked the wind out of her.

"Clark!" she called out, but there was no hope he'd hear in all the commotion.

Then, the first bullet hit.

8:53 a.m.

Adele picked through what was left of the silver platter of fresh fruit and plates of patés, smoked salmon, and caviar delivered by room service. Morgan rolled his eyes as she popped a grape into her mouth, grinning at him as she chewed. Looking out the window, Morgan saw that the motorcade had come in through the garage, leaving only curious onlookers and the police cordon outside.

He heard a beep in his earpiece. *Conley.*

"Did you get the news?" Conley asked.

"What do you mean?"

"You haven't heard?" asked Conley. "Bombs in Penn Station."

"When?"

"A few minutes ago," said Conley. "It's all over Twitter. No way I'm getting inside the hotel now. They're taking extra precautions because of the Iranian president. Doors are locked and security's turning everyone away."

Morgan shot a glance at Adele, who was looking at him as she bit into a pear. "What do you know about the attack?"

"Nothing yet. I've made contact with Bloch at headquarters, but it's going to be bedlam for at least a couple of hours."

"Bomb in New York City, on the day of the Iranian President's visit."

"It's a hell of a coincidence," said Conley.

"I don't like coincidences," said Morgan. "I'm going downstairs to see what I can find out."

8:54 a.m.

Alex didn't hear the shot, just the screaming some ten feet ahead of her, its source and cause concealed by the throng of people. A movement like a riptide dragged her backward toward the station doors.

The next bullet came seconds later, a stream of bloody mist erupting from the back of a freckled-faced woman right in front of her. The woman slumped back, and Alex nearly fell onto the asphalt of East Forty-second Street in an attempt to hold her up. The woman tumbled onto the pavement, blood gushing out right at the bottom of her ribcage, near her spinal column.

The crowd opened up around the fallen woman, giving Alex a refreshing breath of cool air. She saw the entry wound at the woman's chest and made an instinctive calculation that the bullets were approaching from a high angle.

Sniper.

She looked up at the buildings that surrounded them, but there were too many windows to even count, let alone find a single shooter. She cast her gaze down at the woman, who stared up at the sky in wide eyed, uncomprehending terror. Alex moved toward her to administer first aid or at least offer her a measure of solace. But the crowd closed in again as people scrambled for cover, and Alex was swept along with it. It was no use trying to get back to her.

Cover, she thought. *I need cover.* But it was useless—she was now moving with the mass of people around her, whether she wanted to or not, toward the doors to Grand Central Terminal. She was tossed and squeezed and her mind grew foggy with panic. *Focus,* she told herself. But the crowd heaved, and her knees couldn't keep up. She stumbled and fell.

She curled up into a ball as feet hit her back, her shins, her head. She heard another surge of screaming, she didn't know where from. A shoe scraped her ear, and it seared with pain, feeling like it was half torn off. *I'm going to get trampled. I'm going to die.* She screamed.

"Alex! Alex!" Her name was reaching her as if from a distance. "Alex, get up!" A hand on her shoulder. "Come on!"

Clark Duffy pulled her to her feet, with the help of a beefy man with a scraggly black beard who was holding back the crowd as much as he could to give her space. She staggered to her feet and moved, led by Clark, toward the door. The rest of the way was a blur of movement and shoves until she was panting inside the main concourse, surrounded by marble and under the green-painted ceiling. Around her, families and friends drew close to each other, looking around in alarm. She turned to Clark.

"Thanks," she said, giving him a hug. "And thank you," she told the bearded man who had followed them inside. She wrapped her arms around him.

"It's, uh, no problem," he said, flustered. "Bud," he said, awkwardly extending a hand. "Bud Hooper."

"Alex."

"Are you okay?" asked Clark.

She touched her ear, half-expecting to find it dangling from a thin strip of skin. It was wet with blood, but otherwise seemed intact. "Yeah, I'm fine." *So far,* she said. But now, they were trapped inside Grand Central Terminal. Whatever was going on, she had a feeling it was just beginning.

9:01 a.m.

Lisa Frieze pounded the pavement in her uncomfortable dress flats. She hit redial on her phone for the fourth time as she wove around a yellow cab on Park Avenue. Traffic was at a standstill and angry drivers leaned on their horns. She heard the plastic click of the receiver being picked up off its cradle.

"Chambers."

"This is Frieze." She stayed on the street, avoiding the hordes that were plugging up the sidewalks.

"Frieze who?" came the brusque response, then, before she had time to respond, "The rookie. Right. Take it you've heard the news."

"I just caught wind of it on the radio, sir," she said, reaching the small crowd that had gathered around the Waldorf, drawn by the arrival of the motorcade. She tried to plunge in through the outer layer and failed. "I need to know if there's something I should be doing. I've studied the emergency response procedures, I can—"

"Are you at the hotel yet?"

"I'm right outside." A woman in a green jogging suit elbowed her, nearly knocking the phone from her hand. Frieze elbowed her back but couldn't budge the mass of people blocking her way.

"Get me the report I asked for," he said. "And stay out of everyone's way. I can't spare anyone to hold your hand today."

"Sir, I've got experience with forensic—" He hung up before she could finish. Adding to her frustration was the solid wall of bystanders that stood before her.

"FBI!" She yelled out. "Out of my way!"

The crowd parted, finally, and she pushed through to the

police cordon. A young man in aviators wearing the black uniform of the NYPD and holding a Styrofoam cup of Dunkin' Donuts coffee stepped forward to meet her.

"Special Agent Lisa Frieze," she said, flashing her badge. "I need to get inside."

"I can let you through, but the hotel's locked down," he said, lifting and pulling the steel barrier one-handed with a grunt, opening a crack just wide enough so she could pass. "No one's going in or out. There was a bomb, you know. At Penn Station."

"Yeah, I heard."

"Emergency procedures," he said and sipped his coffee. "To protect the president of Iran. Although if you ask me, I don't know why we're trying to protect the bastard, anyway."

"I didn't," she said.

"Didn't what?"

"Ask you. I just need to get inside."

"You can try," he said, shrugging.

She walked up to one of the glass double doors to the Waldorf lobby and knocked on the glass, holding up her badge. A man in a suit who was standing guard, blond and bony-faced, either Secret Service or Diplomatic Security, mouthed *locked down*. She raised her badge higher and raised her eyebrows, but he just shook his head.

She turned back and looked up and down Park, running her fingers through her drawn-back hair. She pulled out her cell phone and dialed. No signal.

Great.

"Looks like you and I are late to the party."

She wheeled about to find the man who'd spoken. He was tall and wiry with a strong chin and nose, in khakis and a blue button-down with rolled up sleeves despite the cold. Handsome, in a sort of professorial way. But he was no professor. The faint scars on the back of his hand pegged him as a man of action. And if he was on this side of the police barriers, he was no mere civilian.

"Peter Conley," he said, holding up his ID. "State Department."

"FBI. Agent Frieze. Lisa." She held out her hand and they shook. "Can you get me inside?"

"No can do," he said, "Secret Service is running point, and they get territorial."

She looked back at the hotel and the stolid agent at the door. "Are you the one in charge here at the scene?"

"I'm way down in the totem pole, sugar," said Conley. "Plus, no one's in charge at the moment, as far as I can tell. But one of the cops had radio contact with someone on the inside. Come on, I'll introduce you."

9:05 a.m.

Dan Morgan walked out into the colonnaded lobby of the Waldorf Astoria. He was glad to see plenty of guests had come down to complain of the lockdown, tripping over each other to scream at a couple of harried hotel employees at the front desk. He counted seven Secret Service agents posted at the doors and corners, solemn and more tense than usual—no guests dared approach any of them. Four others Morgan recognized by their beards as belonging to President Ramadani's security team. One eyed him with suspicion, and Morgan made for the disgruntled swarm until he spotted what he was looking for—a bald man in a cheap suit whose bearing told Morgan he was not a Fed or used to dealing with guests. He was walking across the lobby, keeping his distance from the crowd.

Morgan approached him. "Excuse me."

"Get back to your room, sir," he rasped without making eye contact. "The lockdown will be over when it's over."

"You don't understand." Morgan flashed his Homeland Security badge—one of many fakes issued him by Zeta Division, whose friends in high places guaranteed the credentials checked out against official records. "Dan Morgan," he said. "You work security here at the hotel?"

"Head of," he said without slowing down. "Shane Rosso."

"Spare a word?"

"You wanna talk to me, you gotta walk with me." Morgan liked this guy already. "Now, I've spoken to your people already."

"They're not my people," said Morgan. "I'm here as a guest. Just making myself useful."

"If you say so." Rosso pushed open the door into the service hall and held it for Morgan. "Come on." The hallway was a little small for the two of them to walk abreast, so Morgan let Rosso take the lead. "So what's your question?" He asked without turning back.

"Did anything strange happen between yesterday and today?"

"What, you mean besides a bunch of Bahrainis coming in to take over my hotel? Or the fact that it turns out they were Iranians, and I had their goddamn President arriving right under my nose, making them that much more of a pain in my ass?" Heat wafted out as they passed the door to the kitchen. "Maybe you mean the bomb at Penn Station, and the fact that the Secret Service is shutting up my hotel because of it. Or maybe you mean the fact that the good-for-nothing manager decided not to show up."

"Who's your manager?" asked Morgan. They walked together into a small office with Rosso's name on the door. In it were steel files and a scratched and bent cheap office desk. Rosso hunched over at a computer station without sitting down and pecked at the keys with his two index fingers, navigating some sort of database.

"Angelo Acosta," said Rosso. "He was supposed to come in and help with this crap, but no one can reach him. Fat bastard probably couldn't drag his ass out of bed in the morning."

"Has he missed work like this before?"

"Nah," said Rosso. "Now that I think about it. Not without calling in. Probably going to get fired over this, especially today of all days." The printer on the desk next to the monitor whirred, and then stopped. "Of course, our general manager didn't manage to come in this morning with all the ruckus." Rosso slapped the printer twice with an open palm. "These goddamn things, am I right?"

"Any chance I could take a look at the security tapes between yesterday and today?"

"I got no problem with it," said Rosso, fumbling with the mouse. He double clicked, and the printer started going again. This time, it spat out printed sheets, tables with short words and numbers—guest data, Morgan figured. "But between the Iranians and the Secret Service, I don't even have access to my own hotel's cameras."

"What if I ask them?"

"I gather the Iranians won't take too kindly to it," said Rosso. "Better chance with the Secret Service, if you wave that fancy badge in their faces."

"I know how to deal with them. Meanwhile, can you show me the guest and employee manifests? I need to get them out to my people ASAP."

Rosso grunted. "It's the second time in an hour someone's asked me to do that. You government types really need to learn to share."

9:22 a.m.

Shir Soroush checked his watch one last time, then marched across the Presidential Suite's living room to the office. Navid Ramadani was conferring with his chief of staff and his secretary, huddled over the desk and away from the windows, as they had been instructed after finding out about the shootings at Grand Central. Masud and Ebrahim, who were standing guard in the room, acknowledged Soroush as he walked in.

"Come with me, Mr. President," said Soroush.

"What is happening?" demanded Ramadani, standing up in alarm. Perspiration showed on his brow.

"We are under attack," Soroush said.

"What? By whom?"

Soroush exchanged a glance with Masud, then unholstered his suppressed Beretta .45 and fired. The bullet burrowed through Ebrahim's right eye and burst out the back, showering the desk and the white curtains of the suite in blood. With his silenced pistol, Masud plugged two bullets in the back of the heads of Asadi and Taleb, who collapsed on the carpeted floor.

"Me," said Soroush.

"What are you doing?" demanded Ramadani, standing from the table, eyes ablaze with fury.

Not as weak as I thought.

"Taking back the Republic," said Soroush. "Sit."

"I will not—"

Masud made his move, kicking the President's leg to make him sit on the heavy oak chair. "*Sit,*" Soroush repeated. Then, "Masud."

Masud drew the thin syringe from his suit jacket. In one swift motion he thrust the needle into Ramadani's neck and pressed the plunger.

"What—" the President yelped in surprise. His eyes rolled upward and his spine went slack. Masud grabbed him before his head hit the table in front of him.

"Phase one is complete," Soroush said into his radio communicator. "Phase two begins now."

9:41 a.m.

Lisa Frieze tried to suppress a shiver as she leaned against the cool stone of the outside of the Waldorf Astoria.

She was looking around at the various law enforcement personnel who were milling about within the cordoned zone. The crowd had thinned significantly as news of the attack spread and people hurried to their loved ones or fled the area. She tried her parents again, but it was impossible to get a call through, so she checked the news for updates. Nothing. She looked up again and was startled by Peter Conley, who stood facing her.

"Couldn't find him," he said. "Sorry."

"It's just as well," she said, biting her lip and looking at a policeman waving the crowd back. "It's just busywork. With everything that's going on, this is not really on anyone else's list of priorities."

"You really wish you were somewhere else, don't you?" He leaned against the wall next to her.

"Yes. I should be doing something," she said, exasperated. "The city's under attack, and I'm here twiddling my goddamn thumbs."

"Maybe you should," he said. "Do something, I mean."

She pushed herself off the wall and stood up straight. "I'm not looking to get reprimanded for insubordination on my first day." She stared down Park Avenue toward the Met Life building and wondered nervously whether being under fire would throw her into a flashback. It'd been over a year since she'd had one, but the thought of testing it gave her a sense of foreboding.

"I can't tell you what to do," said Conley. She looked at him. He had light brown eyes brimming with openness and sincerity. Something about him was disarming, some quality that inspired instant trust.

"No," she said. "You can't. Listen, I can't stay out of this fight. I'm going—"

She was interrupted by a muffled *pop pop* coming from inside the hotel.

Her eyes widened. "Is that—"

"Gunfire."

9:47 a.m.

Morgan hung up the phone in Rosso's office after his third busy signal and tried his radio communicator again. "Conley? Conley?" No response. The signal was probably being jammed by the Secret Service. Gunshots still echoed down the hallway. "I can't raise my guy on the outside," he said to Rosso. "Do you have any weapons?"

"The feds locked away everyone's guns," he said. "Only they and the President's security had them."

Goddamn it. So the hotel security team would be helpless. "We have to do something," said Morgan, turning to go. "I'm going to the lobby to see what's going on."

"Wait!" said Rosso. "You don't have to. The surveillance room's next door. We can see what's happening anywhere in the hotel."

Morgan let Rosso lead the way a few yards down the service hall. Rosso pulled out an oversized key ring from under his jacket and unlocked a plain gray door. He turned the knob and pushed it open to reveal two dead Secret Service agents and an Iranian guard, already raising his silenced SIG Sauer semiautomatic to shoot.

Morgan pushed Rosso out of the way of the threshold as the bullet ripped, hearing it pierce flesh, using the impulse to impel himself in the opposite direction. Rosso fell forward on the far side of the door, rolling on his back and exposing a flower of blood blooming on his shirt. Morgan checked himself, but apart from a little splatter from Rosso, he was clean. Adrenaline pumped, and a heightened awareness kicked in. He caught a flash of red in his peripheral vision to his left. He turned to catch sight of a fire extinguisher and axe. The plan formed in his mind faster than he could even think. He lifted the extinguisher off its hinge and, holding it by its base, swung it hard against the wall. The blow broke off the entire discharge mechanism, and white powder gushed out in a constant stream. Morgan then tossed the device into the surveillance room, where the powder spouted into the room, flooding its cramped confines.

Morgan grabbed the axe off the wall as the Iranian inside coughed and loosed a hail of bullets that embedded themselves into the wall opposite the door. Morgan counted six shots, plus, probably, two in each Secret Service agent. The SIG Sauer could hold up to twenty rounds.

Two more bullets sailed out of the room. This told Morgan that the man was desperate and blind, but had enough rounds of ammo to hold them off for minutes that Morgan couldn't spare.

9:48 a.m.

Soroush smiled as he looked out the window at the officers below, running around like cockroaches. Hearing heavy footsteps coming toward the door to the Presidential Suite, he raised his Beretta and saw Zubin appear at the threshold.

"Status," said Soroush.

"The American agents have been taken care of," said Zubin, in a voice breathy from climbing the stairs. "As well as those not loyal to our cause. The doors to the guest rooms have been electronically locked, and all keycards de-authorized."

"Good," said Soroush. "I have word from Aram. Grand Central has been shut down. Thousands of people are still inside. The devices are in place for phase three. We proceed as planned."

"Just one thing," said Zubin. "We lost Shahin. He took a bullet from the Secret Service."

"Have Hossein take his role in the plan." He laid his hand on Zubin's shoulder. "This is our day," he said. "We cannot fail."

"For Allah," said Zubin, breathless, with the wide eyes of the true believer.

"For the Islamic Republic of Iran."

9:49 a.m.

Out in the hallway, standing flush against the wall next to the door to the surveillance office, Morgan clutched the axe and considered his options. The best plan would be goading the man inside to spend his remaining bullets. But that would take time. He glanced at Rosso, propped against the wall across the door from him, blood pooling on the floor. Time was something he did not have. The moment settled into an eerie quiet except for the hiss of the extinguisher still gushing white inside the room. The white powder wafted out into the hallway. Morgan rearranged the weapon in his hands, clammy palms against polished wood. This was going to be a gamble.

He stood by until he heard coughing once more. At that, he pivoted into the room and, engulfed in the white powder of the fire extinguisher, swung the axe in a wide upward diagonal arc. It hit home at Morgan's one o'clock, and he heard the man drop onto the table and then the floor.

Morgan picked up the extinguisher, still spurting gas, and rolled it down the hall. He then crouched next to Rosso. Large beads of sweat peppered his forehead and he wheezed on inhaling. Blood oozed down from his shoulder where the Iranian's bullet had hit.

"You all right?" asked Morgan.

"Can't say much for my left arm," he said, pressing a handkerchief against the wound. The fabric quickly became saturated with red. Morgan helped him to his feet. "Good thing I shoot with my right. Let's take a look at those cameras."

They went back inside the surveillance room and wiped the suspended powder out of the way until they could just make out what was happening in the array of monitors that covered nearly half of one wall, each broken up into a grid of video feeds. It was worse than Morgan had imagined.

He looked at the lobby camera feeds first. People—by the

way they were dressed, mostly hotel staff—were being herded by men with guns into the middle and made to kneel. He counted the seven Secret Service agents, fallen where they had stood minutes before—none of those had even managed to draw their guns, which betrayed the deadly coordination of this attack. Another two lay dying behind a couch in the lobby, where they had taken cover. He counted five more dead from the hallway feeds.

"Jesus Christ," said Rosso.

"I've got nine hostiles in the lobby," said Morgan. He tried his radio again, but the signal wasn't going through.

"Two more in the hallways," said Rosso. "And one coming down the stairs here."

"Do you have a visual on Ramadani?"

"Negative," said Rosso. He motioned to a row of feeds that were completely dark. "Those are for the floor of his suite. His people disabled the cameras. You think Ramadani's men turned?"

"Yeah, they did," said Morgan. "The question is, turned on whom?"

9:50 a.m.

Soroush emerged from the stairwell into the lobby, where about one hundred people—staff and the guests who had been downstairs when they struck—were seated on the floor, hands on their heads. Three of Soroush's men were moving among them, unspooling the wire and securing it to each with a zip tie. Soroush reveled in the hostages' terrified incomprehension, in the tears of the women.

Zubin rushed forward to meet him. "The doors are secured. The bombs will be armed within five minutes."

"Good," said Soroush. "We need precision. The blasts must be timed exactly to our departure. Maoud is getting the President ready to be transported. Ten minutes."

9:52 a.m.

Alex Morgan examined her left ear in a compact mirror borrowed from a Latina girl about two years younger than her who was sitting nearby. The ear was cut up and looked like it might leave scars. Wincing, Alex dabbed at it with a wet wipe provided by the same girl, cleaning out the dirt and congealed blood. Fresh blood welled out bright red. She wiped that away too, and held the sleeve of her sweater against it like a compress until the bleeding stopped. She'd have preferred to do this in the bathroom rather than sitting on the cold marble floor, but the line to the bathrooms went halfway around the downstairs waiting area.

"How are you doing?" she asked Clark, who lay back against the marble floor, staring at the ceiling, phones in his ears. He shrugged, hoodie rustling against the stone beneath.

She reached to her pocket to check if her cell phone was there, but it wasn't. She'd left it in her backpack, which she lost when she was knocked down by the crowd.

"Hey," she said, prodding him. He removed his earphones. "Can I borrow your phone?"

He pulled the earphones out by the wire and propped himself up on his elbows. "Here," he said, pulling out the headphone jack and holding it out for her. "I tried to call the 'rents already, though. Couldn't get through. Maybe you'll get lucky, though."

She dialed her father, then her mother. No luck.

"I'm going to take a look around," she told him, handing him back the phone. She stood up with aching muscles. She couldn't sit still. She was antsy, with a bad feeling something else might happen, something worse. More than anything, she wanted to make herself useful.

The main concourse of Grand Central Terminal echoed with loud voices. People were standing and sitting around the expansive floor, and more were downstairs. She estimated that they numbered at least five hundred. MTA Police had spread out, mostly keeping to the exits and the walls, although she spotted two K9 teams doing rounds, inspecting people's bags. She passed a prayer circle as she made her way around the concourse, people old and young, of all races, holding hands as a middle-aged black man spoke a solemn supplication. "Lord, deliver all your children from harm . . ."

Near the passage to the Lexington Avenue and Forty-seventh Street entrance, she heard the disconsolate sobs of people who had lost someone outside, or who had simply broken down from fear and shock. "My son is out there," one young mother pleaded with a policeman holding people back from the door. She sank to her knees. "Please. My Lawrence, my baby . . ."

From there, Alex made her way to Vanderbilt Hall, which opened into the main entrance. It had been cleared and set aside to form a sort of makeshift hospital. Here, people in everyday clothes were attending to the injured. Only two of the people there had bullet wounds. The rest had been injured in the tumult, trampled, pushed, or had fallen against the pavement.

"Hi, excuse me, dear," said a tiny lady who looked to be in her forties sporting spiky orange-red hair in comfortable pants and a casual sweater. She spoke with surprising authority. "Come over here, we'll have someone look at your ear."

Alex said, "No, my ear's okay. I want to help. I have some first-aid training."

"Oh, that's very kind of you," said the woman. "We actually have enough doctors and nurses here. But we could use some more water, if you'd be a dear and get it for us at the market."

It wasn't the help she wanted to give, but, of course, help shouldn't be about what the helper wants. Alex made her way to the Grand Central Market. The shops all seemed to be closed, but a group of girl scouts and other children were lined up to receive bottles of water and fresh fruit at the door to the market itself, where four vendors were distributing them to the kids for free. Alex approached one of them, a young, brown-skinned Hispanic man in a black cap.

"I need water," she said. "For the wounded."

He set off into the market and came back with a plastic-sealed case of six twenty-ounce water bottles.

"You want me to carry that for you, miss?"

"Don't worry," she said, grunting under the weight as he handed the case to her. "You look like you have your hands full."

9:58 a.m.

Morgan and Rosso watched through security video as two of the Iranians attached the wire, which had been zip-tied to about one in four people in the crowd, to the ten or so black suitcases that were laid along the perimeter of the hostages.

"What are they doing?" asked Rosso. He sat in the chair, clutching his wound, his breathing heavy. His eyes were beginning to glaze over.

"It's a trip wire," said Morgan. "Attached to the bomb in the suitcase. If the wire is cut or detached, they blow."

"They're going to have to cut the zip ties loose one by one," said Rosso. "Evacuation's going to be impossible."

"Yeah," he said. "For the hostages and the terrorists." Morgan reached for the phone on the desk. "I need to talk to my man on the outside." He lifted the receiver, but it was dead.

Rosso pointed toward the dead Secret Service agents. "Whatever they had to communicate with the outside, they're definitely not using it anymore," said Rosso.

Morgan bent down over one of them. He had short, curly brown hair, and he was young, so goddamned young. He had the slightest bit of stubble, and Morgan could tell his beard was still patchy and irregular. "Sorry about this," Morgan said, and popped the earbud out of his ear and followed the line to the transmitter in his breast pocket. Morgan pulled it out and fiddled with it to patch into the frequency he was using to communicate with Conley.

"Conley, Conley, come in," he said.

"Conley here. Morgan, is that you? It's mayhem in there. What—"

"The Iranians," he said. "They took out all the Secret Service agents."

"Shit," said Conley. "There's been shooting at Grand Central, too. Reports say more than one sniper fired at the crowd."

Morgan banged his hand on the table in a mixture of rage and worry. *Alex.* "Conley, I need you to try to call my daughter. She's supposed to be coming into Grand Central this morning. I need to know that she's okay." He gave Conley the number.

"I'll try," said Conley. "But the cell system's overloaded. Not sure I'll get through."

"Any idea what the endgame is here?" Morgan asked. He looked at Rosso, who was stooped on the desk, examining the feeds. "They've got no chance of making it out of this building alive."

"They might try to use the hostages for leverage," said Conley.

"I have no idea what that could achieve. Why here? Why now?"

"I don't know," said Conley. "Listen, an NYPD Hercules team is already on its way."

"Son of a bitch! They're wiring this place up with explosives. You need to hold them back. We need to find out what they want, and how it's connected to the shootings at Grand Central—"

"Did you say," Rosso cut in, "that what happened here might have something to do with Grand Central?"

"Yeah. Do you know something?"

"Maybe it's nothing," said Rosso. "But there's an old train line called Track Sixty-one. It was built for FDR in the thirties. It runs underground between here and Grand Central Terminal."

"Could the Iranians access it from here?" asked Morgan.

"If they know where it is. There's an elevator that leads down there from the hotel."

"Did you get that, Conley?"

"Got it," said Conley. "That's their way out, then. Which means they have no reason not to blow up the lobby of the Waldorf."

"Conley," said Morgan. "Keep the Herc team outside. If they come in here, they're going to get themselves and everyone else killed."

10:04 a.m.

"Do you have contact with any of your people on the inside?" Lisa Frieze asked the Secret Service man, one of two left on the outside. The scene was chaos, as agents of various law enforcement branches moved about frantically outside the Park Avenue entrance to the Waldorf, trying to coordinate with each other. The policemen, instead of trying to keep onlookers away, now surrounded the doors, ready for whatever might come out. She shivered, pulling her blazer tighter around her torso and wishing she'd worn something warmer.

He shook his head. "No response on any of the communicators."

"Do you have any word from the field office?"

"They're mounting a response. That's all I know."

She swore under her breath and dialed the number for the hotel, which returned a busy signal.

"Agent Frieze!"

She looked up from her phone to see Peter Conley making his way toward her. "Have you got anything?" he asked.

"First responders are thin on the ground," she said as he approached, "scrambling to deal with the three-pronged attack. From what I gather, though, the Waldorf attack has priority one. This place is going to be swarming with people from at least half a dozen agencies within fifteen minutes."

"That's going to be a problem," he said. "I've got a man on the inside, and he just made contact. We've got a hostage situation. The people inside are wired with explosives. There's no way to get them out safely."

"You've got a man on the inside? We need to establish reliable contact with him and coordinate with—"

"He's not going to wait," said Conley. "And neither is this situation. We need to buy him time to deal with the situation."

"NYPD is getting a negotiator here," she said. "Plus tactical response teams and snipers. Protocol for defusing this sort of situation."

"That's not going to work here," said Conley. "The hostage situation is just a diversion. The terrorists are leaving through an old train tunnel that goes from the Waldorf to Grand Central."

"How do you know this?" asked Frieze. "Who's this man on the inside? Is he State Department?"

"He's a trained black operative," said Conley. Frieze eyed him, but left it at that. There was no time to quibble about these things.

"How does he know their plan?"

"I'd call it a professional hunch," said Conley. "It's the only plan that fits."

"What if they're suicide bombers?"

"Then everybody would already be dead."

Frieze kicked the ground. "Goddamn it," she said. "What the hell do we do, then?"

"We keep the tactical teams out of the hotel," said Conley.

"If this doesn't pan out, my career at the New York bureau is over on my first day."

"Do you think there's any other plausible explanation?"

The tire squeal of a halting car cut off Frieze before she could respond. A thickset man with side-parted salt-and-pepper hair and the expression of a charging bull sprang out and pushed through the barrier.

"Get these people out of here!" he yelled to the policemen at the scene. "I want a perimeter set up on a one-block radius. You." He pointed at the young cop who had let Frieze through earlier. "Push the crowd back, have the barriers set up on Fiftieth, half a block down that way." The cop stood still like a deer in the headlights. "*Now* would be good."

He charged the few additional yards to the front door of the Waldorf. "I'm taking charge of this scene," he yelled out to all present. "All decisions and new information now go through me. Do we have eyes on the inside?"

Frieze spoke up. "Agent Frieze, FBI."

"Sergeant Pearson." His cheeks were splotchy red, nostrils flaring at the base of his bulbous nose. "Are you in charge of the scene?"

"No," she said. "But I need to talk to you."

10:15 a.m.

"Another camera's gone black," said Rosso, hunched over the monitors in the surveillance room. "The elevator to the Presidential Suite."

Morgan poked his head out the door and looked both ways down the hall. Wisps of extinguisher powder still hung in the air, but it was otherwise empty. "Does that give them access to Track Sixty-one?"

"Yeah," said Rosso. "That's the one."

"Then it won't be long before they blow this place," said Morgan. He sat down next to Rosso. "We need to act. There," he said, pointing at a monitor showing the lobby. Only one Iranian was left there, all the others having disappeared. "In that man's hand, see?" It was something small and black, barely visible in the hotel feed. "That's our detonator. We need to get to him before he blows this lobby sky-high."

"All right," said Rosso. "What's the plan?" He winced in pain.

"You sure you're up to it?"

"I'm not doing this out of heroism," he said, refolding his bloody handkerchief and pressing it again to the wound. He stood up, bracing against the desk. He let go to stand only on his feet and swayed. Morgan was ready to catch him, but he didn't fall. "I'm not getting out of here unless that guy is dead. Saving those people is the only way I make it out alive. So that's what I'm going to do."

"I have an idea," said Morgan. "Let me tell you how we're going to do this."

10:18 a.m.

"That's quite a story," Sergeant Pearson said to Frieze, half turned away from her. He towered above her, heavyset and broad shouldered. Working his bushy gray eyebrows into a scowl, he addressed two newcomers bearing tactical sniper rifles, gesturing to them with a hand like a ham. "I want you on the roof of the building across the street, and *you* at the Intercontinental on Forty-ninth."

"You need to trust us," said Conley, at her side. "Keep the Hercules teams out."

"The Iranians will blow the explosives on the first sign of invaders," added Frieze.

"What the hell do you want me to do?" said Pearson, still looking past them at the wider scene, the lines of cop cars and two fire trucks, and dozens of first responders, moving with purpose in all directions. Some pushed people back farther and several scanned the windows of the hotel with binoculars.

Pearson gestured to someone behind Frieze. "If what you're saying is true, we need to get the Herc teams in there as soon as possible."

"That would be a mistake," insisted Conley.

"So instead I'm supposed to trust that this guy on the inside is going to take care of the situation?" Then he shouted, "Get those civilians back! I want Park clear of civilians!"

"It's our best shot," said Frieze.

"Get me in contact with this guy. We'll see where to go from there, all right?"

Frieze saw two black shapes approaching from Forty-ninth Street—large vans, which halted just around the corner. Men clad in black tactical gear with helmets carrying Colt Tactical Carbines and shotguns spilled out. The NYPD Hercules teams—New York City's elite police special forces. They were running out of time.

"All right," said Conley. "I'll patch you through."

10:21 a.m.

Morgan was checking the magazine of the dead Secret Service agent's gun when he was hailed on the radio communicator.

"Sergeant Pearson here," he said. "NYPD. Is this Morgan?"

"Can I help you?" said Morgan, keeping his voice down and his steps light as he made his way down the hall. It was deserted, and any sound seemed to echo in either direction. A hiss emanated from one of the pipes that ran its length. He glanced backward and saw Rosso disappearing around a corner at the far end.

"I'm told you're on the inside of the Waldorf. I need eyes

and ears to coordinate the tactical insertion for the rescue operation."

"Don't attempt anything yet," said Morgan, looking around a corner.

"Excuse me?" Pearson huffed.

"Stay out until I give the all-clear. These guys are not looking to negotiate. All they want is to keep you busy as long as possible. Come inside and they have no reason not to blow." Morgan made a mental map of the lobby in his head, picturing the enemy's location as shown by the security cameras. Only one had stayed behind. They only had to get the one.

"Who the hell do you think you are? You'd better do what I'm telling you to before I make sure you're held personally responsible for the deaths of any—"

Morgan clicked the communicator off as he reached the door leading form the service hallway into the lobby and waited, looking at his watch.

This had to be perfectly synchronized. He and Rosso were going to get one chance. It had to be a one-shot kill— anything less and the terrorist might squeeze the detonator switch.

Morgan checked his watch again. Five seconds.

He heard gunfire right on cue, and afterward, the screams of the people on the floor. Rosso's diversion having been achieved, Morgan pushed the swinging door out into the lobby, which led him behind the front desk. He found the trigger man hiding behind a column, taking cover from the hail of bullets loosed by Rosso on the far end of the lobby.

Morgan had a clear line of sight, but he was too far away. He couldn't be sure of his shot. He had to get closer.

He pushed off the ground, one hand resting on the reception counter as he swung his legs over. His feet hit the floor as he landed catlike on the other side. The trigger man heard and turned to look.

His eyes went wide under thick black eyebrows. Morgan saw the calculation in those eyes—his chance of not being shot if he surrendered, the life that awaited him if he did survive that day—life imprisonment in Guantanamo Bay, enhanced interrogation. In slow motion, Morgan saw him make his decision—the man's eyes cast on the detonator in his left hand.

But the split-second hesitation was enough to give Morgan the advantage. He put two slugs in the man's chest and one between the eyes. The Iranian slumped against the pillar, leaving a red smear as he slid down onto the ground.

"We're clear!" Morgan yelled out.

"Everyone stay put!" Rosso yelled to the crowd. "We're going to get you all out of here in just a moment."

Morgan turned on the communicator. "That was me," he said. "The terrorist has been taken out. You can bring in your guys to defuse the bomb." He jogged around the hostages, still kneeling with their hands on their heads, until he was near enough to Rosso so that nobody else would hear. "I need to go after the others. Tell me how to get to the elevator."

10:32 a.m.

Soroush was last to exit the elevator onto the dark, dusty Track 61, under the Waldorf Astoria. Floodlights by the elevator illuminated the immediate vicinity, but his men already had flashlights at the ready to traverse the tunnel. The air was cool and stale, with a rich smell of dirt along with a whiff of rotting trash. A few yards into the tunnel, Masud wheeled the oversize black roadie case that contained an unconscious Navid Ramadani. Hossein, Paiman, and the others had already gone ahead to make sure the path forward was clear. They had heard the gunfire on the way down, and there was only one thing to do.

"Disable the elevator," he told Sanjar.

"What about Sadegh?" Sanjar asked as he screwed open the elevator-button panel.

"He won't make it," said Soroush, setting down a briefcase on the floor of the elevator. "He will give his life for the cause."

10:33 a.m.

Pandemonium broke out as police drew their weapons and took cover behind the line of cars in response to the shooting. Frieze pressed her back flat against a dark SUV and found that Pearson was right next to her. Her adrenaline pounded and she felt the creeping numbness that preceded a panic attack. She closed her eyes and focused on her breathing.

"Herc teams, move out!" Pearson yelled beside her. "Park and Forty-ninth Street entrances! Clear the lobby! Bomb teams, follow!"

Her panic receded. She opened her eyes with a renewed sense of confidence and security. Frieze ran as the Herc team breached the door. Glass cracked and shattered and they filed in, fanning out onto the open lobby.

A chorus of "Clear!" "Clear!" echoed from inside. Pearson took the lead through the door, and Frieze went in after him.

The elegance of the lobby of the Waldorf Astoria was transformed into a scene of terror and chaos. What seemed to be the entire staff of the hotel plus a number of guests were kneeling on the carpet. Most were crying, and a few had dropped to the fetal position. One woman wailed and a middle-aged, balding businessman rambled incoherently. A couple of the Herc team members were asking them to keep calm, reassuring them that help had arrived.

"The trigger's over here," yelled out a man wearing a white button-down half-red with blood, leaning against a pil-

lar and panting. Frieze heard Pearson calling in an ambulance on his radio. "There are no hostiles in the building, but
these bombs are live," said the man. "In the briefcases." He
staggered, and Conley rushed forward to help ease him onto
a couch.

"Who are you?" asked Pearson as the man lay back.

"Rosso," he said. "Head of security."

"I'm looking for Morgan," said Conley. "On the short
side, dark hair. Bit of a Boston accent. You know who I'm
talking about?"

"Yeah," said Rosso, "You just missed him."

10:36 a.m.

Morgan reached the art deco elevator door that Rosso had
said led to Track 61. In his right hand was the Secret Service
agent's handgun, which he stuffed in the waist of his pants
after activating the safety. In his left was the fire axe.

He pressed the button for the elevator, and was not surprised by the lack of movement. He would have to do this
the hard way.

Morgan took two steps back and swung the axe, wedging
its cutting edge between the steel elevator doors. He grunted
as he pulled the handle, working it as a lever. The doors
groaned open a crack, then a few inches. He then dropped
the axe and pulled one door open with all his might until he
had opened it just enough to get through.

He looked into the ominous blackness of the elevator
shaft. He always hated this part.

10:39 a.m.

Frieze looked at the wire running from the briefcases af-
fixed with zip ties to the hostages' arms. Those who weren't
tied down were escorted outside.

"I want to stay," said a woman, pointing at a child of
about ten whose wrist held a zip tie. "My son."

"We'll get him out," Conley told her in his deep reassuring voice. "Please, come with me."

One woman who was also outfitted with the morbid bracelet, a sixty-something blonde in housekeeping uniform, was convulsing with sobs. Something welled up inside Frieze—the old familiar anxiety, rising up toward panic. She had contained it, but this particular woman's fear, her distorted, plaintive face, touched something deep in Frieze.

She closed her eyes, ignoring all noise, and walked over to the crying woman. Crouching down so that they were at eye level, she put her hand on the woman's shoulder.

"We're going to get you out of here," Frieze said. "It's going to be okay."

The woman, whose small eyes were almost lost in wrinkles, drew a ragged breath.

Frieze stood up and turned to the emergency responders who were now flooding into the lobby. "We need wire cutters to get these people free," she called out. "If you're not engaged in bomb defusal, help me here!"

"Get alligator clips to redirect this wire," she heard Pearson telling one of the bomb squad.

Someone put a wire cutter in her hand and she began to snip. "Conley!"

"I'll start escorting them out," he said, intuiting what she was going to say. She cut loose the woman she'd comforted first, directing her in Conley's direction. Frieze then went on to release others one by one, from the mostly young men in kitchen uniforms to attractive men and women in dress shirts who worked reception to the guests, in business and leisure attire alike, who'd been caught in the lobby when the terrorists hit. She continued to send them toward the officers who Conley had enlisted to direct people to the outside. Conley had now turned his attention to the explosives.

"The bombs have got to be synchronized, which means there's going to be a single receiver," he said when Frieze approached.

"They're locked," said one of two bomb technicians kneeling by the suitcase. "It'll be a few minutes before we can get them open."

"Allow me." The speaker was Rosso, wobbling up off the couch. He held up his hand and knelt down next to the nearest briefcase. He fiddled with the lock, and had it open within a few seconds.

"Zero zero zero," said Rosso, with a smirk. "They never know how to change the codes on their damn briefcases."

The bomb technician opened the briefcase carefully, exposing the five pipe bombs laid out and fixed to the bottom of the case, along with an electronic detonation mechanism.

"Leave this to us," said the bomb tech. "Just get everyone out."

10:40 a.m.

In the dark of the elevator shaft, Morgan held on to the steel cable, making slow progress down. The cable bit into his hands and thighs, but inch by inch, he moved down until his feet touched the elevator. He felt around for the trapdoor into the elevator car. On finding it, he undid the latch and swung the door open.

Light shone from the tunnel beyond the elevator and an updraft blew dust in his face. He coughed and rubbed his eyes, then peered into the trapdoor, listening for any sign of the Iranians. There were none—they had come this way and gone already. Morgan slipped onto the floor of the car, hanging from the edge of the trapdoor, and then dropped another foot into the elevator.

It was only then that his attention was drawn to a black briefcase on the elevator floor.

Bomb.

Without a second thought, Morgan dashed out into the dark tunnel, down a dirt path between thin steel supports illuminated only by the floodlights at the elevator door.

10:43 a.m.

Frieze jogged along Park Avenue with the last group of hostages leaving the hotel, accompanied by firefighters and policemen. She caught sight of Peter Conley closing the doors to one of at least fifteen ambulances at the scene and banging on it twice to alert the driver. He turned and saw Frieze.

"That was the security guy, Rosso," he said. "He says Morgan went after the attackers into Track Sixty-one."

"Is there any way down there?" asked Frieze. "We need to cut the Iranians off before they reach Grand Central."

"I need to find—Pearson!"

The sergeant was coming out of the hotel. He searched for the source of the voice.

"What's the status on the bombs?" asked Frieze.

"Squad says they're clear," said Pearson. "We're evacuating guests now."

"We need to get down to the track," said Frieze. "Follow the Iranians into Grand Central."

"The elevator's out of commission," said Pearson. "But the tunnel has street access. It's right—"

The pavement rumbled beneath their feet. The door he had just pointed out blew off its hinges and flew ten feet to cave in the side of a police car. A plume of gray dust shot out halfway across Park Avenue.

"—there," said Pearson.

10:45 a.m.

The blast knocked Dan Morgan off his feet, sending him sprawling on the dirt. Engulfed in darkness, he heard the dull crash of falling masonry. He rolled onto his back, dazed.

He tried to get up and lost his footing.

He noticed something—a pattering sound, or many, thousands. He made out a squeaking noise. And then they were on him.

He just felt the scratches, at first. It took him a few seconds to figure out what it was.

Rats. Thousands of them, running from the blast.

Morgan picked himself up and ran, the rodents scratching his legs as they tried to use him as a ladder. He needed to get off the ground or he'd be overrun.

As his eyes adjusted, ahead he saw a rusting black train car, which he recognized as Roosevelt's own train—today, a tourist attraction. It would do. He made a running jump, grabbing the ladder and pulling himself up. He reached the top and flopped onto his back, against the rough, dirty metal. He allowed himself to lie there as he caught his breath, waiting for the deluge of rats below to pass him by.

10:47 a.m.

Outside the Waldorf, Frieze tried to contain the chaos, directing the people coming out of the hotel north on Park, where a group of NYPD officers were gathering the hostages to sort out who needed medical attention and to get their names and personal information. She glanced at the hotel front doors, half expecting to see a ball of flame emerge. Instead, she saw Sergeant Pearson.

"Pearson!" she called out, running toward him. "What's the status?"

"The guests who were locked into their rooms are coming down," said Pearson. On cue, people started streaming out of the lobby doors.

"Have you contacted your agents at Grand Central?" she asked.

"I'm not getting through," he said. "Communications are down. I've sent some guys over there to warn them."

"What about the passage to the tunnel?"

"Blocked," he said. Something caught his eye and he yelled out, "No, *this way*! Direct them *this way*!" He jogged off toward the hotel doors.

Exasperated, she looked around the scene. She found Peter Conley talking to a gorgeous blonde who had been among those coming out of the hotel. She felt an unaccountable pang of jealousy as she walked towards him. He handed the woman a black box about the size of a book, and she put something small into the palm of his hand.

"Adele, your services are, as usual, much appreciated," Frieze heard him say.

The woman noticed Frieze, and looking her up and down, turned with a "Ta-ta!" Conley turned to face Frieze. She shot him a quizzical look and shot a glance at the woman as she swayed up Park Avenue. Then she shook her head. Nothing mattered at that moment except the crisis.

"We need to warn my people. Whatever these guys' plan is, we need to be waiting for them."

"Tell me who to call," he said.

"Chambers," she said, and gave him the number. He handed her the phone. Straight to voicemail.

She looked down the length of Park Avenue in the direction of Grand Central Terminal. The whole street had been sectioned off by police and was nearly deserted between there and the Met Life building. "I can't wait and hope the call gets through," she said. "It's only half a mile or so. You keep trying."

She took off running, glad that she had chosen to wear flats that day.

10:53 a.m.

Soroush checked his watch in the dim light as Hossein and Paiman carried the case containing President Ramadani up the rusting steel steps from the subbasement, the metallic clanking of their footfalls echoing in the tight quarters. Three of his men had already reached the upper landing, and Zubin was at his side. Now that they were not as deep underground, Soroush tried to hail his man on the radio communicator.

"Touraj," said Soroush. "Come in."

"This is Touraj." The voice came faint and distorted. "I hear you."

"Status."

"You have a clear path to the control room. Enemy communications are jammed."

"We are coming to you," he said. He checked his watch again. "Ten minutes. Have the others stand by for my signal."

The box containing Ramadani hit the steel steps with a clatter. Soroush saw that Hossein had let it slip, and the box had fallen on Paiman's hand, pinning it against the step. Wincing in pain, Paiman managed to keep it from tumbling down.

Zubin walked down three steps to Hossein and backhanded him across the face.

"Idiot." He turned without another word. Soroush looked down on him. "We have come too far to be done in by incompetence." He turned forward once more and resumed walking. "Zubin, run ahead and take the lead," he said. "Remember, we wish to avoid firing before we are ready to take the terminal. Sanjar?" This last he called to the man below Hossein and Paiman. "Get ready. You know what to do."

11:01 a.m.

Frieze pushed her way through the crowd of onlookers to reach the perimeter that the NYPD had formed around Grand Central at the corner of Vanderbilt Avenue and East Forty-sixth Street. She flashed her badge at the officer, who let her through the barrier. She turned back just long enough to see Conley, out of the corner of her eye, gaining admittance behind her.

No time to wait for him. She ran down Vanderbilt Avenue,

which was empty of pedestrians except policemen enforcing the cordon. When she had traversed a block down to Forty-fifth, she saw that, along the Grand Central building, cars had been left abandoned on the street by people escaping sniper fire. She caught sight of a dark bloodstain on the pavement and chills ran down her spine.

She turned onto East Forty-second Street to find a cluster of first responders, some thirty in total, not only wearing NYPD uniforms but black suits and dress shirts, under the Park Avenue overpass, which provided at least partial protection in case the snipers returned. She searched the crowd, circling it until she saw who she was looking for.

"Chambers!" she called out. He was conferring with Nolan, who was speaking into his phone at the same time.

"Frieze? Jesus Christ, the Waldorf is still an ongoing terror scene. I need someone—"

"Sir, this couldn't wait," she said, panting. "The Iranian president's been abducted. They're coming here."

"What are you talking about?" he said, motioning to a man carrying a rolled-up piece of paper some three feet long. He unrolled it on a table that had been dragged out of the Pershing Square Café. It was a floor plan of the terminal.

"To Grand Central! The terrorists are bringing him here. We need people on the inside to intercept them."

That got his undivided attention. "How do you know this?"

"Head of security for the Waldorf says he saw them go down to an underground track that runs between the Waldorf and Grand Central."

"Why am I only hearing this now? For God's sake, Frieze, why didn't you call?"

Frieze motioned to his cell phone, still in his hand, with a call still active.

Chambers stabbed the phone with a meaty finger to disconnect. "Our teams are tied up searching the buildings for the snipers," he said. "Nolan," he called out, and Frieze noticed that he was standing against the window of the café, texting on his phone. "Update on tactical."

"Sir," said Nolan. "The snipers haven't been found."

"Divert the teams," he said. "I need word sent to the officers inside. All resources need to be on finding those kidnappers."

"What about the people inside Grand Central?" asked Frieze.

"We can't risk letting the Iranians slip out," said Chambers. "They stay inside until our people inside get a grip on the situation."

11:06 a.m.

Soroush's ten-man team invaded the Grand Central Control Room bearing MP7 submachine guns, spreading through the elongated chamber with its two rows of desks facing giant monitors built into the wall, reminiscent of Mission Control at Cape Canaveral. Masud and Paiman raised their firearms to the two security guards in the room. "Guns on the ground!" yelled Masud. "Now!"

Seeing themselves outgunned, the guards placed their semiautomatics on the ground.

"Hands on your desks," Soroush yelled out. "Do not attempt to fight back and do not attempt to contact anyone, or you will die. Is that understood?" Then, in a measured tone, he said, "Touraj." A young man sitting at the back desk, about three-quarters of the way to the far end of the room, stood up and walked to face Soroush. His hair was close-cropped and he wore a short-sleeved pale yellow shirt. People watched him as he stood, astonished. "Is everything in place?" asked Soroush.

"The communications jammers are in trash cans around the terminal," he answered in Farsi. "They are ready for deployment."

"And the other device?"

"It is ready to be triggered," said Touraj.

"Good," said Soroush. "Contact security. You know what to do."

11:16 a.m.

Standing against a shuttered ticket booth, Alex Morgan watched the MTA policemen. There'd been a marked change in their mood. The tension had transformed into urgency in the past five minutes. And now, she noticed, they had all gotten the same piece of information. Around three quarters of them seemed to be heading in the same direction, toward the western end of the terminal.

"Clark," she said to the distracted boy, sitting with his back against the wall next to her. "I'll be right back."

He nodded without pulling out his earphones.

She made her way through the crowd, careful to make it seem like she wasn't following them, although it hardly mattered. All were too preoccupied to pay her any attention.

She walked to the edge of the throng, which spilled a few yards from the main concourse into the corridor, and sat down, pretending to belong to a group of young women. Out of the corner of her eyes, she watched the policemen pass.

"The subbasement power plant," she heard one of them say. "Looks like we've got hostiles."

So that was it. Terrorists were in the building.

She knew she should stay with everyone else. She knew they were trained professionals, and she was just a kid. She knew that she would probably get hurt if she got involved.

Knowing all the reasons that she shouldn't, Alex Morgan slipped away from the crowd into the empty hallway, after the policemen.

11:19 a.m.

Dan Morgan heard the rush of movement as he was coming up from the Grand Central sub-basement. He ran off the stairs into a dark tunnel and ducked behind a steam pipe. Through a crack, he saw that they were MTA police—not as bad as the alternative, although he wondered if he might get shot if they found him there, anyway. He waited until they had passed, and then emerged and resumed his way up. His legs burned as his khaki pants rustled against the fresh scratches from the wave of rats that had tried to climb him in Track 61.

He ran up and turned the corner at the top of the stairs so fast that he couldn't stop before bumping into a figure who stumbled back at the impact—small, light, female, svelte athletic frame, short brown hair—

"Alex?"

"Dad? What are you doing here?"

"Getting you away. Come on. We're going to find a way out." He pulled her by the arm down a dark and dank service hall.

"Dad, come on," she said, pulling against him. "I know you're here for a reason. An important reason. I can help you."

"This is no place for you," he said. "You're getting out. Now."

"But Dad, I can—"

Morgan staggered as the ground quaked beneath his feet, and a deep rumble shook him to his bones.

11:23 a.m.

Soroush felt the blast before Sanjar told him that the bomb had been detonated. Unbolted objects shook against the desks. A mild commotion erupted among the control room staff, which Zubin silenced with a shout.

"The policemen have been taken care of," said Sanjar. "Those who are not dead will be trapped underground."

"There are still those left on the main concourse," said

Soroush. "Move out. Touraj, give the order. We will hit them swiftly and give them no opportunity to resist."

He took the lead out of the control room, and all his men followed but Touraj and one more, who stayed behind to guard the hostages. MP7s in hand, they stalked toward the main concourse. "Touraj, are your men ready?" Soroush spoke into his radio communicator.

"Just waiting for the signal, sir."

"Stand by." He gestured for Zubin to lead half the men to the north passage while he took four men through the south. "Now, Touraj."

The gunshots rang out just as Soroush turned the corner, making himself visible to everyone inside the terminal. Then the screaming started. But no eyes were on them. Instead, they were focused on the nine men Soroush had planted in the terminal, who had now drawn their weapons and were taking out the MTA police who remained in the concourse. Hossein loosed a volley of bullets, shepherding people away from the western passage. Soroush pushed his way through the crowd and got up on the balcony, from where he could see the entire scene of mayhem.

"Sir," said Touraj on the radio. "Outside. Their people are getting in position. They will be inside within minutes."

"It's time then," said Soroush. "Activate the device."

"Activating," said Touraj, "in three, two, one."

11:27 a.m.

"Get those doors open!" exclaimed Chambers.

Frieze ran to the padlocks to the chains that were holding the Forty-second Street doors closed. People were banging against the glass, crushed by the swell of people trying to escape. "Who's got the keys to this thing?"

The tactical teams were assembling behind Chambers, twelve men in black gear and helmets carrying submachine guns and shotguns. One of them produced a two-foot-long bolt cutter.

"Here!" Frieze called out to him, and he ran toward her.

A siren broke out above the noise.

"What the hell?" yelled Chambers. Frieze saw what it was. Gigantic steel doors were descending on the passage, right above her. She rolled out of the way as they hit the ground with a deep and metallic sound. She got to her feet and drew close to inspect the barrier. Thick, steel, impossible to get through.

"Are any of the other doors open?" yelled Chambers.

"It's the automatic lockdown system," said Nolan. "Big steel blast doors on every entrance. Subway, trains, everything. No dice. They come down automatically in the event of—"

"Chemical attack," said Frieze. "They released a chemical weapon inside Grand Central Terminal. We need to get those people out."

"If they really detonated a chemical weapon inside," said Nolan, "everybody in there is already dead."

11:35 a.m.

With Alex behind him, Morgan opened the service doorway a crack, just enough to see the men with MP7s herding people through the Vanderbilt Passage toward the main concourse. A whine reverberated throughout the terminal as the PA system came online and a voice was broadcast throughout the building.

"Silence!"

Morgan retreated back into the service hallway, letting the door click shut.

"There is no way out," said the voice. It spoke in a light British accent. "Those on the outside believe you are dead. They cannot open the doors, they cannot get inside. No one is coming for you. Your only chance to make it through this

day is to cooperate. You will all return to the main concourse. You will remain calm and follow orders. If you do,
you will survive. If not, you will all die."

Morgan furrowed his brow. "Alex," he said, "tell me you
have a cell phone."

"Sorry. I lost it when the snipers started shooting people
outside."

"Damn," he whispered. "Okay, we need to get you out of
the way first."

"And then?" she asked.

"And then you stay put," he said. "Now, how do we get to
the basement?"

11:56 a.m.

Lisa Frieze felt the urge to run, to *do* something, but
nothing could be done. An awful lull in the activity at the
Forty-second Street entrance had set in as others came to the
same conclusion. The doors could not be opened—the automatic lockdown lasted six hours. People were working on
overriding the system remotely, but nobody at the scene
could help in that task. Chambers had also sent for teams of
workmen with blowtorches to try to get through the doors
the hard way.

Frieze sat down on the curb in the sun as exhaustion
began to creep in. She closed her eyes, just for a moment,
and when she opened them she saw a pair of legs in front of
her. She looked up to see Nolan standing there with a white
cardboard box.

"Local bakery sent us some bagels," he said. "Plain,
whole grain, or everything?"

"Whole grain."

He handed her the bagel on a napkin. "We've got some
cream cheese packets and plastic knives, too, if you want
'em."

She shook her head no as she bit into the oven-warm bread,

realizing that she hadn't eaten since the night before, when she'd had cold lo mein straight from the delivery box in her as-yet unfurnished studio apartment, which, among many other things, still lacked a microwave.

"Thanks," she said through a mouthful of bagel.

"Don't mention it," said Nolan. "Hell of a first day, huh?"

"You said it." She chewed her bagel in a state of fatigue. She barely acknowledged Peter Conley when he walked over and sat down next to her.

"Hell of a first day, isn't it?"

"People keep saying that."

Conley chuckled. "I guess it can't be very original of me." He stretched and yawned. "Do you think an actual chemical weapon detonated inside?"

"No," said Frieze, swallowing a bite of her bagel. "It makes no sense at all. These guys are not out to cause simple destruction. They're executing a carefully orchestrated plan. There's no reason they couldn't have set off a chemical weapon in the first place, if that was their ultimate purpose. No reason to go through all that."

"So it strikes you as strange?" asked Conley.

"Of course this strikes me as strange," said Frieze. "The terrorists lock themselves inside Grand Central? What the hell is their plan?"

"I don't know," said Conley.

"Yeah," said Frieze. "That's exactly what worries me."

12:08 p.m.

Morgan opened the door to the utility closet and stood aside for Alex. It held a couple of mop carts and steel shelves fully stocked with cleaning supplies. It smelled of bleach and lavender. "Here," he said. "Your accommodations, until I come get you."

"Not exactly the Waldorf, is it?" she said with a dubious expression on her face.

"Believe me, I was at the Waldorf today. This is a lot better."

"I don't understand why I can't come with you," she said. "I could really help."

"No, Alex. What you would do is get in the way and get yourself killed. Now, *stay here.*"

"Fine," she said with a pout, sitting on a ratty old wooden chair that had been stowed away in there. "I'll wait in the wings while people need saving."

"That's a good girl," said Morgan. He glared at her, then closed the door. He was in a service hall on the west side of the terminal. He needed to contact Conley. The people on the outside needed to know what was going on inside. Along with the gun, he had lost his communicator after the subterranean blast. What he needed was a cell phone. And there was one place he could be sure to locate one.

Lost and found.

It was on the other side of the main concourse. The terrorists had gathered everyone there, spilling up the balconies. But the upshot of that was that the lower level had been emptied out. Morgan made his way there via the escalator. He crept past the deserted food kiosks. Out in the waiting room, he saw one of the Iranians carrying a semiautomatic, patrolling. Morgan calculated his chances of taking him on alone, then decided against it. He didn't want his presence known just yet. The odds were not in his favor. Surprise was one thing working in his advantage.

Morgan took off his shoes and waited, listening for the footsteps. When the man left the waiting room for the other hallway of the dining area, Morgan sprinted, shoes in hand. His sock-clad feet made no noise as he traversed the waiting room, making for the closed-off tracks.

He jumped onto the counter and crouched through the Lost and Found window. As he hopped to the floor on the other side, he heard a clatter of multiple objects hitting the ground—he had knocked over a pencil holder. He heard footsteps from the hall behind him coming in his direction.

Shit. Morgan knelt and rolled parallel to the window.

"Who is in here?"

Morgan stood flat against the wall. If it came to gunfire, he would lose the element of surprise, and probably die, which he was trying to avoid, if at all possible. On steel wire shelves were boxes upon boxes of forgotten objects, dominated by cell phones, small bags, and retractable umbrellas—the non-retractable kind were stacked on the top shelf. A little to his left were the various bags and backpacks in cubby holes. He sketched a plan in his mind.

Morgan reached out and grabbed an umbrella from the shelf—a long, non-retractable one with a heavy curved wooden handle. Then he waited.

The man climbed through the window and hopped to the floor like Morgan had done, his sidearm in his hand. When his feet hit the floor, Morgan swung the umbrella, connecting with the terrorist's hand. The gun was sent rattling on the floor. Morgan swung the umbrella back up, hitting the curved handle against the man's chin. He tried to raise his submachine gun. In close quarters, Morgan had the advantage. He couldn't take the gun—it was attached to a strap slung over the man's shoulder. Instead, Morgan activated the safety. The man pulled the trigger, and the gun clicked to no avail. His look of surprise was all the time Morgan needed to release the detachable magazine, which fell to the floor, and remove the chambered round, reducing the weapon to a paperweight.

The man responded with a head butt. Morgan staggered back. The man grabbed a golf club and drew back to swing. Morgan grabbed a plastic container full of cell phones from the shelf and tossed it at him. The man fumbled against the rain of forgotten phones and dropped the club, but returned with a kick.

The heel hit Morgan square in the solar plexus, knocking him backward and leaving him winded. He saw the man bending down to pick up his gun. Morgan saw that his own was too far out of reach. His attention turned to the lost items. He fumbled through the boxes until his hands closed around cool metal.

Ice skates.

He grabbed the laces to one and pushed himself up onto his feet, swinging the skate like a flail as the man raised the gun. He brought the blade down hard, piercing skin and crushing bone to embed it in his forehead. The man fell forward with the weight of the skate. Morgan panted over him, face spattered with blood.

He raced over to the shelves where the boxes were stored and rummaged for a cell phone. Once he found one he set it on a counter, out of sight of the window. He was looking for something simple, durable, and with as close to a full charge as possible. After sifting through a number of them, he settled on a Nokia with a monochrome screen and three-quarter charge, along with a similar Samsung model as backup.

He tried to make the call on the Nokia, but got no signal. He tried the Samsung next, but no dice. He was going to have to reach higher ground.

12:19 p.m.

Morgan backtracked to the west end of the terminal, now equipped with the MP7 submachine gun and CZ 110 pistol of the man he had killed and two cell phones.

When Alex was ten, he'd brought her to a behind-the-scenes tour of Grand Central Terminal. She'd hated it, he recalled. But at that moment, he was thankful that he had dragged her to it. Because of that tour, he knew how to get where he needed to go.

The Tiffany clock. If there was one place he could get a signal, it'd be there.

The way to the clock was through the Metro North control room, from which the entire rail network was managed. It was also a likely place to find the terrorists.

He crept along the corridor, listening hard for any sign of the enemy. The way was clear until he reached the door marked CONTROL ROOM. Access required a key-card reader, but it was propped open by a fire extinguisher. He pushed the door open just far enough so that he could get a look inside. The control room had two long rows of tables facing two enormous boards, and the passage to the clock was on the far end.

His eye caught movement and he retreated, then popped out for another look. On the far end of the control center was a meeting room of some sort with an enormous window overlooking the entire chamber. Two men were hunched over a desk near the far end.

This could only be a bad idea. But he could think of no other way through.

Morgan assessed his options. Long room, no appreciable alternate routes. No possibility of avoiding exposure. Usually subterfuge, instinct and careful planning won the day. But sometimes, you just had to run at the enemy with a big gun.

Morgan gripped the MP7 and visualized the layout of the room and the men's position in it. They were far, but he could cover half that distance before they even looked up. The gun would do the rest of the work.

Morgan burst into the room and ran, full tilt. They looked up at him in stupid surprise. He unleashed a burst of bullets, which sailed over them to hit the far wall, but it was enough to make them flinch, which gave him enough time to make it near enough to hit the first man. He pulled the trigger, sinking two slugs into his left arm and one in his neck. The other man scrambled over the desk, knocking down a monitor, then over the second desk, to put space between them. Morgan turned the gun on him and fired, but the bullets flew over him and hit the far wall, splintering wood. He ran toward the door, faster than Morgan would have expected. He fired and fired again, but all bullets missed their target, hitting the wood paneling. He reached the door, and Morgan ran after him.

Morgan erupted out into the hallway and took aim. But something made him hold fire.

Alex.

She was in the hallway, frozen as the man ran right past her toward the main concourse.

"Alex, get down!" he said. She dropped, and he pulled the trigger. Too late—the man was rounding a corner. Morgan had no hope of catching him now.

"What—" he began, fuming. She was a deer in the headlights. "You know what, I don't even have anything to say to you. Come. Now."

She followed without a word back into the control room.

"Where are we going?" she asked. "This is the first place they'll come looking."

"Up," said Morgan. He led the way up a flight of stairs into the situation room, which was furnished with expensive office chairs and an sizeable conference table, and had a broad window overlooking the entire operation of the control room. At the back was a brown wooden door. Morgan opened it to reveal a low passage under an X-shaped structural support that led to a tunnel of bare concrete.

"Is this what I—" Alex was interrupted by a muffled yell. Morgan turned his attention to a large wheeled black case, the kind used by musicians to haul equipment. Morgan's first thought was that it was big enough to fit a man inside, and his second was that a man was exactly what was inside it.

"Help me out here," he said to Alex. Together, they laid the box on its side and undid the latches. Morgan pulled open the lid.

"Shit!" he said. "Is that—"

"President Ramadani," said Alex.

The Iranian president, rolled up into the fetal position in the confining box, groaned and blinked glazed-over eyes. "Mr. President, my name is Dan Morgan. I guess I'm here to rescue you."

12:32 p.m.

Shir Soroush surveyed the main concourse from the western balcony with satisfaction. The police presence had dwindled, with the few surviving officers stripped of their guns and sent to join the other hostages. The sun, filtering in through the enormous windows, projected rays on the captives seated within the central rectangle of the main concourse, while Soroush's men patrolled the perimeter. It would not take long now to prepare their escape, as soon as—

Soroush's thoughts were interrupted as Touraj huffed up the balcony stairs.

"Sir," he said, "Mansoor is dead. There is a man with a gun. He came into the control room. It was so fast, I—"

"Where is Ramadani?" Soroush demanded, full of righteous anger.

"I—the man with the gun—"

"You *left* him there?"

Soroush swore under his breath as Touraj explained himself. "He came out of nowhere. I barely made it out of there alive."

"Inshallah. Zubin. Stay. Take care of the hostages. Hossein, Paiman, with me."

Soroush led the way, Beretta in hand, down from the balcony. The hostages recoiled in fear as he passed. He walked with purpose to the control room, and then down its length and up the stairs to the situation room. The box was on its side, open and empty.

With a cry of rage, Soroush overturned the case. "Where is he?" Hossein and Paiman gave him blank stares. "I want you to comb the place. I want Ramadani found!"

12:34 p.m.

Morgan brought up the rear behind the Iranian president, going up the ladder past exposed pipes and ducts and concrete. Alex took the lead. Ramadani, still groggy from the drugs, climbed slowly. More than once, Morgan had to hold him up so that he wouldn't fall.

Morgan heard the deep, loud clicking of the Tiffany clock before he saw it. Still, it dazzled him when he caught sight of it. The stained-glass sun radiated from the center of the clock face, glowing bright gold against the sunlight. He helped the President onto a corrugated steel platform with a final push, and then sat down next to him. Ramadani rubbed his eyes and studied Morgan.

"I owe you my life," he said.

"Don't speak too soon," said Morgan, checking the cell phone he had taken from Lost and Found. "We're not out of the woods yet."

"Still, you did rescue me," he said. "I am grateful. What is your name?"

"Morgan," he said, dialing Conley's number. "Dan Morgan." The phone rang. No answer.

"Who are you with?" asked Ramadani. "Secret Service? FBI?"

"I'm just a guy, Mr. President," said Morgan.

"Just a guy. Of course."

"What can you tell me about the men with the guns down there?" Morgan asked.

"The ones who took me captive?" said Ramadani. He bent his limbs, working out the aches from his cramped confinement. "Their leader, I believe, is Shir Soroush, my head of security."

"Do you have any idea why your own head of security would take you hostage?"

"I have a good idea," said Ramadani. "Though I never thought he might actually do it. If you follow the politics of my country, you know that the Supreme Leader is not happy with me. The Ayatollah is losing his influence on the nation. He will be strengthened by renewed conflict with the United States. I don't know if he is directly involved, but he would certainly be the beneficiary if I were to die."

Alex, Morgan noticed, was listening with keen interest. "What's the angle here, though?" he asked. "What can he gain from this? If he wanted to kill you, why didn't he just do it at the hotel?"

"I believe his purpose was not just to kill me," he said, sitting down against a railing. "See, if it is believed that my assassination was connected to him, the people would take to the streets. The Ayatollah himself might fall. But if I were to disappear, and Soroush and his men were able to vanish as well, the truth could be warped and massaged. A propaganda campaign could well convince the majority of Iranians that I was abducted by the United States government, thus ensuring decades of hatred between our nations."

"But the people would find out the truth!" Alex exclaimed. "They couldn't pull this over the eyes of everyone in Iran like this."

"I fear they could convince enough people easily enough," said Ramadani. "Many are ready to believe the worst of the United States. This could very well lead to war between our nations."

"That's why we're going to stop them," Morgan said, and dialed again. This time, Conley picked up.

"Conley," came the voice on the line.

"I've got Ramadani," said Morgan. "I need you to get us out of here."

12:38 p.m.

Lisa Frieze was jogging back from the northeast doors to the Forty-second Street entrance to give Chambers the bad news. The three-man team of workmen who were trying to cut through the steel barrier into the terminal reported that it would take at least another three hours to make a man-sized hole. She turned the corner at Forty-second and ran toward the space under the Park Avenue overpass when she heard her name called out.

"Frieze!"

It was Peter Conley. He strode over to her. "I've just made contact," he said. "My guy on the inside. He says he's got Ramadani."

"*What?*"

Conley explained that the man had rescued the Iranian president and gotten him to the Tiffany clock, where they were now awaiting rescue.

"Hell!" said Frieze. "Who *is* this guy?"

"Just a helpful citizen," said Conley with a grin.

Frieze shot him a withering look. "We need to tell Chambers," she said. "Come on."

Chambers was inside the Pershing Square Café, which had been converted into the nerve center of the operation. Blueprints were spread out among the many tables, and rows of laptops had been set up. People yelled and rushed around. Chambers himself was conferring with a young agent at a laptop when Frieze called out his name.

"Frieze," said Chambers as he saw her approach. "Tell me you have good news."

"Better than you might expect." She relayed the information, with Conley, who was standing next to her, breaking in and adding details here and there.

"Do you have him on the phone now?" asked Chambers. Frieze looked at Conley, who shook his head.

"Then get him. I want to speak to this Morgan."

12:46 a.m.

Morgan undid the latch and pulled open the window that held the number 6 on the clock face, a white Roman numeral in a red circle against a blue background. Bracing cold fresh air rushed in and he breathed deep. Up above him, the clock's mechanism ticked away, second by second. As he noticed the time, he was glad that the tower had no bell.

"This is our exit," he told Alex and Ramadani.

"How?" asked Alex.

Before Morgan could answer, the phone rang, and Morgan picked up.

"Is this Morgan?"

"Who is this?"

"Chambers, FBI. I understand you have the president of Iran with you."

"You understand right," Morgan answered.

"I'd like to speak to him to confirm."

"It's for you," said Morgan, holding out the phone for Ramadani. They exchanged a few words, then Ramadani handed the phone back to Morgan.

"We have rescue on the way," said Chambers. "We'll have a helicopter drop down a ladder for you at the clock window. Meanwhile, we're going to need you to tell us whatever you know."

"The terrorists belong to Ramadani's security team," said Morgan. "Although I think there might be others helping them. The leader is a man called Shir Soroush." Morgan looked at Ramadani to confirm he'd gotten it right. On the line, he heard Chambers relay the name to someone else.

"Morgan, I need more from you. Tell me what's going on inside."

"I'm not in a good vantage point to see what's happening in the main concourse," said Morgan.

"We are planning an operation to take out the terrorists," said Chambers. "We need to know roughly how many there are and their positions."

"I'll see what I can do," said Morgan. "I'll call you back." He hung up, then said to Alex and Ramadani, "I need to scope out the place. I'll be back soon."

"Dad," said Alex. "Let me go."

"Alex, there is no way—"

"I'm smaller and quicker than you," she said. "And they won't shoot me if they catch me. Probably."

"No," said Morgan. He checked the CZ pistol and tucked it into his pants waist, against the small of his back. He handed the MP7 to Ramadani. "You know how to use this?"

"Well enough," said Ramadani, holding it to get a feel for the weapon.

"Dad," said Alex. "The catwalk. From there you can get a clear view of the main concourse. That's where you should go."

12:59 a.m.

Morgan crept down the ladder from the clock, taking each rung slowly so as to make the least noise possible. It was all too likely there would be men in the control room, and he didn't want to give them advance warning of his coming.

He touched on the concrete floor and crouched, listening against the door to the conference room. He heard no sound of voices or footsteps. He waited for a few minutes to be sure. Then he swung the door open.

The conference room was deserted. Crouching, Morgan made his way forward so that he could just see through the window overlooking the control room. A stroke of luck, for once—no one was there. He stood up straight, clutching the sidearm two-handed as he moved down the stairs and out onto the control room. He walked toward the door, gun raised, then listened for noise out in the hall. Silence. *Good.*

Morgan had only a vague memory of the backstage layout of Grand Central, but his sense of direction took him up stairs and down deserted hallways to the catwalk above the main concourse. He had to crouch to see through the semi circular window. He counted seven men, standing guard on the far balcony, and four more on the floor of the main concourse guarding the east passages. He knew more men would be directly below him. He had to find a better vantage point.

He went farther down the catwalk, where a door opened onto the main concourse, to a narrow passage along the edge of the curved ceiling. Morgan emerged, crouching, stretching his neck to see what was hidden from him on the catwalk. A cluster of men stood against the leader—Soroush, Ramadani had called him—on the near balcony. Morgan whipped out his phone and redialed, counting the hostiles in his head. At least sixteen were out in the concourse—certainly more than had been at the hotel. The others would have been at Grand Central from the beginning.

"Chambers."

"I've got the count," Morgan said into the phone. "There are—"

Morgan heard the shouting first, and then gunshots. It took looking down for him to notice that they were firing at him.

Shit.

He bolted back into the catwalk, running past the window as bullets cracked the glass and sailed by.

He thought of Alex. The clock was the one place he couldn't go. Whatever he did, he had to draw the men away from her. He had to give her and Ramadani enough time to get rescued.

He ran down hallways and stairs, gun drawn, down, down, down toward the Iranians.

1:14 p.m.

"Morgan? Morgan?" Chambers swore and hung up the phone. The Pershing Square Café was silent, hanging on his reactions.

"What is it?" asked Frieze, who was standing beside him.

"We've got gunfire inside!" yelled a freckled, redheaded man wearing a headset.

"I lost contact," said Chambers.

"Do you think he's dead?" Frieze asked. Conley seemed to be disturbed by this possibility—a look of concern and vulnerability came over his face. Whoever this Morgan guy was, this was personal for Conley.

"I don't know," said Chambers. "Where the hell is that chopper?"

"Delayed, sir," said a short curly-haired woman in a black button-down. "Ignition issue. We've got a second one preparing for takeoff as we speak."

"Not fast enough," said Chambers. "It's time to use explosives to breach. Frieze, set it up. I want this ready within the hour. Let's get those hostages out of there."

1:16 p.m.

The clock ticked on. The passage of each second held unbearable meaning to Alex Morgan, who with clenched fists tried to do what her father had asked of her and stay put. But when she heard the gunfire, she knew it could only have been aimed at him. Her father needed help, and she was the only one who could offer it. She stood up on the catwalk.

"Mr. President," she said to Ramadani, who had been lost in thought. "I'm sorry, but I'm going to need the gun."

"You're going to go help your father." He exuded a deep serenity.

"The rescue helicopter should be here any minute," she said. "You don't need me, or the weapon, anymore."

"You're right," he said. "I don't. But I am not about to let a young girl go up against armed men." He stood up with a quiet groan. "I will go. You stay."

Alex laughed. "Save it," she said. "Chivalry's one thing,

but you're President of an entire country. It's more important for you to live than me, any day."

"That is very noble," he said. "But I would be no kind of man if I did not go instead of you."

"I'm not saying this just to seem noble," she said. "It's true, and you can't deny it. No, I won't let you go. And you can't stop me unless you shoot me. And if you don't give me that gun, I'm going without one."

He chuckled. "There is no way—"

"I *will* wrestle you for it," she said. "With all due respect."

Ramadani unslung the MP7 and handed it to her. "You are a brave young woman," he said. "And persistent. Do you know how this works?"

"My father taught me," she lied, checking the safety and feeling its weight in her hand.

"He's a good man, your father."

"The best," she said. "So you know why I need to do this. Wish me luck, Mr. Ramadani."

1:19 p.m.

Morgan dashed through Vanderbilt Hall, six of Soroush's men in hot pursuit. He took the ramp down looking to lose them on the lower concourse, but he heard shouting from below—some of them had gone around to intercept him. Only one place to go now.

Morgan pushed open the heavy wooden door to the Oyster Bar. He made a running jump over the counter, knocking over a pile of glasses to shatter on the floor. He checked the magazine in his gun. Five rounds.

Morgan figured he was worth more alive than dead—they needed him to tell them where the President was. He just had to keep them at bay long enough for Alex and Ramadani to be rescued.

For his own sake, he intended to be captured. It was his best chance at survival. But he was damned if he wouldn't take at least one of them with him.

He heard the squeak of the door opening. Morgan stood, gun raised, and emptied the magazine, sending four of the bullets into the man in front, with the fifth missing its target. Morgan continued to pull the trigger and feigned surprise when the bullets ran out and the gun clicked again and again. Sure that he was no longer a threat, the two remaining Iranians just trained their weapons on him, stalking in his direction. Morgan dropped his empty piece and raised his hands.

1:24 p.m.

Zubin brought up the stairs to the balcony the man who was causing so much trouble—a short, muscled, dark-haired man in a soiled and torn white undershirt whose eyes bore a look of wild defiance. One less man was returning than had gone.

"What about Hossein?" asked Soroush. Zubin just shook his head.

"And who are you?" asked Soroush once the American was brought to face him.

"This is the man, I think, who took the President," broke in Masud. "He killed Behdad in the Lost and Found, I believe—he had his gun."

"That is him," said Touraj. "He killed Davar as well. That is the man."

Soroush walked a few paces forward to face him head-on.

"Is that true?" Soroush asked, looking the prisoner square in the eye.

"I didn't really bother to learn their names."

"And what is yours?" asked Soroush.

"Morgan," he said.

"Mr. Morgan," said Soroush. "You need to tell me where you took Mr. Ramadani."

"The only people who tell me what to do are my wife and my doctor," said Morgan. "And even then—" Soroush backhanded him across the face. Morgan ran his tongue over his split lip.

"Insolent," said Soroush. "But we have ways of dealing with insolence. Get him to the control room."

1:43 p.m.

Under the Park Avenue viaduct, Frieze tried Morgan's phone for the twelfth time. Again it rang with no response.

"Frieze," came Chambers's pissy voice. "I need you to tell me something good."

"No answer from Morgan," she said. "He's not going to pick up."

"Goddamn it," he said, kicking a plastic Gatorade bottle down the street. "And where is the goddamn rescue helicopter?"

"On their way," said Nolan. "ETA ten minutes."

"It should have been here *twenty minutes ago.* Nolan! Do we have the information on Soroush?"

"The Iranian embassy is not forthcoming," said Nolan. "State Department is pushing on that front. Meanwhile, we have CIA reports. I'm sending them your way now."

"What about the explosives teams?" asked Chambers.

"We're a few minutes from being able to breach," said Frieze.

"Have them ready to go on our signal. We're timing this to the rescue of the President. I don't want those hostages in there one minute longer than is necessary."

1:48 p.m.

Alex Morgan clutched the MP7 in clammy hands as she stood flat against the wall of the flight of stairs that led up to the catwalk. She had gone all the way up there looking for her father, only to find that he was downstairs in the concourse. She made her way down slowly, so that she wouldn't be heard or bump into the attackers.

The MP7 felt awkward in her hands. She had gone with her father to the shooting range before, but this was heavier than a handgun, and she had no idea what the accuracy or recoil would be like. She hoped she wouldn't have to fire.

She was out of her depth.

She heard the movement ahead of her, right outside the control room. She listened as they passed, counting three, from the sound of the footsteps.

She waited until they had gone through the threshold to creep around the corner and stand at the door. In the control room, mere feet from the door, were two armed men and her father, with their backs to her.

"Freeze," she said. "And drop 'em." She punctuated this by cocking the handle. The men tensed up but didn't turn around. "I said drop them."

The men unslung their submachine guns. A victorious grin was forming on her lips when rough hands grabbed her from behind. The MP7 was wrenched from her hand and she was pushed aside, stumbling into a desk.

"Now, who is this?" said the man behind her in a cool British accent. "And what is she doing here?"

Alex turned to look at him, the tall, steel-gazed leader of the terrorists. The man who Ramadani had called Soroush.

She stood in defiant silence against his cold authority. He ran his hands over her pockets, and she pushed them away, which led him to punch her in the stomach. Pain rang in her head and bile surged up her throat, leaving her doubled over and retching. He reached into her back pants pocket and pulled out her student ID.

"Alexandra *Morgan*," he said, looking at her father. "Do I detect a family resemblance?"

Through tearing eyes, Alex saw the fury on her father's

face. Soroush grabbed her by the hair and bent her over against the table, cheek against the cool smooth surface. An *I love New York* snow globe sat inches from her face, obscuring most of her view. She struggled but couldn't get free. Soroush then gripped her left arm and pinned her hand. He released her hair, and she looked back at him to see that he had drawn a black serrated folding knife from his pocket.

"I was going to torture you," Soroush said to her father. "But I like this better." He grabbed her index finger, pulling it back so hard it felt like he'd broken it, and she screamed in pain. He set the knife against the base of her finger. "Where is Navid Ramadani?"

"Don't tell him *shit,* Dad," said Alex, through sobs of pain and fear.

"Quiet, love, the adults are talking," said Soroush. "Morgan. Where? And if you send me up a blind alley, I will cut off her finger. Next, it might be her pretty little nose."

She could hear her father's heavy breathing.

"Don't," she said. "Don't tell him."

"Suit yourself," said Soroush. Alex took a deep breath and braced for the pain.

"No!" Morgan roared. "Don't. I'll tell you. I'll tell you. Just let her go."

"No, Dad," she said. "You can't do this. Not because of me."

"Quiet," her father said. "You're not the one who decides. He's up in the clock. You get up there through the door in the conference room up those stairs."

Soroush relaxed his hold on her and drew the knife away. "If you are lying, it will be more than a finger."

"What did you do?" Alex said. "Dad, what did you do?"

Soroush spoke in Fasrsi to one of his men, who ran toward the situation room. Soroush and the other guard backed off, giving them some space. Her father bent over her and ran his hand through her hair. "I would cause World War Three if it meant saving you," he whispered to her.

"Dad, no . . ."

"Now I'm going to get you out of here," he said. "Get ready to run."

He took the snow globe from the desk and threw it at the man with the submachine gun. That was her cue. To the sound of shattering glass, Alex Morgan ran out the door with her father close behind.

2:09 p.m.

"The chopper's making its approach," said Nolan. They all moved outside, everyone who was not engaged at their workstation, all looking up with nervous anticipation. Frieze could hear whispered prayers around her. She turned and saw that Peter Conley was standing next to her. He caught her eye and took her hand in his. They were large and calloused. The gesture carried more comfort than she'd like to admit.

Squinting against the blue sky, she spotted the chopper once it cleared the surrounding buildings, an AS365 Dauphin painted red and white. It began its slow descent until it came to a stop, hovering in place a few yards above the ornate Tiffany clock. The window on the clock face was already open, but no one came out.

They waited interminable minutes for the figure of the President to appear. It was Conley who said it first.

"There's no one there."

The undeniable fact sank in. Chambers threw a clipboard against the pavement.

"What the hell do we do now?" asked Frieze.

"Now we hit them hard," said Chambers. "Nolan, are the teams ready to breach the entrances?"

"Yes, sir. The explosives are in place."

"Have them be in position and hold for my order. Let's smoke out those sons of bitches."

2:18 p.m.

The desk squealed as Paiman pushed it against the outer door of the control room. Soroush watched from the window of the situation room. He had decided not to have him go after Morgan and his daughter, but to wait for Masud to bring down Ramadani. That was the prime target. Morgan was nothing more than a distraction, a rock in his shoe. From behind him, Soroush heard the clamor of the two men descending a steel ladder. Ramadani emerged first from the door, visible through the floor-to-ceiling window of the raised situation room. Masud came next.

"Give me the cell phone you took from Morgan," said Soroush as Masud escorted Ramadani down the stairs. Soroush took the Nokia brick phone from Paiman and hit redial. It rang twice, and then a man picked up.

"This is Chambers. Morgan, where is Ramadani?"

"I'm afraid I have some bad news," said Soroush. "Morgan is gone, and we have custody of Navid Ramadani now."

"Who is this?"

"I will now offer you proof," said Soroush. He held the phone near Ramadani's mouth. "Speak."

"This is President Navid Ramadani. I am a hostage to—"

Soroush pulled away the phone before he could say the name and backhanded the President. "You come in now," he said, "and he dies. Along with as many other innocent bystanders we can take with us."

2:34 p.m.

Morgan led Alex to the safest place he could think of inside Grand Central—underground. He tramped down the steel staircase toward the basement from which he'd come, above Track 61. He felt tired. His legs were weak. Now that they were away from danger, his pace slowed and he felt the deep weariness of the day.

"Dad," Alex whispered. "I'm sorry. I didn't mean for that to happen. I swear, I—"

"Don't," he said. "You risked everything to save me. I can't blame you for that. I did the same. I did worse."

"Dad . . ."

They reached the short service hallway where Morgan had hidden from the MTA police earlier that day, with its twisting pipes. It seemed so long ago now.

"It's okay," said Morgan. "I just need to sit down for a while."

He rested against the cool concrete wall, shirt clinging to his back with sweat. He closed his eyes, shutting out the dim light. The only sound came from Alex, sitting opposite him and sobbing.

2:49 p.m.

Soroush sat at the conference table and reclined in the mesh office chair. Morgan's cell phone continued to ring, as it had for the past half hour. He regarded Ramadani, sitting across from him, and his lips broke into a victorious grin. Ramadani sat, impassive, no emotion etched onto his face. But Soroush saw that he was tired, shoulders low, bags under his eyes.

"You haven't won," said Ramadani.

"Haven't I?"

"You are stuck in a train station with the entire United States security apparatus parked outside," said Ramadani. "How do you think you will fare?"

Soroush grinned.

"Give up, Shir. Turn yourself in. I will fight for extradition and give you a pardon in Iran. The madness can stop here."

"You are weak," said Soroush. "And a traitor. It is no wonder you cannot discern real devotion."

"You can't possibly survive this."

"Even if I don't," said Soroush, "the Islamic Republic will prevail." He took up the ringing cell phone and picked up. "Your persistence is touching," he said.

"We just want to start a conversation," said Chambers, the FBI man. "Find out if you need anything in there. Maybe get some of the injured hostages out."

"I am not an amateur bank robber," said Soroush. "I don't make conversation. I don't make compromises. I make demands."

"And we'd like to know what those are so we can start working on getting you what you want."

"I want you to send in a representative," he said. "With a cell phone, nothing more. No guns, no wires. We will open the Lexington Avenue passage for this representative to pass, and we can begin our 'conversation.'"

"Okay, we can work with that," Chambers said.

"Good. Let me remind you that we have access to all CCTV feeds. If you attempt to come in, we will begin killing hostages, starting with Ramadani. Is that clear?"

2:55 p.m.

The Pershing Square Café was in an uproar, people trying to shout over each other to get the information out to every one of the agencies represented there.

"Give me a list of hostage negotiators!" Chambers yelled out to an NYPD liaison. Lisa Frieze tapped Chambers's arm

"Let me go, sir," said Frieze.

"What?" he turned to her in surprise, his blond mustache twitching.

She adjusted her poise toward greater confidence, shoulders back and chin up. "I want to go in. With your permission, sir."

He shook his head and opened his mouth to speak, but

she interrupted him. "I've trained for this. I'm close to the situation. I've been here at the heart of it from the beginning. I'm the right one for the job."

He turned to Nolan. "Am I insane for considering this?"

"She makes a strong argument," said Nolan. "She knows everything that's going on. It'll be hard to get an outside negotiator up to speed on all these details."

Chambers frowned and rubbed his temples. Staring her in the eyes, he said, "I need to know that you're ready for this."

"I'm ready, sir," she said.

"If you break down in there, it's my ass."

"Send me in," she said.

3:11 p.m.

Frieze took timorous steps through the Lexington Avenue doorway to face the thick steel door. She gave an "OK" signal to Nolan, who stood at a distance outside, flanked by dozens of NYPD officers and more than a few sharpshooters. She stood there a few seconds before the door rumbled open, only about waist high. She crouched and passed underneath it into the granite interior of the terminal, and the door rumbled closed behind her.

She hurried past the deserted shops, so eerie in their emptiness. Her footsteps echoed in the silence. A man appeared at the end of the passage, by the looks of him Iranian, holding an HK MP7.

"Arms out," he said. She complied, cell phone in her right hand. He pawed at her shirt, her breasts and between her legs, looking for a wire. There was no lewdness in the act, just callous disregard. "Turn around. All the way, like a ballerina." He finished his inspection. "Good. Follow me."

He took her to the south side, into a service hallway and up to the control room, and into some kind of conference room, all of which she recognized from poring over photographs and floor plans outside. At the conference room table, seated in fancy office chairs, she saw Soroush and a face she recognized.

"Ms. Frieze," said Soroush. "Meet Mr. Navid Ramadani, President of Iran."

"It's an honor, sir," she said.

"I wish it had been under less strange circumstances, Ms. Frieze," said Ramadani.

"I'd like you to confirm to your people outside that Ramadani is alive," said Soroush. He looked like he did in his pictures, with carefully trimmed facial hair, all sharp angles. There was a coolness about him, even in this situation.

Wasting no time Frieze made the call.

"Chambers."

"This is Frieze," she said. "I'm inside. Ramadani is alive and in one piece. I'm with him now."

"Good," said Soroush. "I would like you now to relay our demands to your people on the outside." He picked up a clipboard from the table and tilted it toward him. "First, fifty million dollars in unmarked bills. Second, ground transportation to John F. Kennedy Airport. Third, a private jet, fully fueled, and safe passage out of United States airspace."

She repeated the demands into the phone. "Did you get that?"

"Got it," said Chambers. "You know what to do."

"I've put through the request with my superior," said Frieze. "Now we'd like a show of good faith from you. Release some of your civilian hostages—the wounded and the children."

"This is not a negotiation, Ms. Frieze," said Soroush. "These are demands."

"My superiors—"

"I know precisely how your superiors operate," said Soroush. "They will stall until they get a chance to strike. So we will do this. You will bring the money by four p.m. or I will start sending out the children in pieces. The transport will be arranged by five p.m. or the same will happen—ten children every ten minutes until the demands are met."

Soroush waited until Frieze relayed this to Chambers.

"Goddamn it," said Chambers. "Tell him we'll work on it."

"He says they'll work on it."

"The lives of the hostages are in his hands," said Soroush, holding up his palms.

4:00 p.m.

The blast door opened once again waist high, and Lisa Frieze bent down to pass under it. She found the two black duffel bags at the entrance, as they had promised. Nolan was there, looking at her as if to ask her, *Are you okay?* She nodded, then turned her attention to the bags. She tried to pick them up, but some quick mental math told her that they weighed about one hundred pounds each. She settled for dragging them through the threshold one at a time. The door closed, shutting out the grayish light that filtered from the outside, leaving only the yellow illumination of the Vanderbilt passage. Two men grabbed one bag each and carried them away, back toward the control room.

4:02 p.m.

Dan Morgan opened his eyes to his daughter saying, "Dad. Dad," in a persistent and level tone.

"I'm awake," he said, blinking in the darkened underground hallway.

"Dad, what are we going to do?" she demanded, urgency in her voice. "They have the President."

"We need to find out what they're planning," he said, bracing against the wall to stand, voice thick from sleep. "We're unarmed. There's no use coming at this blind, too. You wouldn't happen to have a mirror, would you?"

"No, I—" Alex began, then remembered she did—she

never returned the mirror she'd been lent earlier to fix up her ear. "Will this do?"

"Perfect," he said, grabbing and pocketing it. He then held her arm tight. "Do I even have to tell you to stay?"

"No, Dad. I won't budge from here, I promise."

"Good girl," he said, hugging her. He then turned to go upstairs. He made his way to the control room, keeping to the service passages. At each turn, he held the mirror around the corner to check whether it was clear. On the hallway leading to the control room, he saw two men, lurching with the weight of the duffel bags they were carrying. They were so heavy that the men needed both hands to carry them, leaving them disarmed, MP7s dangling at their backs.

Like candy from a baby.

Morgan waited for them, flat against the wall. They passed, too concerned with the weight of the bags to spare a glance his way. Once they were ahead of him, Morgan stepped out and grabbed the nearest man's submachine gun, still attached to the strap, releasing the safety and sending a burst of bullets into his back point-blank. The bullets erupted in a mist of blood. Morgan held on to the man's sidearm, which he pulled from the holster as the man fell. Morgan raised the gun and shot just as the other terrorist wheeled about to face him. The bullet burrowed in his neck. He gasped and gurgled.

Morgan took this second man's MP7 and tucked the handgun into his waist.

Then he got the hell out of there.

4:07 p.m.

Soroush was just as surprised as she was, Frieze noted, to hear the gunfire. He and two of his men set off at a run from the situation room toward the door to the service hallways, and he motioned for her to follow. They halted halfway down a corridor, and she soon saw why. The two men who had taken the money were lying dead on the ground. One of the submachine guns was gone.

One of the men, whom she heard called Zubin, turned to her with fury in his eyes.

"It wasn't my guys who did this," said Frieze, intuiting his thoughts.

"Liar," he said in a hushed whisper.

"I'm the only one you let inside, remember?"

"Back to the control room," said Soroush. "Everyone."

They brought the bags with them, Frieze walking forward with a gun pointed at her head.

She turned first into the control room to find four more of Soroush's men inside.

"Two more dead," said Soroush behind her. "Vahid and Ilyas."

"Was it Morgan?" asked one of them.

Soroush just glared.

"It no longer matters," said the man named Masud. "The bombs have been planted along the perimeter of the main concourse."

"Good," said Soroush. Frieze had no time to react before the knife pierced her gut just over her right hip. Soroush pushed it deeper and upward, then pulled it out. It was an odd feeling, the knife tearing up her insides. She gasped at the pain and wondered which organ he had breached.

She braced her fall with her arms, hands hitting the carpet. A wave of nausea washed over her and she retched, but nothing came out. She flopped on her back, and the world swam before her eyes. Who would have thought, being stabbed brought no flashbacks. She even felt a strange calm, staring blankly at the ceiling, eyes drawn to a lightbulb, bright and searing.

"Zubin," she heard Soroush say, as if far away. "It's time to prepare our escape. Bring the drivers together at the platform. Time to tell them what their part in this will be."

Frieze didn't have the energy to turn to see the men file

out, taking the Iranian president with them. All she could do was stare at the light as it seemed to become brighter and brighter.

4:13 p.m.

Morgan waited inside a utility closet for the procession of terrorists to pass him by. Noting the absence of the FBI woman, he made his way to where they had come from—the control room, where he found Frieze on the ground, a small puddle of blood thick and almost black on the gray carpet.

"Still breathing," he said to himself.

Morgan further ripped open the tear that the knife had made on her shirt and pressed down on the wound.

"Who are you?" she wondered.

"Dan Morgan," he said. "Nice to meet you."

"You're Dan Morgan?" A faint smile played on her lips. "Peter Conley speaks highly of you."

"I need to get you out of here," he said.

"No." Her voice was breathy and weak. "You need to stop them. They're taking the trains. That's how they're getting out. You need to stop them."

Morgan bit his lip. "I can't leave you," he said.

"Send someone in for me, then. But you can't let them win. You can't, Morgan. They've planted bombs. They're not going to leave any survivors. Tell my people. We need to get the civilians out."

"Hang in there," he said. "I'll send help for you."

Morgan looked around the room until he found a cell phone that had been left behind in a jacket by one of the staff. He then dashed off to get back to Alex, running through service tunnels until he was at the landing of the stairs that led down to the basement.

"It's me," he called out to her. "I'm coming down."

She emerged from behind the steam duct. "Dad, are you okay? Are we leaving now?"

"I'm all right," he said. "You're leaving. I'm not. You really wanted to do something? Here's your chance."

"Anything, Dad."

"You remember Peter Conley," he said. "I want you to call him at this number." He drew the cell phone he'd taken from the Control Center and dialed in the call function. "Have them come in by any means necessary. All the hostages need to be evacuated, and they need to send in the bomb squad. Do you understand?"

She nodded.

"Then go," he said.

"What about you?"

"I'm going after them."

4:19 p.m.

Alex Morgan ran upstairs to the Grand Central catwalk. Panting and catching her breath, standing flat against the corner, she dialed the number her father had given her.

"Conley."

"Peter! It's Alex. Alex Morgan."

"Alex? Where's your father?"

"He went after Soroush and the President," she said.

"Are you safe?"

"Safe enough," she said. "But I need your help. They've wired the main concourse with hidden bombs. I don't know where they are. But I know the Iranians plan to blow all the hostages up when they leave. Peter, there's more than a thousand people in here."

"Wait a second."

It wasn't one, but forty seconds, all of which Alex spent drumming her fingers on the reinforced glass of the catwalk window.

"Okay," said Conley. "We're going to blow the doors open. I need you to talk to the people inside. Can you get to the PA system?"

"I think so."

"Tell everyone to stay clear of the doors until after the blasts, and only then start evacuation."

"Okay," she said. "Peter, there's one more thing. There's a woman in here. Her name is Lisa Frieze. She's been stabbed. She's in the control room, bleeding out."

"I know her," he said. "I'll send someone for her as soon as we get inside."

4:24 p.m.

Shir Soroush walked down the line of eleven drivers like a drill sergeant carrying out an inspection. They stood in fear, some frozen, some fidgeting, some outright trembling.

Fear was a good thing to inspire in people.

Facing the drivers was a row of eleven children chosen from among the hostages—one for each driver.

"Each of you is going to take your train, and you're going to go to your destination," he said. "You will not stop at any stations, and you will not make contact with anyone on the outside."

He motioned to the children.

"Look at the child directly in front of you," said Soroush. His man, with a Sharpie, began writing a number on each child's forehead—each, Morgan realized, corresponding to a platform. "That is *your* child. You, and only you, are responsible for it. We will be taking them with us on our train. Each of your trains has been equipped with a GPS device." He held up a tablet with a map on it, each train represented by a glowing green dot. "If you stop your train, for any reason, we will kill this child. If you contact anyone, we will kill this child."

Soroush let it sink in as each man looked in the face of the child he would be responsible for.

"It's time to go to your trains now," he said. "We leave in two minutes."

4:30 p.m.

Dan Morgan, flat against the wall that separated the lower concourse from the platforms, looked at the Lost and Found window. He needed outside support if he hoped to stop the Iranians from escaping. Which meant he needed a phone.

He sprinted to the Lost and Found window and jumped through. He rifled through the cell phones as fast as he could, holding the power button of each for two seconds to see which would turn on. Finally, he found an LG flip phone that turned on, batteries charged to more than half.

Morgan heard the whining of the trains as they began to move all at once. He'd seen Soroush board the train on Track 114, halfway across the lower level. He turned into the passage to the platforms so fast that he banged into the wall. The train was already moving.

Morgan raced down the platform after it. In a few seconds, it would be moving faster than him, and gone beyond all hope.

Morgan sprinted, closing the distance between him and the last car, but less so as the train picked up speed.

He reached the back, so close he could touch it, when he realized that he and the train were moving at the same speed, and the train would only be going faster. This would be the last chance he'd get. Morgan swerved to the right, sailing off the platform and grabbing hold of the bar next to the back door of the train, landing his feet on the narrow ledge that jutted out, swinging and banging against the train with his right side.

Stabilizing himself, Morgan looked through the scratched window and made eye contact with one of Soroush's men, guarding the last car of the train.

He swung out of the way, holding on to the bar with his left hand. The bullets from the man's MP7 pierced the door and shattered the window of the back door.

Not bulletproof. Good to know.

Hanging on, Morgan reached with his free right hand to his back, where the Glock 37 he'd lifted from one of the Iranians was tucked into his pants.

He raised it and let loose two bullets against the glass of the side window, swinging away to avoid the shards of glass that rained down onto the tracks. He looked inside the train car to see that the man had fallen on the train aisle. With a little more time to look, he checked to see that no one else was there. At least he had the time to work this out now.

Morgan tried the door, but it was locked. He had no way of entering gracefully. *Window it is.* He cleared the broken glass that was stuck to the window frame with the barrel of the gun. Then he raised his leg and, crouching, hopped through.

Morgan hoped that the noise of the moving train had masked the gunfire.

He walked to the man, lying faceup on the train floor, panting like a wounded animal. He looked up at Morgan with fear in his eyes. Morgan took his MP7, tugging at the sling to get it over the man's head, and put it over his own shoulder. He also took the earbud from the terrorist's radio communicator and inserted it into his own ear. No one was speaking, which meant they had not heard the noise.

Morgan then pulled the cell phone from his pocket and checked for service. No bars. That would have to wait until they were out in open air.

No way to go now but forward.

4:33 p.m.

Alex Morgan scanned the crowd, which was already restless and loud. A few of the braver souls had already stood up, though they were reluctant to move. It took her some thirty seconds to find who she was looking for. Grateful that he wasn't far away, she ran among the kneeling people until she reached—

"Clark!"

The boy turned to look at her in surprise.

"Alex! I thought you were dead, you were gone so long! Where were you?"

"Never mind that," she said. "Come on."

He followed her away from the crowd. People looked at her in puzzlement, and several were emboldened by her presence to stand up as well and start walking. *Damn it,* she swore. *Should have thought of that.* Some people called out to her, but she paid them no heed.

"Listen," she said to Clark on her tail, "I need you to do something for me." She gave him his instructions. "Got it? Think you can do that?"

"Yeah," he said. "Where are you going?"

"Just something I got to do." She ran upstairs back to the control room and found Lisa Frieze, gasping for air and losing blood, holding her bunched-up jacket against the wound. She was trembling, although Alex didn't know whether it was from cold or shock.

"Hi," she said. "I'm Dan Morgan's daughter, Alex. I'm here to help." She took over the compress, letting Frieze relax her slack hand. It frightened Alex how pale she looked.

The tri-tone of the PA played over the loudspeakers, and Alex heard Clark's voice begin. "I, uh . . ." Then, with a burst of confidence, "Help is on the way. The police are going to get everyone out of here soon. But for now, we need everyone to get away from the big steel doors. Please help anyone who needs it to stay clear of them. You should put at least thirty feet of distance between yourselves and the doors. I repeat, for your own safety, *stay away from the doors.*"

Alex cradled Lisa Frieze's head. Her lips curled into a smile of pride. *Well done, Clark.*

"It's going to be okay," she told the FBI agent. "Help is on its way."

"You're a good kid," pronounced Frieze.

4:42 p.m.

Morgan made his way toward the front of the train at a half-crouch. It was him against seven remaining men, and the element of surprise was all he had to keep him and the President of Iran alive.

He saw the movement two cars ahead. People. Gunmen. He had to wait. He stood no chance without help and without a plan. He sat in the corner seat and waited for two minutes until, from the darkness of the tunnel, the train emerged out into the blue light of evening.

He took out the flip phone and dialed Conley.

"It's Morgan," he said when his friend picked up. "I need your help. Soroush sent out lots of decoy trains. I'm on the right one—the one Ramadani is on. Can you trace my location from this call?"

"No problem," said Conley. "I'll have Zeta run it and send the choppers to converge on it."

"No!" said Morgan. "Do that, if you want to get a whole bunch of children killed."

"What should I do, then?" he asked.

"Find the train first," said Morgan. "But don't move in. Leave it to me, at least for now. If I don't contact you within ten minutes, that means I'm dead, so by all means, send in the cavalry."

"Okay," said Conley.

"Meanwhile, I need you to do something for me."

4:58 p.m.

Alex Morgan felt more than she heard the serial blasts that brought down the emergency doors. A cheer from the concourse filtered in dim and faraway through the service hallways to the control room.

"Hear that?" she said to the delirious Frieze. "That's our rescue. That's the sound of us being saved."

Frieze mumbled something through pale, trembling lips.

It was some three minutes before Alex heard the sound of heavy boots approaching. Three firemen appeared at the door carrying a stretcher.

"Here," called Alex, waving to get their attention. They tramped over to her and laid Frieze on the stretcher. They lifted in a smooth practiced motion and carried her out. These guys weren't wasting time, and she felt like she shouldn't, either. She walked after them, keeping pace. Once they emerged into the concourse, they ran into the crowds, which were packed at every exit. The firemen moved toward the Lexington passage, Alex following. The crowd parted for the stretcher to pass, but Alex didn't feel right taking advantage, so she hung back. She looked backward toward the main concourse, where the last stragglers were moving into the passage. She ran back to help usher everyone out to the exits.

That's when she saw him. A little boy, about six, wandering out from the ticket machine nook across the concourse. Somehow, he'd been missed, left behind, and he was ambling toward the giant clock. The bombs would go off at any moment.

There was no time to think. Alex tore out at a dead run toward the kid. Hardly slowing down, she bent down to pick him up. She grunted and he squealed at the impact. He was crying as she ran after the evacuees in the Vanderbilt tunnel. The kid wailed in her left ear. She was sweating, her legs feeling heavier and heavier.

She was within sight of the outside doors, people still funneling outside, when the blast knocked her off her feet and sent them both sprawling. She looked all around her, woozy and disoriented, but in one piece. The child she had saved was a few feet ahead of her, sitting down, crying, but there was no blood. She looked back at the main concourse, where concrete and twisted brass littered the ground. No one was there.

A fireman helped her to her feet while another scooped up the child. They ran together until she finally reached the street, into the blessed cool air and the darkness of the city illuminated in yellow light.

5:13 p.m.

Morgan stood against the far wall of the train car, next to the door that would lead to the restaurant car. From what he'd gathered, the children were being held there, guarded by two men. The phone vibrated in Morgan's pocket. He flipped it open and held it to his ear.

"The chopper is ready to broadcast the signal you asked for," said Conley. "Are you ready?"

"Just waiting for your okay."

"Ten seconds," said Conley.

Morgan hung up and turned the volume to his radio receiver to the lowest setting short of muting it. He put the MP7 in his right hand.

The noise came as a quiet high-pitched hum—a feedback loop broadcast to every one of Soroush's men's communicators, each, if turned to a reasonable volume, now playing an intolerable loud feedback tone. He pushed the handle on the first door between cars, which sprung open on its own, then the second.

The two men, as expected, were distracted by the noise. One of them was to Morgan's right, having looked up from tapping the device just long enough to see down the muzzle of Morgan's handgun as he fired two bullets right-handed. With the MP7 in his left hand, Morgan took aim at the other, who was near the middle of the car, behind the bar. He had removed his earpiece, which he dropped onto the counter as he reached for his gun. Morgan already had the MP7 trained on him, and released a burst, hitting the man full in the chest.

That's when he registered the high-pitched screaming of the hostages.

"I'm here to rescue you," he said. "I need you to do what I say. Go back the way I came, all the way to the back of the train as fast as you can."

One girl, taller than the rest, got up with a determined look on her face. "Come on, everyone," she said. "Let's get out of here."

Morgan kept an eye on the far door, edging his way toward it against the current of children. Someone was bound to come investigate the noise. He crouched behind the bar for the inevitable. It was thirty seconds before he heard the door to the front of the bar car sliding open.

All he had to do was wait. He felt their footsteps on the floor as they passed him. He stood once their backs were to him and shot two bursts from the MP7. The men fell to the floor of the train.

Two were left, one of them Soroush. Who would be expecting him, with the President of Iran as a human shield. The odds were stacked against him, and Morgan couldn't trust this to chance.

He dialed Conley again.

"Conley? Surprise is blown. We're going to have to take this in a different route. This is going to require some preparation."

5:31 p.m.

Morgan, still crouched behind the bar, shifted his weight from his right to his left. He had spent a long time crouched here, waiting as the gears turned outside the train and as everything was being made ready for the plan. Soroush didn't come, as Morgan had expected. It was too big a risk. All that was left was him and his second-in-command. He was scared and cornered, which made him equal parts vulnerable and dangerous.

Morgan checked his watch again, although he didn't have to. He knew it was time. He dialed Conley.

"Are we ready?" Morgan asked.

"As we'll ever be."

Morgan dropped the MP7, the Glock, and the cell phone on the floor of the train and stood up. Two cars between him and Soroush, no more. He raised his opened hands and crept forward through the first intervening car, hands raised and visible. Soroush's second-in-command caught sight of him while he was barely halfway down the first car and came through the double doors to meet him, MP7 raised chest high at Morgan.

He hadn't shot on sight. That was something.

"Hey," said Morgan. "No weapons, see?" He turned around to show his back.

"Zubin!" Soroush yelled out from the other car. "Bring him here."

Zubin tilted his head for Morgan to go, keeping the MP7 trained on him. "Go," he said. Morgan did, moving into the first train car where Soroush sat with Ramadani. The Iranian President met Morgan's eyes for half a second, nothing left in his eyes but resignation. He was preparing to die.

"Take a seat," said Soroush. "You've had a good run, Morgan. I think we can sit together and salute your defeat."

"Is that right?" he said, taking his seat opposite Soroush. He rested against the seat back, crossing his legs in a lounging position. Zubin sat a few seats back, clutching his gun, not taking his eyes off Morgan.

"Of course," said Soroush. The triumph in his voice was palpable. "What, are you talking about the men you killed? They were expendable, everyone is. All that matters is the cause, and the cause will succeed. Surveillance is divided among the different trains. We will make our escape soon, and we will not be found. And even if we are . . . When I say lives are not important, I include myself. I am willing to die for my cause, Mr. Morgan. All I need to succeed is for people to believe I was innocent of this. And they will. The US government will be blamed. The CIA. Even if we are all killed, Mr. Morgan, we win."

"That's one way things can go down today," said Morgan.

Soroush shook his head with a condescending expression on his face. "You are a man of action, Mr. Morgan. But I am a man of intellect. My planning has been impeccable."

"You didn't count on me."

Soroush chuckled. "In the game of chess, it is common for the novice to take a few important pieces from the expert player. It is the sacrifice the master knows he must make to achieve his victory. You may have taken some of my pieces off the board, but even those moves were steps along the way to my checkmate. The only reason you are still alive is so that you can witness your ultimate defeat before you die."

Morgan felt the tug of inertia pulling his body forward, and suppressed a grin. Ramadani looked up in alarm, and Morgan saw a flicker of hope in his eyes.

"Why are we slowing down?" asked Zubin. "What is happening?"

"Go ask the driver!" Soroush demanded.

Zubin opened the door to the driver's cabin. "Why are we slowing down?"

"There's another train in the way, up ahead in that station. If I don't stop, we'll ram it."

Soroush looked at Morgan with smoldering rage in his eyes. "What did you do?"

"I invited a few more people to witness my ultimate defeat," said Morgan.

The train rolled into the station and slowly came to a stop. A barrage of camera flashes hit the car. Video cameras—at least half a dozen—were pointed through the windows

"Game over," said Morgan. "If you kill him now, everyone knows it was you. It'll be on every news channel, on every website, uploaded a thousand times on the Internet. You could have called it an American conspiracy if you did it quietly, away from the media. You can't kill him for the whole world to see."

Soroush was a deer in the headlights for a split second. Then the cool, cruel clarity that ruled his mind came into focus once more.

"Maybe you are right," said Soroush. "But I can kill you." He raised his Beretta level with Morgan's head.

5:55 p.m.

Morgan heard the sound of cracking glass behind him as he saw the bullet burrow itself in Soroush's left shoulder, splashing the window behind him with a curtain of red. It was followed by two others, taking out Zubin.

Morgan lunged for Soroush, knocking him against the train's window, but he held tight to the gun, trying to bring the muzzle against Morgan's head. Morgan brought his head down hard against Soroush's nose. This knocked the Iranian back and Morgan grabbed at the gun with his left hand, pinning it against the train window. In close quarters, he felt something hard against Soroush's hip. *Knife.*

Morgan swiveled, opening up space for him to reach for Soroush's holster, but lost his hold on the gun. He pulled out the knife as Soroush swung the Beretta back around against Morgan. Morgan plunged the knife upward, deep into Soroush's neck. He gurgled, face contorting in fury, struggling to bring the gun up to hit Morgan. The gun dropped first from his slack hand, and then he fell to his knees and landed facedown on the floor of the train car.

Someone opened the door to the outside, letting a blast of cold air into the car.

"On the ground!" said a man in full tactical gear. Morgan kneeled as he saw others moving down the length of the train.

Morgan knew the drill. He put his hands on the back of his head and lay prone against the corrugated floor of the train car, a piece of gum trampled into flatness inches from his face. He was handcuffed while he sensed the movement of the Iranian President being ushered out by heavily armed men.

He grinned against the cold train floor. *Checkmate, asshole.*

6:05 p.m.

"How was that for a day out with your old man?" Morgan asked his daughter.

Alex, riding next to Morgan in the ambulance, cried through a smile. She looked haggard, about as bad as he felt. Her short brown hair was thick with sweat, and she had dark bags under her eyes. Her left ear was bandaged. "You troll," she giggled.

"Did you call your mother?"

"I did," said Alex. "She said she was worried sick. She'll meet us at the hospital."

"How about a steak house instead?" asked Morgan. "I'm starved. Tell the driver. If we turn around now, we might still make it to Peter Luger in time for dinner."

"Much as I'd like to," she laughed, "the government guys were pretty adamant that you needed to go to the emergency room."

"Wouldn't want to contradict the US government, now, would we?" Morgan lay back and closed his eyes. "Do you know anything about Lisa Frieze?"

The ambulance swayed. "Peter said she's in ICU, but stable," she said. "I guess they're saying she'll make it."

"She's a tough one," said Morgan. "I'll give her that."

"And what about me?" Alex asked. "I think I've earned some extra privileges today, haven't I?"

"Are you kidding? After today, you're not leaving the house again until you're forty."

They laughed, and then sat in silence together in the swaying ambulance until sleep overtook them.

ACKNOWLEDGMENTS

First I want to thank my beautiful and patient wife, Lynn, who has been the driving force behind my writing career from the beginning. She had the foresight to believe in my storytelling ability, is always willing to listen to all my ideas, and has kept me motivated over the past five years. Lynn, without you Dan Morgan would never have made it to the page.

I need to express my gratitude to my dear friend, Dr. Rodney Jones, who has been one of my staunchest supporters for the past four years. He has been a sounding board for many of my ideas, and has read some of the early manuscripts. He traveled with me to New York to do research on this novella, *Twelve Hours*. He has also attended all of my book launch parties and has been at many of my library presentations. I am truly honored to have him as a friend.

Thank you to Dan Brucker, manager of Grand Central Tours. He took us on a two-day tour, showing us many of the secrets of Grand Central Terminal, along with some of the sublevels and secret track that went from Grand Central to the Waldorf Astoria, and much more. Dan, you are amazing!

My appreciation to Special Agent Chris Sinos, from the FBI Office of Public Affairs in New York, for all your help and information as to how the FBI responds to a terror attack as part of a first responder team.

Thanks to both Dan and Deb Sullivan, owners of my local independent book store, The Book Oasis, in Stoneham, Mass. They have been a huge help getting my books out to my readers, both in their shop and at many of my library events.

A special thanks to Mayur Gudka, my webmaster and social media consultant, who has made my life so much easier; and to Sky Wentworth, my local publicist, who has been with me for five years, preparing press releases and arranging for radio and newspaper interviews. You are both valued members of my team and true friends.

Thank you, Lisa Frieze, who I am lucky enough to have as a huge fan. She has not only reads all of my novels but also had beautiful custom cakes decorated with the likeness of the front covers of *Silent Assassin* and *Black Skies* for each of the launch parties. She also started an international fan club for me and developed a website for it. Since we happen to live in the same Massachusetts suburb, we have met several times and have become good friends.

I am extremely grateful to have such a wonderful team at Kensington Publishing. Michaela Hamilton is not only the best editor I could possibly hope for, she has also become a trusted friend. I can't thank Adeola Saul, Arthur Maisel, Alexandra Nicolajsen, and Michelle Forde enough for all their hard work and the invaluable guidance they have provided. Thank you to Steve Zacharius, owner of Kensington, for your vision with the company and for accepting me as part of the Kensington "family."

To my first and only agent, Doug Grad, thank you for all your hard work, persistence, and excellent advice. I consider myself very lucky to have you representing me.

I would also like to recognize and thank bestselling authors Lee Child, John Gilstrap, Mark Sullivan, Meg Gardiner, Michele McPhee, Ben Coes, and Hank Phillippi Ryan for taking the time to read my manuscripts and provide quotes for my books.

I would be remiss not to acknowledge everyone who has bought my books and thank them for being faithful readers of the Dan Morgan thriller series. Without your support I could not continue to write. I always enjoy meeting you at conventions and other events.

Finally, I want to thank my partner in writing and creating my novels, Caio Camargo. He has helped me to translate my stories and characters to the printed page. Again I am fortunate that someone who started out as a consultant is now a dear friend.

I hope all my friends know that like Dan Morgan, I feel that one of the most important attributes in someone is loyalty . . . and I will always be loyal and grateful to them.

For Duty and Honor

This book is dedicated to my daughter, KATIE, who has been the joy in my life since the moment she was born. She is beautiful on the inside and outside. She's kind, considerate, and simply an all-around good person as well as a wonderful mother to my three granddaughters, KATHERINE, CECILIA, and GRACE, whom I adore.

I also want to dedicate this book to my niece LIANNE, who has always had a special place in my life and heart. She has been an unfailing supporter of my writing endeavor.

Chapter One

The prisoner's body was a brick of exhaustion and pain.

Steel cuffs chafed against his raw wrists and ankles, the rough uniform scraping the burns and cuts that lined his arms and legs and pocked his torso. Even under the blackness of his hood, the prisoner smelled stale sweat mingled with his own breath: iron from the blood, acetone from the starvation. He could barely hold himself up against the jolting ride. All that was keeping him upright were the two thick guards at his sides boxing him in.

At the outset, hours ago at the landing strip, the guards were in high spirits, joking and jesting in Russian, which the prisoner could not follow. Whenever he couldn't hold himself up anymore and leaned into one of them or into the front seat, they would box the prisoner's head and laugh, forcing him to sit upright again.

But as they drew nearer to their destination, and the car's heating lost ground against the cold, the guards grew quiet, like there was something grim about the place even to them.

The prisoner swung forward as the jeep came to an abrupt stop, tires on gravel. The doors opened and the spaces on his sides cleared as the men got out, leaving him exposed to the frigid Siberian air. Against this cold, the canvas uniform felt like nothing at all.

The guards unlocked the cuffs and yanked the prisoner out. Too tired to offer any resistance, he walked along, bare feet on the freezing stony ground. Someone pulled off his cowl. He was struck by a hurricane of light that made him so dizzy that he would have vomited, if there were anything in his stomach. It took a moment for the image to stop swimming and resolve itself into the barren landscape of rock and creeping brush lit by a sun low in the sky.

The Siberian tundra.

They prodded him forward. He trudged toward the Brutalist conglomeration of buildings surrounded by tall mesh fences and barbed wire. Prison camp. Gulag.

The prisoner's trembling knee collapsed and he fell on the stony ground. A guard gave him a kick with a heavy, polished leather boot and pulled him to his feet.

They reached the top and entered the *vakhta*, the guardhouse. He passed through the first gate and was searched, rough hands prodding and poking at him. They then opened the second, leading him through, outside, into the yard. His gaze kept down, he saw guards' boots, and massive furry Caucasian shepherds, each taller than a full-grown man's waist. He didn't look up to see the bare concrete guard towers that overlooked the terrain for miles around or at the sharpshooters that occupied them.

He was pulled inside the nearest boxy building, walls painted with chipping murals of old Soviet propaganda, apple-cheeked youngsters over fields of grain and brave soldiers of the Red Army standing against the octopus of international capitalism. On the second floor, they knocked on a wooden door.

"Postupat'."

The guards opened the door, revealing an office with a vintage aristocratic desk. They pushed him onto the bare hardwood.

A man stood up with a creak of his chair. The prisoner watched as he approached, seeing from his vantage point only the wingtip oxfords and the hem of his pinstriped gabardine pants, walking around his desk, footsteps echoing in the concrete office.

"Amerikanskiy?"

"Da," a guard answered.

The man crouched, studying the prisoner's face. "You are one of General Suvorov's, are you not?" His voice was deep and filled with gravel and a heavy Russian accent.

The prisoner didn't respond—not that he needed to.

"You are tough, if he did not break you." He stood, brushing off unseen dust from his suit jacket. "And if he had broken you, you would be dead already. I am Nevsky, the warden. Welcome to my prison."

The prisoner looked up at last and saw a thickset jowly man, with a nose like a potato, bloodshot eyes, and the ruddy swollen face of an alcoholic.

"We have no official name, but we call it *Pokoynitskaya*. Do you know what that means?"

The warden opened a cabinet and poured himself a glass of vodka.

"Charnel house. Because everyone in here is dead meat." He emitted a grotesque throaty laugh and tipped the glass into his mouth. "Stand up," he said, slamming the glass onto the side table. The prisoner couldn't muster the energy to. "I said *stand up*."

Oxford wingtips sunk into the prisoner's side. He doubled in pain, groaning.

"Up!"

Bracing himself on the desk, he staggered to his feet.

"You will learn to do as you are told here." He poured another glass of vodka. "Look out the window. What do you see?"

A broad barred window overlooked the tundra, where it was too cold for any trees to grow. A vast bare expanse of low grasses, with mountains rising from the flatness far in the distance.

"The answer is nothing. I will not tell you my prison is impregnable. In fact, we have had breakouts. If they get past the fence, we take bets on who will hit him. But the few that get away, nature takes care of. We find them dead in the wasteland within a few days."

The warden grabbed the prisoner's arm, feeling his muscles. "Strong. That will not last." He slapped the prisoner hard on the buttocks. "This is what your life will be. You will mine all day—and the days of the Arctic summer are long. You will be questioned, if the order comes. That will not be pleasant. But mostly, you will work." As he spoke, the warden circled the prisoner, who kept his eyes down. "You will waste away, and your mind will break." The warden knelt close to him and whispered in his ear, his rancid alcoholic breath filling the prisoner's nostrils. "And one day, you will die here, forgotten."

The prisoner's face contorted in fury. He lunged for the warden, who stepped back to avoid him. The prisoner stumbled under his own weakness and fell back to the ground.

Nevsky sat down and signed the prisoner's intake papers. "We are done here," he said. He squinted to read the type. "Show Daniel Morgan to his cell."

Chapter Two

Two guards pulled Morgan on shuffling feet outside, back onto the cold-hardened earth, where the harsh wind whipped against his skin. They were in the yard now, a squarish space surrounded by various freestanding structures on all four sides, although he was too dazed to get any kind of clear picture of it. He thought he caught a whiff of something cooking and sheer instinct led him to turn toward its source. The guards yanked him, pulling him into another building, this one squat and single-storied. Like the others, it was built out of worn concrete and had heavy metal doors and thick bars on the windows, all covered in rust.

There were two more guards in there who stripped him of his tattered, bloody clothes and tossed them aside. They shoved him, naked, against a wall of chipped porcelain tiles and stood back as one opened a hose. He gasped as ice-cold water blasted him in the chest, sputtering when it hit his face. They tossed a rough moldy sponge and a cracked bar of caustic soap at his feet and hollered at him, pointing down at them. He bent and picked them up with shivering hands, running the sponge against skin reddened by the cold, his wounds smarting with the chemical burn as he scrubbed himself of weeks of dirt and blood and sweat. The pungent scent made his eyes water as he trembled and flinched from every new blast of frigid water.

When they were satisfied, they shut off the hose and tossed him a thin towel, which he fumbled and dropped on the wet tile floor. They laughed as he ran the now-sodden towel over his skin to get off whatever excess water he could manage. The guards then pulled him, still damp, to the next station, where they sat him down on a splintering stool. One of them turned on a clipper that was at least twenty years old and buzzed like a bumblebee the size of a poodle.

They started with the hair on his head, dense and black with wisps of gray at his temples, which fell on the tiles in thick tufts. They shaved his mustache, the machine tugging at his split lip so that it began to bleed again, and the beard that had grown in since his capture. They worked his way down his body, his hair—*all* his hair—falling about the feet of the stool. Once the guard finished Morgan's legs, he clicked off the machine. Another guard poured a white acrid-smelling delousing powder onto his head and back. It clung to his damp skin and raised a white cloud around him. The guards cackled at Morgan's ensuing coughing fit.

Finally, they handed him a folded-up jumpsuit to put on. It was tan canvas, rough and coarse against his skin, and provided little protection against the cold. After he put it on, they shoved a stinking coat in his hand and gave him cheap cloth shoes, which he pulled over his feet. They were, like his hands, numb from the cold. The guards got impatient at how long the operation was taking and boxed his ear for good measure. Morgan pulled on the coat, which at least offered cover from the wind.

From there he was escorted into the blockhouse. It was single-story and much larger than the building he had just left, with only tiny windows letting precious little light in. There were scratches on the wall, the writings and designs of prisoners with no one else to talk to, who wanted to leave their last mark on the world before disappearing, in an unmarked grave thousands of miles away from home, where those they left behind would never find their bodies, never know what happened to them.

They led him to a room where there were rows of bunks that looked more like shelves, each bed only two wooden boards held up by vertical beams. It smelled lived in, of sweat and piss and mildew. The guard pushed him inside, and he stumbled onto the bare concrete floor.

The guard shoved a blanket, woolen and reeking, into his hand and pointed him to a bare wooden bunk. His, Morgan guessed. Then he gave him a bent tin bowl. "This is your bowl," he said. "You have bowl, you get food. No bowl, no food."

"Where do I keep it?"

The man shrugged. Not his problem. The other men seemed to store them under their bunks, so Morgan put it on his.

"Rest," the guard said.

Morgan didn't need telling twice. He got onto his bunk and collapsed onto the wooden boards. They were hard and uncomfortable, but he was exhausted beyond caring. He pulled on the reeking blanket and slept, clutching the food bowl tight, and dreamed of home.

Chapter Three

Alex Morgan reached upward into darkness and found a handhold in the jutting bricks. She pulled her weight up, finding a new foothold for her left foot. *One, two. Easy does it.*

The warm summer wind lashed against her at this exposed height. One upward gust pulled off her black knitted cap, leaving her short hair whipping against her head. She followed its progress against the light of the streets below as the wind carried it away.

Then she looked down.

Mistake. Big mistake. She grew dizzy and weak and felt her grip slipping. She slapped her face with her free hand.

This is no time to lose your nerve.

She closed her eyes, using the sting on her cheek to center herself, and kept on going. *One, two. One, two.*

Not that she had too much to worry about. She had a slim body and strong arms and legs, and she left everyone else in the dust back at the training camp when it came to climbing. Height aside, this was routine for her.

Alex climbed one more floor and looked to the right at the balcony on level with her. Was this it? She counted from the top. Yes. Twenty-second floor. This was it.

She edged along the jutting bricks the few feet to the balcony and reached out to grab the railing. She stepped onto the ledge and then swung over, breathing a sigh of relief as her feet landed on solid ground.

"Hello, Alex."

She was so startled she leapt six inches into the air. If she had been on the other side of the railing, she'd have fallen off the building.

Diana Bloch, in a maroon silk robe, stood up from a deck chair. "I'd just like you to be aware that one of our snipers had you in his crosshairs by the time you reached the third floor." She opened the French doors into the apartment and stood aside for Alex to walk through. "Come in. I have chamomile tea steeping for you in the kitchen."

"Thanks," Alex mumbled, entering the apartment, "but I don't drink tea."

The place was bigger than any apartment Alex had ever seen in the city. She looked back out past the balcony at a breathtaking night view of the bay. Being the head of Zeta Division came with its perks. The interior was obsessively clean and decorated within an inch of its life to look like a design catalog.

Even here in her own home, Diana Bloch was a facade, a front.

"I think you could do with some calming down."

"Sure." Alex rubbed her triceps, sore from the climb. "Whatever." She followed Bloch into the kitchen, where a steaming mug was waiting for her, the string of a tea bag hanging off the side. Bloch pulled it out, letting the excess liquid drip back into the mug before placing the bag in the trash.

"Sugar?"

"Four."

Bloch dropped in four cubes and stirred. "This was quite unnecessary. You could have severely hurt yourself, or died. We've already invested much in your training. It would have been a serious loss."

"I wanted to see you," said Alex. "And you kept stonewalling me." She sipped at the tea. Too hot.

"You are supposed to be in training. Skipping out was quite a feat, by the way. It seems you've got your fellow recruits atwitter, wondering how you did it."

"Bloch, *where is my father?*"

Bloch's face took on a pained expression. "Come into the living room," she said. She sat down at a white leather Barcelona chair and motioned for Alex to sit across from her. "We don't know where he is. But we're doing everything we can to find him."

"Tell me what happened."

"You know I can't divulge details of the mission. But he was caught while on assignment."

"Where?"

"Does it matter?"

"*Where?*" Alex's tone took on a hard edge.

Bloch seemed to consider whether to chew her out. She could pull rank at any moment. But instead, she said, "In Moscow. Does that make it better? Does that lessen your pain?"

Alex bit her lip and scowled in anger. "After everything he's done for the organization. You could move heaven and earth to find him, if you wanted to."

"There are limits on what we can feasibly do. Your father knew the risks going in, as you will when it's your turn to go out into the field. But we are doing what we can—"

"Not. Enough."

Bloch's eyes went cold. "I'll be the judge of that."

"I'll go on my own if I have to."

"That's not a good idea, Alex."

"I didn't ask."

Bloch stood from her seat and dropped ice cubes tinkling into a glass. Then she uncorked a bottle of whiskey and poured. "I know you think you're ready. Your help has been valuable to us in the past, and you'll make a hell of an operative someday. But you're still green. If you go out on your own, I'm afraid you won't survive."

"Are you going to stop me?"

"No. I'm not."

"Then I think we've said all we have to say to each other."

"I suppose," said Bloch. She unlocked the front door and held it open for Alex. "Why don't you take the elevator down?"

Chapter Four

Morgan woke to the bark of a guard yelling at him in Russian. His immediate reflex was to punch the man's lights out, but he was still too tired. So instead he lay disoriented until the guard, impatient, wrested the bent bowl from Morgan's hands and tossed it down the sleeping quarters. It tumbled, clattering, toward the door.

The message was clear enough.

Morgan stood, shaky from the interrupted sleep but also renewed, if only a little. How long had he been out? The sun was still in the sky, still low, but that meant little out here. The sun was always low. And the wind, even in summer, carried a chill.

He picked up his bowl and went outside into the yard. Men were filing in from the double gates that led outside the camp. The whole procession was hairless like him, although none so recently shaved, so that stubble was already growing in on their scalps and faces. They were shuffling, exhausted from a day of forced labor at the mine. All were skinny, their overalls and coats hanging loosely from their bodies. Their faces were pale, with deep dark bags under their eyes.

These men were broken. Morgan recognized the signs.

Guards oversaw the whole process, carrying their Kalashnikovs, holding dogs on leashes. Even the guards, though young, were stooped, with gloomy, lifeless eyes. Morgan didn't know if it was from the dreariness of the place—no women, no entertainment, nothing to do but drink in cramped rooms, if they were allowed that much— or the violence they committed against the prisoners. Something about torturing and brutality made men into miserable monsters. He'd seen it often enough.

He wondered whether this was a punishment assignment.

Morgan scanned the group. All were in the same clothes and had the same (lack of) hair, so all he had to go by were faces, and even these looked similar, with sunken eyes and pale skin. It proved just about impossible to pick out an individual from the crowd.

Food was distributed out of a single window by prisoners on meal duty. Morgan wondered if they had spent the day in the kitchen or come back early from work. In any case, it would be a prime position in the camp, the work light and pleasant in comparison to the mines. There was a little more color on their cheeks, too. Morgan guessed that they sneaked food as they cooked.

Morgan clutched his bowl. His stomach growled. He hadn't realized how hungry he was.

The men lined up at the window and Morgan took his place at the end. There was a scuffle to see who would get closer to the front, but at a shout from a guard, under fear of violence, the men took their places, those behind resigned to their position.

As he stood in line, Morgan noticed a group of three prisoners glowering at him, and he felt like the only unattached girl at a singles bar. The men exchanged words and turned away.

He didn't like it. Any kind of attention in this place was unwanted.

Morgan drew closer to the meal window as the prisoners got their dinner rations. When his turn came, he held out the bowl. The prisoner who was serving, wearing a jumper like his but stained with food, dunked a ladle into the big pot and spooned the contents into Morgan's bowl—a stew with vegetables, heavy on onions and potatoes, a few wisps of meat and bits of animal fat, and a thin layer of oil at the top.

The man motioned for him to move along.

Resisting the urge to swallow the portion whole right there, Morgan shuffled off, away from any grouping of prisoners, and sat against the cell block, holding his hand as steady as he could so as not to spill a drop. He'd not had any food in several days.

He tilted the bowl against his lips. They were cracked and split from the beatings he had taken in the past week, but the stew, thin as it was, filled him. Even with the faint odor of rotting potatoes and onions, even with the stringy, gristly meat, it was the best thing he'd ever tasted. He wanted to down the whole thing in one gulp. But he knew that if he ate too fast he'd puke it all up again, so he chewed each solid mouthful twenty-five times before swallowing, and took small sips of the liquid. In his hunger, he lost awareness of everything else around him. All he could focus on was the next mouthful.

He finished the scant portion, tilting the bowl against his lips to get the last drop. It felt warm and full in his stomach, after days of nothing but a trickle of water. He felt invigorated, power flowing back into his muscles. But at the same time he was aware that it wasn't enough. Two of these a day would keep a bedridden man alive and comfortable, but for men working all day in the mine, this was a starvation diet.

He wondered how long anyone lasted in here. Every one of the thousand or so men milling around in the yard looked withered and wasted, some more than others.

As he looked around, Morgan caught sight of the three who had been staring at him before. They were crowding around a man—Arabic, of around forty years old. Morgan had noticed him before, off in the corner making his prayers to Allah as others waited in line for food.

The three punks circled him, pinning him against the wall of the prisoner barracks. He was backing off from them, shaking his head. They stepped forward, holding out their hands. Morgan saw the Arab had his bowl in his arms, protected as if it were a baby. The goons wanted it, his only means of getting food, an extra portion for them. Without it, he would starve.

The prisoners around them couldn't be missing it, but they made a point of not raising their heads. A guard looked at the scene with no more interest as if he were seeing a dog scratch himself. One of the men slapped the Arab in the face and screamed something in Russian.

Morgan pushed himself up off the ground, his own bowl in his hand. Bad idea, getting into trouble on his first day. Plus, he was sore and exhausted. He had every reason not to get involved.

He walked the diagonal over to the men, inserting himself between them and the victim.

"Step off."

They first looked surprised, then glanced at each other with a blend of confusion and amusement. The oldest of them, a man slender and short like a weasel, spoke to him in Russian.

"No Russkyi," he grunted. "*Amerikanskyi.*"

A different man broke in, the youngest and tallest of them, fair-skinned and blond, who looked like the Russian equivalent of an Iowa farm boy except for the tattoo of a snake that peeked out of his overalls on his neck. "American, eh?"

"That's right. And you're going to leave this man alone."

He translated for his confederates and they shared a laugh. "Americans like to think they are cowboys. New sheriff in town, come to do justice. Move away, cowboy, or you die."

"*Step. Off.*"

The farm boy turned sour. "This is not funny anymore."

"Never was."

"You do not want to pick this fight."

"Maybe I do."

The man mugged at his comrades as if to say, *Can you believe this asshole?* and took a swing at Morgan, trying to catch him in a sucker punch. Morgan was slowed by hunger and fatigue, but not enough to fall for that tired trick. This was a bully, untrained at fighting anyone who knew how to fight back. Morgan dodged and grabbed his arm, using the man's own momentum to drop him to the ground. Weasel man growled and pounced on him. Morgan pivoted out of the way, kicking his leg at the knee so he fell face-first on the dirt ground of the yard.

The third hesitated, casting his eyes on his two confederates. He'd learned his lesson not to rush in. He balled his hands up into fists.

Morgan didn't give him the opportunity to get close. He rammed the sole of his foot into the man's chest, causing him to stagger back. Morgan then moved in to deliver a punch that would lay him out flat when someone grabbed his right arm. He saw a prisoner's overalls in his peripheral vision. He twisted to break free, but someone else grabbed his left. Morgan struggled, but he wasn't in any shape to wrest himself free of two men who, in spite of the conditions, had been sleeping and eating better than him for weeks now.

Someone new came up to him. He was older than most, as old as fifty. He was skinny as anyone else, but Morgan could tell he was thickset and jowly, with once-fat cheeks. His eyebrows were like two hairy gray caterpillars. He carried himself with all the dignity of a mafia don.

He moved in and punched an immobilized Morgan in the gut.

"You tried to be a hero. But this is not a place for heroes." He followed this with a meaty right hook to Morgan's cheek.

He'd have done worse, but the guards sprung into action at last, pulling the men apart from each other and knocking them to the ground, along with Morgan himself. The guards set upon all of them them, kicking them with heavy boots. Morgan took a painful kick in the ribs.

The man who had hit him, the don, was merely shooed away. Morgan went limp as they dragged him off. He didn't need any broken bones in here.

"You are dead, American!" the don yelled after him. "You hear me? Dead!"

Chapter Five

The siren woke Morgan in the solitary cell they had tossed him into after the fight the night before. With no room to stretch out, he had slept leaning against the far corner of the cell, feet resting against the door. This took its toll on the form of a throbbing pain in his lower back. His left cheek was sore and tender from the punch he took from the don. He stood with difficulty and tried to stretch the pain away to little avail.

Almost on cue, the dead bolt on the door was undone and the door opened, letting daylight flood into the darkness of the cell.

"Time to work, American!"

They pulled Morgan out and escorted him down an L-shaped hallway lined with cells and then out to the yard.

It was still dark, the sky leaden in the horizon where the sun was about to come up. The morning air chilled him to the marrow. The yawning, drooping prisoners lined up outside again, first for the morning count, and then at the food window, this time to get a dollop of potato porridge, bland and lumpy. But it was food, and it was warm.

Morgan kept an eye out for Bortsov's men, who paid him no attention. Morgan would assume they'd give him extra scrutiny after the day before. This raised alarm bells in his head, but he didn't have time to ruminate on it before another siren sounded and they lined up for the morning's meal.

Lacking any kind of utensils, Morgan followed the others' lead and ate with his hands. Once everybody had gotten their ration, they were lined up again, three abreast, in front of the double gates. An escort of guards surrounded them, one for every twenty or so men. A smaller siren rang out and the double gates swung open. With a shout from a guard, the men set to marching. They filed through the no-man's-land between the inner and outer perimeter fences. Morgan knew how it worked. Anyone caught there would be shot without ceremony or a second thought.

This was not an army, and their march was slow and plodding. Stuck near the back, Morgan couldn't see where they were going, so he settled for keeping his eyes down on the stony ground to keep from stumbling or stepping on the heels of the man ahead of him.

"You are American, right?"

It was good English, a young voice, right next to Morgan. He turned to his left to look at the man, in his early thirties by the look of it, with baby blue eyes and dark blond hair coming in on his head. There was something still unbroken in him despite his having the same sunken cheeks and sallow eyes as everyone else.

Morgan didn't have a mirror. He wondered whether he had the look yet. He would.

"I saw you back there." His English sounded like he

might have been educated in the US. "Standing up to those thugs. Not just anyone would do that for another man."

Morgan squinted into the dawning sun. A hawk shrieked far above.

"My name is Grushin. I am a journalist. In today's Russia, that's enough of a crime to get me sent to prison, but I got a little too inconvenient for even the usual holes they stick us in. So they put me in the gulag." He kicked a rock, which rolled diagonally and nearly hit a guard's boot. The guard turned, searching with a scowl for the culprit. Morgan looked away to deflect suspicion. "What are you in here for?"

Morgan didn't respond. The kid was nice, but as they say in reality shows, he wasn't here to make friends.

"All right, Uncle Sam. I should know better than to ask."

Morgan felt the spot where he took a boot the night before. It was aching anew with the strain of the march. He wondered whether he had a broken rib. "You *should* know better."

"But I can talk," he said, grinning. "The guys you attacked. They're all ex-mafia people. The one who punched you was their leader, Leonid Bortsov. They don't have much power, although I think their people bribe some of the guards from outside, so that gives them privileges in here. They run the laundry, which gets them away from the worst of the forced labor. One of the perks. The other is that they steal the others' food and blankets." He sighed. "Somehow, even this place is not bad enough that men like Bortsov can't make it worse."

They marched for forty minutes across the tundra, on cold hard ground. The path was well beaten, so that the low grasses that covered the plains around them did not grow there. Everything around them was flat. Even if he could run, there was nowhere for him to run to, nowhere that would put him out of the line of sight of the guards' rifles.

The sun had risen above the horizon by the time they arrived at the mine. It was a handful of shacks surrounding a hole cut into the rock, sloping down to a set of double steel doors. The men fanned out, each seeming to know where to go.

A guard approached Morgan. "New prisoner," he said. "You go with Vanya's team."

Vanya was a tall man, wrinkled and with heavy scarring on half his face. Morgan guessed it was a chemical burn, probably from torture. Vanya argued with the guard. After a brief back-and-forth, the guard gave what from the tone was an ultimatum. Vanya swore and said, "Come, American."

He walked off, and Morgan followed. "What was that about?" he asked.

"We have a quota per man on the team," he said. "More men, higher quota. If we do not meet quota at the end of the week, we get lash."

"Sorry about that."

"You look strong," he said. "You will pull your weight. We do not do your work for you. If we get the lash, you get worse. And then you will be very sorry."

"Got it." Morgan was making friends left and right.

Vanya led him to the toolshed, where men were crowding around, elbowing each other, trying to get their hands on an implement. Morgan followed Vanya's lead, fighting to the front of the line to look at what was on offer.

No modern mining equipment. No machines. Hand-held implements was all they had, goddamn shovels and mallets and chisels. Nevsky must have a penchant for the vintage.

There weren't enough for everyone, Morgan now saw. The smaller and weaker men were pushed aside. They would be getting the lash at the end of the week.

"Get *kirkomotyga*," Vanya told him. "Pickaxe." Morgan he forced his way and took one. He held it close to his chest, smelling the rich iron, holding it tightly against the grabbing hands until he got clear of the crowd. Then he examined it. The wood was old and grooved, the head covered in rust. But it would do its work.

A guard unlocked and swung open the heavy metal doors that led into the mine with a prolonged creak. He pulled down a heavy switch on the other side of the door, and dim lights came on. The wooden struts were old and seemed like they could cave in at any minute. Convenient way to bury a group of men the Russian government wanted disappeared.

The prisoners filed into the mine, two by two. Morgan walked inside with Vanya's six-man team. Being the new guy, he was given wheelbarrow duty, his pickaxe sitting inside as he struggled to hold the wheel steady on the uneven ground. There was no explicit order or direction, but Vanya and the men moved forward without hesitation. As the tunnels branched out, the men thinned until their group was alone.

Morgan wondered how often men got lost in here. He wondered how many corpses had been forgotten in the mine.

They walked for several minutes before Vanya said, "You go with Sergey here. He doesn't speak English. If you need help communicating, get lost." Sergey motioned for Morgan to follow him a ways down the tunnel to a small hollow. There, the Russian showed him how to wield the pickaxe, chipping stone from the cave wall.

They worked in silence for a while, only the dull clang of metal hitting rock. It was hard to gauge the passage of time in the darkness of the mine, so Morgan had no idea how much time had gone by when he heard footsteps coming down the tunnel. He turned, assuming it was Vanya and the others.

It was not. From the darkness, the three men he had fought on the yard the day before approached. They said something to Sergey, who dropped his pickaxe and took off running down the passage, the sound of his dash fading in the tunnels.

The three men advanced on him.

"No guards to save you here," said the young, tall man. "You are going to have a little accident."

Morgan didn't like his odds. Someone could get hurt.

He thought about shouting for help, but he doubted that anyone would hear him, except perhaps Vanya's men. Also, it would do him no good in the long run. Bortsov's little gang would just wait until the next opportunity.

Morgan knew one thing. He wasn't going to die in that mine. So he was going to put a stop to this here and now.

He tightened his grip on the pickaxe. This wasn't going to be pretty.

The tunnel was too narrow for them to come at him all at the same time, which gave him a strong defensive position, but also hamstrung his swing of the weapon.

The first, the younger tall guy, came at him with another pickaxe. He was slow. Morgan moved out of the way and swung his pickaxe against the man's back, calculating the force to crack a few ribs. The tip connected, and the man fell forward with a cry of pain.

The next man held a shovel, which had a longer reach

than Morgan's pickaxe, putting him at a disadvantage. The man thrust it like a spear, hitting Morgan in the belly. He winced. It was going to leave a nasty bruise.

The man moved to thrust again, and Morgan locked the shovel into the curved head of the pickaxe. He pushed the head of the shovel back against the attacker. The handle caught him in the chest and he staggered back. This gave Morgan his opening. He swung the shovel to the side. It fell from the man's weakened grip and clattered to the stone on the cave floor. Then Morgan swung at the man's head with the side of the pickaxe, which slammed into the man's temple. He hollered, clutching at the bleeding wound. Morgan kicked the man's leg out from under him and he dropped.

The third attacker, the tiny, weasely man, came at him, roaring, wielding a long-handled mallet two-handed. He swung downward and Morgan parried, almost losing his grip on the pickaxe. The man swung again, and Morgan dodged out of the way, inches from taking a blow that would crush his jaw.

Morgan kept backing away as the swings came. The man had too much reach, and Morgan couldn't get an opening in the tight quarters. He could rush his attacker, but only at the expense of leaving himself open to a bone-crunching strike. And soon he'd be backed up against a wall, a sitting duck.

Morgan took stock of the environment as he stepped back. Was there anything he could use? Narrow tunnels, held up by struts too strong to break, not high enough that climbing would give him any advantage. But connected to it . . .

Hanging from the strut above him was the last bulb of the tunnel. Without pausing to think twice, Morgan swung the pickaxe upward, shattering the lightbulb and plunging the passage into darkness.

Morgan could see the man's silhouette against another lightbulb up the passage, but Morgan himself was concealed by a pall of murk. The man swung the hammer blindly. Morgan waited for a wide swing and brought the pickaxe down on the hammer's handle. Without expecting it, weasel man lost his grip. Then Morgan rushed him with a running tackle that knocked the man off his feet.

Morgan took up the hammer from the ground. He raised it, and the man, seeing Morgan by the dim light he was no longer blocking with his body, raised his hand in defense.

Morgan dropped the implement next to the man on the floor, panting. "It's a very, very dangerous thing to attack me. I'm not looking to kill anyone today. That makes this your lucky day. Try again and I guarantee your luck will run out." He brought his foot hard against the man's side. "And tell Bortsov that if he pulls this shit again, I'm coming for him."

He walked away, leaving all his would-be killers writhing in pain on the cave ground.

Chapter Six

They marched back to the camp after ten hours in the mine, the sun still glaring in the Siberian summer sky. A truck drove alongside them, carrying the day's haul in tin ore. Bortsov's three goons limped along with everyone else, keeping the pace in spite of their injuries.

No one said anything about the fight. Morgan watched as his attackers were questioned by hostile guards in the yard as the mess window opened and men struggled to be among the first to eat. Morgan asked Grushin what the men were saying.

"They say it happened in an accident. That they fell."

The guards didn't look like they were buying it for a second, but Bortsov's men said nothing that would connect the occurrence to him. Stonewalled and not interested in taking this any further, the guards let it go. It wasn't skin off their backs if a couple of inmates wanted to give each other shiners, as long as the ore was flowing.

Morgan had expected as much. They were already under scrutiny for the fight the other day, and would not want to call any more attention to themselves. The whole point of attacking him in the mine was to do it in secret, where no one would see. And with renewed suspicion because of their injuries, they would have to lay low before making their next move.

But it was clear they wouldn't let this go. Especially not now.

"You are a lightning rod for trouble," Grushin said.

"I don't know what you're talking about."

"I'm sure you don't," he said. "It was just natural curiosity that you were so interested in the men's injuries, which I'm sure have nothing to do with the fact that you're trying to hide a limp."

"Did anyone ever tell you that you're too smart for your own good?" Morgan asked.

"What do you think got me in here? Anyway, don't worry, no one will tell the guards. I'd be more worried about Bortsov, myself."

"You think they'll try something else?"

"You are challenging the pecking order. They can't let that stand. If he can, he will kill you. But not yet. Eyes are on him now. I don't think he can afford to make a move."

"Sure you still want to be my friend? It can be dangerous to your health."

"Can't sink that much lower." Grushin surveyed the yard, the line for dinner organizing itself out of disorder. "You know, if we all attacked together, at the same time, we could take their weapons and take over the prison. There are almost a thousand of us and, what, maybe a hundred of them?"

"A hundred with Kalashnikovs," said Morgan.

"Still. We get a hold of one or two, and with a decent tactician . . ."

"I don't like the way you're looking at me."

Grushin rested his back against the wall. "I'm not going

to die in here. I refuse to. If I am to die, I want it to be trying to escape. Fighting against oppression, instead of collapsing from exhaustion or starving like a dog."

"Careful with that talk. There are people in here who'd sell you out for an extra dinner ration."

"But I don't think you're one of them," he said.

"Why do you figure?"

"I'm a journalist. My job was—*is*—to see things. So I see people around here. Most of them keep to themselves. Those are your basic survivors, the ones who are focused on getting through the day. Some find God. They tend to stick together—that's them over there. You got your standard bullies, like Bortsov's men, who try to get the upper hand even in here. There are the flight risks, too, although it's harder to figure out who they are beforehand. But they are the ones who will just take off running one day. Usually they get shot. Some get brought back."

"And the rest?"

"You don't want to know."

Grushin was probably right about that. "Sounds like you've got this place figured out."

"There are the specific cases," Grushin said. He pointed out a small man, very thin and middle aged. Morgan couldn't quite tell, but there seemed to be something wrong about the way he carried himself. "They say that is Kolya the Cannibal. He terrorized St. Petersburg some ten years ago. Ate at least thirty people, most of them children, before they caught him. They found the bones in his basement."

"He's been in here since then?"

"It's what they say. Honestly, I don't know how he survived this long. He has never said a word to anyone here. Maybe that's his secret."

"And you? How long you been in?" Morgan asked.

"It's been five months. Feels like as many lifetimes."

"I'm done with this place after a day."

"You won't stay long in here," Grushin said. "Your government wouldn't allow it."

"I wouldn't count on it. I'm dead, as far as my government is concerned."

"I see," said Grushin. "So what are you? CIA? Identity disavowed in case of capture?"

"No. Not CIA."

"But something, right? There's something about you."

Morgan didn't respond. He wondered whether he was that transparent.

"I am going to write about this place when I get out," Grushin said. "The world needs to know what is going on in here. When they take you away, remember us here, okay?"

After dinner, the guards lined up all the prisoners on the yard for the evening count. One guard marched down the line counting aloud while another ticked each number off on a clipboard.

Twilight was setting in by the time they finished, and the men filed into barracks. They distributed into their respective rooms. Morgan was relieved to find that none of his twenty-odd cellmates were the men he had confronted in the yard. The man he had saved, the Arab, was not among them either.

Morgan lay down on his bunk. He was still tired enough that he felt sleep coming on, but he wasn't about to drift off before making sure the others would, too. Sleep left him exposed, and he didn't like it. But soon enough, his exhaustion got the better of him and he fell into dreamless sleep.

Chapter Seven

"How are you holding up?"

Karen O'Neal, with her pretty half-Vietnamese face, fussy, socially awkward and a bit off-putting, sat across from Alex in a downtown Boston Starbucks drinking a triple-shot espresso. They had just missed the morning crowd, who left newspapers and coffee rings behind, and were sharing a table during the tranquil midmorning lull.

"Not well." Alex emitted a hollow laugh. She was nursing an iced hazelnut macchiato with an obscene amount of sugar in it.

"I'm glad you called," said Karen. "Sometimes this job sucks, and sometimes it's hard on the people close to us."

"I think it was harder on my father this time," said Alex.

"I know. I was being polite."

This was why Alex liked Karen. Sometimes she was honest to a fault. "What happened to him?" Alex asked.

"I don't know much. Zeta's keeping this mission on

the down-low, even from people on the inside. They're even boxing *me* out of looking for him."

"What? Why? Bloch said they were doing everything they could."

"I guess that's not literally true," Karen said. "I need to know more."

"I'm sorry, I'm just not in the loop."

But Alex had a last resort, a trick up her sleeve. "Was Lincoln working on this project?"

Karen blushed. "Yes."

Lincoln Shepard was the resident computer tech at Zeta, a brilliant nerd who had been dating Karen in secret for months now. Alex was among the few who knew, having found out by accident.

"He never told you anything?" Alex asked.

"No, but . . ." Karen looked left and right, as if someone might be listening. "There's a name I heard him say several times," she said. "Apparently in connection to this case. Suvorov. Some sort of military officer."

"Suvorov . . ." Alex echoed as she committed the name to memory.

"You're not actually thinking of getting involved, are you?"

"No, of course not. I just wanted some closure, I guess." *Liar.* "Anyway, what are you working on now?"

This was enough to get Karen to go off on a tangent about trying to find contraband through recurring patterns in shipping containers. Alex picked Karen's brain about how data models worked as they finished their coffees, and then Karen said she had to go. They parted on the street with a wooden hug.

"He might not be dead!" Karen called out as Alex waved good-bye.

Alex rode her motorcycle home. She pulled off the highway to the suburb of Andover, Massachusetts, where kids on summer vacation populated the streets on bicycles and on foot. One group was playing in the spray of a hose on the lawn. Alex felt a pang of nostalgia for her own childhood.

She found the house empty except for their German shepherd, Neika. Her mother was out at work, as usual. Diving into her work was her coping mechanism, and as such things went, it wasn't a bad one.

Taking advantage of her solitude, Alex opened the door to her father's office. She found everything still, the air slightly stale, a light dust settled on the gun display case, the model cars.

It was eerie being in there with him missing.

But Alex had purpose, and the heebie-jeebies were not going to stop her. She opened a cabinet behind his chair and removed two piles of old tax and personal documents. Then she felt around the corners for the button, and removed the back panel.

Stashed there was nearly fifty thousand dollars and a Rolodex. She drew out the money and the old apparatus, shuffling through the cards. They were written in a simple cipher, an idiot code that Alex had over time taken pains to decipher.

Now, she was looking for a specific card. She went through them until she found it. A name, which deciphered read Valery Dobrynin. And a phone number.

She picked up the phone in the study and dialed the complex country code and then the number. It rang ten times before she got an answering machine message. She had been studying Russian, but she didn't quite get what the recording said. She only knew she had not heard the name Dobrynin.

She heard the beep, her signal to start talking. "I'm not sure I have the right number. I'm calling about my father, Dan Morgan. I—he needs help. I think you know who he is, and I think you can give me that help. Please, if you care about him, call me back."

She left her number, finished off with another plea for help.

It could be nothing. A total mistake, a man long gone. But she would take anything at this point.

Chapter Eight

Days went by and Morgan had no more trouble from Bortsov's men beyond angry looks. He shared most of his meals with Grushin, who told him about life on the outside, about his political radical girlfriend, and about how he was worried about her and how much he missed her. Morgan said little in return, and next to nothing about his life back home. But the young man was glad enough just to be listened to.

Morgan would've preferred to think he was above it, that he was better as a lone wolf. But the young man's company was humanizing, in a place where most other interactions were opportunistic at best, cruel at worst.

It was about two weeks into Morgan's internment when Vanya interrupted a dinnertime conversation with an announcement.

"Detonation tomorrow. If we're lucky, we won't get picked to do it, and have a day of rest."

They got picked. It was a random draw, and theirs was the short straw—Morgan's team and another, which Morgan saw that morning included the man he had defended on his first day there, the Arab. The twelve of them marched alone to the mine, along with six armed guards. The rest of the prisoners stayed behind and enjoyed a rare day of rest from hard labor.

On their arrival at the mine, the guards unlocked the dynamite shed and told them to get to work.

"Come," said Vanya to Morgan.

"Why me?"

"What, you want me to do it? You are new. You do it."

Seniority applied in the mines, apparently.

Vanya first took a satchel from a shelf and stocked it with wires, detonators, and tape. He then opened a green arms chest, packed with sticks of dynamite. "You carry." He loaded it with eight sticks as Morgan held it.

Morgan lifted it carefully over his shoulder and walked with smooth and precise steps, trying to jog the volatile cargo as little as possible. Vanya led all of them into the depths of the mines, where two spots had been marked for detonation. Once they were there, Morgan set the satchel on the ground and the Arab came forward and drew out three sticks.

With deft fingers, he connected the detonators. While Morgan unwound the wire toward the mouth of the cave, the Arab set the sticks at the second site.

Once everything was ready, they unspooled the wire all the way to the outside. Vanya closed the heavy steel door and everyone stood clear. The Arab activated the charge on a car battery and the ground shook. Dust shot out from the corners of the door, which rumbled on its hinges.

The guards gave them a few minutes to wait for the dust to settle. They were smoking cigarettes, and in a rare moment of empathy offered each prisoner one. The Arab waved it away. Vanya smoked his with relish. Morgan took one and pocketed it. He might be able to trade. At least it might be a treat for Grushin.

They went back inside, coughing at the dust that was still thick in the air, dimming the reach of the electric lights. Vanya surveyed the collapsed rock.

"We did not do enough here," he told Morgan. "We will need to do a second detonation."

On the way back up, he knelt at a spot where stones had been knocked loose. The wire had been cut on a sharp edge.

"Shit. We do not have more. We will have to use fuses. I hate fuses."

They went back for more dynamite. Morgan was given the job of carrying the satchel again. He, the Arab, and Vanya made their way back down, the dust now a bit clearer, to the first detonation site.

"This doesn't look too safe," Morgan said as the Arab set the sticks in the recess of the rock where they wanted to blow the new passage..

"Do it right this time," said Vanya. He was pissy about all the extra work.

"Lighter," said the Arab. Vanya reached over and lit the fuse.

"All right, clear the cave."

They ran single file away from the hissing fuse. Ducking under a low passage, the Arab put his hand on a strut. Weakened by the explosions, it shifted, groaning, and then cracked. Morgan pushed him out of the way, and they rolled together on the ground. A section of the passage wall collapsed on top of Vanya. He was knocked forward and screamed. His leg was pinned against the ground.

"Help me!"

Morgan looked at the light of the fuse, burning not

fifty feet away. How long did they have before it reached the stick of dynamite?

Morgan owed this man nothing. The sensible thing to do was to run away with everyone else and get clear of the blast before it went off.

Instead he grabbed a shovel. "Come on, help me!" he said to the Arab. He wedged the shovel under the rock and pushed down on the handle. It didn't budge. "*Help me!*"

The Arab stepped forward and helped Morgan push the shovel down. They grunted at the exertion. With a creak, the stone moved a fraction of an inch. Under their combined strength, it rose, little by little, rocks shifting as it moved.

"Get him out!"

The Arab let go. Morgan held, giving every ounce of strength he had, as the man pulled Vanya's considerable bulk backward, clear of the rock. Morgan let go, dropping to his hands and knees with exhaustion. The rock hit the cave floor, sending up a plume of dust.

"Move it!" cried Vanya.

Morgan and the Arab helped Vanya to his feet, and he limped, weight resting on their shoulders, as they moved together down the passage.

They had walked barely ten paces when they were knocked off their feet by the blast. They collapsed into a pile on the cave floor, hot air running all around them. The passage behind them caved in, raising a cloud of dust. If they had gotten out five seconds later, they would have been buried.

"Is everyone all right?" the Arab asked.

Vanya didn't answer, but he was moving and moaning, which was good enough.

"Let's not do that again," said Morgan.

Chapter Nine

That evening, Morgan sat to eat with Grushin at dinner, as usual. From their regular seats against the laundry building, he caught sight of the Arab doing his evening prayer halfway across the yard. At the back of the food line, Vanya was limping on an old-fashioned cast. That poor bastard. With a fracture like that, he needed to be in bed, but hell if Nevsky was going to be that compassionate.

At least Vanya caught something of a break. He was, Morgan found out, taken out of the mine and put on latrine duty.

Someone else was eating with them that day. An older man, his face deeply lined, what hairs were left him wispy and patchy. His eyes were sunken and haunted, but there was spirit in the geezer yet.

"Morgan," Grushin had said when Morgan sat down. "This is Milosz. He is something of an institution around here. He has been here for many years, longer than anyone can remember. Even him."

"How you like our home, young man?" Milosz said, in a raspy, guttural English.

"You speak English?"

"I learn in here. Sometimes there is British or American inside. They die or go away fast. But I learn. I learn good."

"That you did," said Morgan. "What are you in for?"

"I was fighter in Czechoslovakia," he said. "In—" he turned and asked something of Grushin in Russian.

"Velvet Revolution," Grushin said.

"Velvet Revolution!" Milosz said with a flourish of his hand. "I was leader."

He related stories of his glory days before his capture, of beautiful women and killing Communists and daring escapes until he announced, "I go take a piss." He rested a hand on Morgan's shoulder. "Don't get old. You piss all the time."

"I'd rather that than the alternative."

He helped Milosz to his feet and watched as the man walked toward the latrines. He commanded rare respect in the camp. Even the guards seemed to have some deference to the old man, and Bortsov's men steered clear of him. No, there was something left of the outside in here after all. Respect for elders was too deeply ingrained to be rooted out all the way.

As he watched Milosz, Morgan saw the Arab walking over in their direction, a bowl of stew in his hand.

"I think that's for you," said Grushin. Morgan stirred to stand up. "No, I was just leaving. Got some important business to attend to at the other side of the yard."

Grushin made himself scarce, and the other man took a seat next to Morgan as he tipped the bowl of stew into his mouth, fatty broth filling his stomach. Both were facing forward and didn't look one another in the eye.

"My name is Badri," he said.

"Morgan."

"American," he said. "We should be enemies."

"I guess we should."

"There is honor in you. Perhaps you are a good man."

"Nah. I'm just like every other asshole in here."

"No. You are not. Most people here are criminals. People who are lost, who have no hope of righteousness. But you. I have been watching. You have a mind for justice, even in this place where there is none, not for any."

"Those are big words," Morgan said. "I see someone in trouble, I do something. It's an instinct or something." He sipped from his stew. It carried an aftertaste of rancid onion.

"Even one who should be your enemy."

"Even." Badri was testing him. He could tell.

"You have family?" Badri asked.

"Wife and daughter back home," he said. "My daughter, she's college-aged. You?"

"Wife, too, and two children. But I haven't seen them in a long time. I don't know what has happened to them." He rubbed his face. "Are you from the CIA? I do not know why else an American would be in here."

Lying was going to do him no good. Plus, given the circumstances, it hardly seemed like it mattered. "I'm not CIA," he said. "But I did work for an intelligence agency. Something clandestine. Totally secret. Not even working for the government, technically."

A flash of ice-cold hatred passed across Badri's face. "Then you are the enemy."

"Well, I'm done with them anyway. I gave everything for my country, for the agency. And they betrayed me. Left me for dead. What are you here for?"

"For fighting the Great Satan," he said. "For making jihad."

They stared at each other in silence. *Natural enemies, then?*

Morgan scratched the scalp behind his ear. "Look, Badri, I've seen things. I've *done* things. I know what my country does, has done. Wars and bombing and assassinations for profit and ideology. Covering up war crimes and manipulating our people. I'm tired. I'm tired of the hypocrisy." He leaned back and closed his eyes. "I saw something. In my most recent mission. I was doing reconnaissance in northwestern Syria. Town called Sarmada. A mission against the Islamic State. I was supposed to give my people the location of a group of leaders for a targeted bombing.

"Except when I got there, I saw a wedding. Women, old people, children. I told them not to fire. I told them to hold off." He spit on the ground. "An entire family killed by a drone strike. A wedding party. Should've been the happiest moment of those young people's lives. Instead, they died." He gritted his teeth. "I'm sick of it, Badri. This has been festering in me a long time. I'm not one of them anymore."

"Perhaps you see things as I do," said Badri. "Perhaps you understand."

"Well. It's not like all that matters in here, does it?" He looked at the desolate wasteland surrounding the prison. A treeless wilderness, with no animals to be seen, cold and barren. "All that's washed away. This is a corner of the world that God's forgot. All we are in here is muscle and bone waiting to die." Morgan took another mouthful of soup. "So I don't see the harm in mortal enemies on the outside sharing a meal."

"Perhaps you are right," he said.

"Screw being right. I'm tired."

Chapter Ten

Alex's feet pounded pavement, a light summer shower cooling off her overheated body.

These days, she couldn't do without her morning run. She'd long gone past the point when it was something she had to force her body to do, and now it was something her body craved, and would revolt if she did not.

She thought of her batch of recruits back at the training camp. They'd be at the range at this time, she reckoned. She realized she missed holding the rifle, missed shooting at a target, missed the endurance exercises and slogging through the mud and practicing first aid on her mates and stealth maneuvers.

She was thinking about checking out a local gun range when the music cut out in her earphones and the ringer sounded.

She stopped, catching her breath for three seconds before drawing her cell phone from its waterproof case and picking up.

"Hello?"

"How you get this number?" Through a heavy Russian

accent, the man's voice was nervous, slathered in a sort of manic paranoia.

"I'm sorry, who is this?"

"Don't ask who it is. You called me."

"I did?"

"You leave number."

Then it hit her. "Is this Dobrynin? Valery Dobrynin?"

"Who are you?"

"Alex, I—Dan Morgan is my father."

"How did you get number?"

"I found it in his things."

The man swore in Russian. "The *mudak* was supposed to forget me."

"Well, he didn't. And you didn't forget him either."

"What do you want? You say he needs help?"

The rain started coming down harder and she turned to make her way back home. "He went missing in Russia a couple of weeks ago. I want—I need to find him."

"And what is this to me?"

"You knew him, didn't you?"

"A long time ago. I do not know anything about him."

"You know he needs your help!"

The man muttered something in Russian she did not catch. "What kind of help?"

"He was on a mission to—"

"*Stop.* Watch what you say over the phone, child. These things I do not need to know."

"Okay," she said. "He's missing. I have a name in connection with it, and not much else."

"And what do you want me to do about this?"

"I want to find him. I want your help."

The man did not answer right away, and all Alex heard was water hitting the pavement. "Is not my problem. Forget this name and this number."

"You owe him!" It was a gamble. She didn't know if it was even close to true.

"What did you say?"

"I said you owe him."

"What do you know about that?" he hissed.

Time for another bluff. "I know enough. You want to get even? This is your chance."

"*Der'mo*. Get even. Okay. You come here? To Moscow?"

"Yes. I'll come to Moscow."

He dictated the address for her in Cyrillic, which she was familiar with enough to write out on her cell phone's notepad app.

"I will be waiting. If this is trick, I gut you with knife."

Nice guy.

She went home and made straight for her father's hiding place. She took out the duffel of cash. Then she looked up flights online. She could leave on one early the next morning. She paid for it with a credit card her father had left behind.

Her mother was out of town for a couple of days, so Alex just left a note.

> *gone to find dad. be back soon.*
> *love you.*

–A.

Chapter Eleven

Alex's plane touched down in Moscow in the late morning. She converted two thousand dollars to rubles and took a cab out of the airport.

She had the driver drop her off a few blocks away from her destination and walked the rest of the way. She was in an old neighborhood, where the buildings were quaint but run-down.

She counted the numbers until she was standing in front of a store window. She didn't need to read Russian to know what it was. The hanging salamis and two massive pigs' heads on display announced with crystal clarity that this was a butcher shop. It looked like something that belonged to the Soviet era and had frozen in time in the late eighties.

She checked the address again and walked all the way back to the corner to verify she had the street address right. Then she walked back and checked the number.

There was no doubt. This was the address the man had given her.

Her face burned with embarrassment. Had this been a

cruel trick? Something to get her off his back? She might be able to trace the phone number, but what was the point of tracking down a man who wanted nothing to do with her?

Still, she had come this far.

A bell rang when she opened the door. A miasma of butchered meat hit her at once, not helped in the least by the heat of the summer.

A woman of about sixty waddled in from the back, cleaning her hands with a filthy rag, and asked Alex something in Russian.

"Sorry, I don't . . ." She closed her eyes and took a deep breath, swallowing her embarrassment. "I'm looking for Valery Dobrynin?"

She tossed the rag and hollered, "*Valyerey!*"

A man came out of the back, grumbling under his breath, wearing a bloodstained apron. He had a long face with gray curls that were once black, and a long, thick nose. He exchanged bickers with the woman, and she retreated inside, spitting a last curse at him and slamming the door behind her.

"*Chto ty khochesh'?*" She could smell the alcohol on his breath from across the counter.

"*Ya ishchu kogo-to.* My Russian's not very good. Mr. Dobrynin?"

"That is me. Who are you?"

"Alex. Alexandra." Dobrynin didn't make a sign of recognizing her. "Daniel Morgan's daughter?"

"Ah, the girl," he said, grumbling some more, and looked over her shoulder at the street behind her. "Did anyone follow you?"

"I don't think—"

"Never mind. Come in." He pulled a hinged section of the counter, motioning for her to follow him.

They walked into a different door from the one the woman had disappeared into, and emerged in a tiny dark kitchen. Its sink held two chipped ceramic plates, two forks and knives that had seen better days, and two aluminum cups. He sat in one of the two chairs and motioned for her to sit in the other, across a table covered in peeling vinyl.

"Put your suitcase down and sit," he said.

"Thank you. You have a lovely home."

He burst out laughing, which transitioned into a hacking cough. "I do not. Agrafena is a worse decorator than I am."

"Is that your wife?"

"What did you come here for?" Dobrynin asked her.

"I told you," she said. "I need your help. I need to help my father."

"And who took your father?"

"I have a name," said Alex. "Suvorov."

Dobrynin whistled. "That is quite a name. If this is true, then your father is in heavy trouble, little girl."

"Who is he?"

"General. Very nasty man. Not known for being polite to prisoners."

Alex felt a lead weight in her chest. "Do you think he's dead?"

"Most probably."

"I need to know for sure," she said. "If there's even a chance—"

"Will you die for a chance?"

She narrowed her eyes. "If I have to."

He stood up from his seat and turned his back on her. "Foolish girl." He turned on the faucet and rinsed the dishes.

"Either you help me, or I'm going on my own."

He circled his way around her and opened a cabinet behind her back. She watched the dripping faucet, thinking of what she was going to do if he sent her away. And then his thick arm was around her neck, and the point of a thin knife touched her neck. "Do you know what they do to little girls in Moscow?"

Alex squirmed, gasping for air.

"You will be gutted like a pig, girl."

Alex calmed her panicking lizard brain and assessed the situation. His form was sloppy, and sloppy meant vulnerable.

She kicked herself back in her chair, knocking her head into his chest. The chair tipped over and she fell back, on the chair, on top of him. Before he could recover his bearings, she took the knife that he had dropped on the ground and swung to her right, landing on her feet. She held the knife inches from his face.

"I'd like to see them try."

"I am old," he grunted, pushing the knife away from his face and standing up. "Others will not be so easy."

"I'm ready," she said.

"You are not. But I will help you with what I can. Daniel Morgan deserves this much."

Chapter Twelve

Morgan pulled his weight and more in the mines. It was backbreaking work, long hours of breaking and hauling, to the steady sound of pickaxes echoing through the tunnels. Guards would patrol, passing every so often to make sure no one was slacking. Getting caught not working warranted anything from a cuff to the back of the hand to a summary beating, but Morgan, like the others, quickly learned the tricks. Work as slowly as possible while still keeping the quota, listen for the sound of the guards' boots on the ground, get whatever rest you can when you can.

Weeks passed, although Morgan did not keep count of how many, and Bortsov's men kept their distance, except for bumping into him on occasion, or pushing him when the guards weren't looking. One day, they knocked a bowl of stew out of his hand and it went clattering to the ground, spilling its precious contents on the dirt. There were no do-overs at the camp. Morgan went hungry that night.

But Morgan didn't want to start trouble, and they didn't

seem to want to escalate, for fear of Nevsky's retaliation. That was a fragile détente, and a reckoning was coming.

One night, the lights went out. It was nearly completely dark by this time, the sun having disappeared in the horizon. There was a commotion among the prisoners, who had been lined up for the evening count, and Morgan's mind went to escape. But the guards were ready, flashlights in hand, and circled the perimeter, carrying automatic weapons and loosing the dogs, still tethered to their chains but with free rein to run the length of the perimeter fence.

The prisoners were made to kneel with their hands on their heads—Morgan was well familiar with the procedure.

Men were going into the building that housed the generator. Ten minutes passed, then another ten. Nevsky emerged from his building and walked across the yard, swearing in Russian.

"Hey!" Morgan called out to him. "Hey! Is it the generator?"

"Shut your mouth, prisoner!"

"I can fix it!" Nobody responded. "Grushin, tell him I can fix it."

Grushin did, calling it out in Russian to the warden, who changed his trajectory to stand before Morgan.

"Are you a mechanic, American?"

"I know my way around an engine."

Nevsky waved him over. "Okay, you try it." He waved Morgan inside the shed. "If you screw it up any worse, it's your ass."

"I need a flashlight," he said. Nevsky took one from the nearest guard and handed it to Morgan.

The generator reeked of diesel. The make wasn't one that he recognized. It was Russian (along with any instructions or identifiers) and old. The panel was already open. He went through the troubleshooting checklist, starting with gas and coolant levels. Next he checked the breakers.

"Jesus H. Christ, who's your mechanics guy? These wires are a goddamn mess."

"Are they the problem?" Nevsky asked.

"No, electrics look like they're working. They're not the issue this time." He found the problem soon enough. "Fuel line's blocked. I need to replace it. You got supplies?"

"Whatever there is in here."

He found an old hose that seemed in one piece. It was a simple substitution, something he'd done plenty of times before.

"That should do it," he said. "Let's start her up."

The generator came to rumbling life. The lights in the camp flickered on.

"American," Nevsky said. "You're out of the mine. You're now on mechanic duty."

Chapter Thirteen

Morgan and Grushin settled into a routine of sitting together at dinner. It was mostly Grushin who spoke, but it made Morgan feel good to talk to him. The journalist reminded him of Alex, who was just as idealistic and headstrong. He missed her so much it hurt physically.

"You got yourself a cushy position," Grushin said.

"Same as you." Grushin was on the rotation to work laundry.

"I get to work all day in the stink of men," he said. "And then the stink of chemicals. They burn my hands and make my eyes water. Not very pleasant."

"Well, it ain't the mines."

Grushin chewed absently. "You know, I think I would actually murder a man for a cigarette and a cup of coffee."

"I've seen some of the inmates with cigarettes," Morgan said. "I guess they get 'em from the guards."

"Yeah. And you should hear the things they'll trade for 'em." Grushin emitted a hollow laugh. "I would kill a man. But I wouldn't do that."

"Can't say I sympathize. About the coffee and cigarettes, I mean. I don't partake."

"What about vodka? Whiskey? My God, a tall glass of German beer."

"Never been much of a drinker," Morgan said.

"So what do you miss?"

"I miss my daughter," he said. "Every single goddamn minute of my existence here. And I miss my wife. I miss how warm and soft she was. The idea of our bed—it seems like another world. Another life."

"To women," Grushin said, raising his bowl and clinking it against Morgan's. "That we might see one again someday."

"God hear you."

They ate in silence for a few minutes. Grushin looked off into the setting sun. "I'm not going to die here."

"Careful with that," said Morgan. "They say hope's what kills you faster. You don't have hope, despair is just a dull ache. But if you keep that fire alive, it'll burn you."

"I'd rather blaze bright, even if it consumes me, than turn to ash in this place." He stood up, raising his voice. "Look around, Morgan! All these defeated men. All fed to and being slowly digested by this place." His voice dropped to a whisper. "I'm going to escape from this place."

"You sound like you almost have a plan."

"I almost have a plan," Grushin said.

"You'll die," said Morgan. "Look." He gestured to the wastes of the tundra.

"I can't do it alone. But I wanted to know if I could trust you. I think I can. And you've shown yourself to be very resourceful. Seem to know what you're doing. The kind of guy I'd want at my side for this. You can handle yourself in a fight. You're quick on your feet. Plus, you're a good man. Not many to be found around here. And you got one big thing going for you."

"What's that?"

"The cars," Grushin said. "You have access to the motor pool. It might be the only way to escape far enough along the tundra not to get caught by the dogs or the guards coming after us. If we disable the other cars, we got a good shot at getting away."

"Into the Siberian wilderness, with no food or shelter and one full tank of gas."

"One step at a time," said Grushin. "First we get out, then we think about how we survive. I like our chances out there better than in here anyway. Hell, I like the idea of dying out there better than another day in here."

"Maybe I can do it on my own," said Morgan. "Maybe I'm the one who doesn't need you."

"You can't," he said. "Trust me. You need me for this."

"What makes you think you're such hot shit?"

"I've got a way out of the prisoner barracks," he said. "Secret way. None of the guards know about it, or, as far as I know, any of the other prisoners."

"Yeah? What's that?"

"I'll keep that one close to my chest, thank you very much. Plus, there's something else. A kind of trump card."

"Yeah? What's that?"

"Two sticks of dynamite, hidden away safely somewhere here in the camp."

Morgan raised his eyebrows. "No shit?" Grushin nodded. "And you know where they are? You can get to them?"

"Yeah, I know where they are, and I have access to

them any day. They've been there a while. No one's found them, and no one's going to."

"How did you happen to come by two sticks of dynamite?"

"There was a prisoner here who was in charge of detonations, down in the mines. Dangerous job. They give it to the people they *really* don't like. Anyway, he lifted these two from two separate detonations where they wouldn't be missed. Tucked them into his uniform, marched all the way back to camp with them, along with a length of detonator fuse, without any of the guards noticing, and then put them away."

"Won't he miss them?"

"Wouldn't think so," Grushin said. "He died a couple weeks before you got here. Got into some trouble with Bortsov's men and met with an unfortunate accident in the mines."

"I see," said Morgan.

"He never knew how to use them to get out. I don't either. But I think you might come up with something."

"Yeah," said Morgan. "I got some ideas."

Chapter Fourteen

Working in the garage changed Morgan's life at the prison. He went from the empty, monotonous drudgery of breaking and carrying stone to something he loved. And the cars needed it. As little as he liked helping his captors, working out clever solutions, fixes, and enhancements with limited materials and tools was a welcome distraction from daily life at the prison.

But as he did, Morgan also compiled a mental inventory on their condition. There were three trucks and two jeeps in the garage, all military, in varying states of disrepair. One of the trucks was broken down. It took Morgan a few minutes to figure out the problem. The fix was simple enough, but no one else needed to know that. One jeep was in good working order, although it was some five years old, and the other was held together with duct tape and a prayer.

The thought of escape filled Morgan with a hopeful energy that he hadn't had since he'd arrived at the prison. Watching and planning took up every waking moment as he studied the rhythms of the prison, its procedures and inner workings, the dogs that circled the perimeter, the guards in the towers, the patrols. The outlines of a plan were slowly forming in his mind.

But there was one thing he had to talk to Grushin about.

"All right," said Morgan. "Let's game this out. We get out of the barracks your secret way. That gets us out in the yard. I can make the generator give out at a crucial moment. This throws us into darkness. Let's say we have our opening in the confusion. We're left with two problems."

This was over their morning meal, before work, one of two times they were able to talk with any kind of privacy.

"First, we have to clear the perimeter fence. The gate's guarded, and the guards have flashlights, and the gate is where they'll concentrate their force. Plus, they're going to loose the dogs. Darkness gets us some cover, but not much.

"Second, we need some means of transportation. If we try to run for it, they'll just come after us as soon as they notice we're missing. We won't get twenty miles out."

"The solution to that is obvious," said Grushin. "We take one of the cars. You have access to the garage. Can you sabotage the rest so that they can't follow us?"

Morgan nodded. "Piece of cake. I can make it so that none of the engines have any hope of starting. But we need to get past the gate. That's where the dynamite comes in." Morgan ran his fingers through the short bristles growing in on his head. "There's something I wanted to talk about. I want to get someone else in on the plan. Badri."

"The Arab?"

"Yeah."

Grushin frowned. "I don't want to bring anyone else into this," he said. "Every person we add to the plan makes it more likely that we will be caught."

"Let me ask you this. Do you know how to deal with dynamite? Do you think you can get it to do what you want it to do, with certainty, without blowing both of us up?"

Grushin had nothing to say to this.

"I want to bring him in," Morgan insisted. "We can't do this without him."

"I don't like it," said Grushin.

"I don't think we have a choice."

"Do you trust him?"

"I trust he wants to escape as much as we do. And I trust he wants nothing to do with his interrogators."

Grushin furrowed his brow, trying to resist the conclusion. "Shit," he said. "Okay. You're right. Talk to him. Feel him out first. Don't reveal more than you have to. But see what he has to say. And I hope you know what you're doing."

Chapter Fifteen

The next day was shower day. Grushin told him that parasites had once grown to be a serious problem in the camp, which the guards wouldn't care about except lice, ticks, and bedbugs weren't too good about telling who was a prisoner and who was a guard. So they made the prisoners shower every week, along with shearing off all their hair and dusting them with chemical powder. It wasn't enough to keep the barracks from smelling like a month-old gym sock. But it kept the critters in check.

The men tossed their uniforms and shoes into a series of plastic tubs, to be taken away for laundry, and waited, naked, as men scrubbed themselves under the cold showers with rough lye soap.

Morgan approached Badri there, as they waited in line. The sound of the showers provided cover so that no one would hear them.

"Goddamn smell, huh?" said Morgan.

"In all my time in this prison, this here remains my least favorite part of it."

"Aren't you glad you can experience it for the first time again through my eyes?"

Badri chuckled. "Truly, it is like regaining my child-like wonder."

"So how bad do you wanna get out of this place?"

"You mean the showers? Very, very much."

"I mean this prison."

"Who does not want to get out of this prison?"

"Well, let's suppose we had a way."

Badri's eyes narrowed. "Are you making conversation or do you have an actual plan?"

"The beginnings of one," said Morgan. "Plus a confederate with some cards up his sleeve."

"Grushin."

It was obvious, of course. The person Morgan spent most of his time with in the prison. Who else would it be?

"What do you need from me?"

"We might be able to get our hands on some explosives. Dynamite. I want to know if you'd know how to use it to help us get out of here."

Badri thought about it. "A distraction, of course, could be useful. We could take down the towers. Perhaps open the gate. Yes, I could help with that."

"Think about it. This isn't going to be easy, and more likely than not we'll end up dead."

"I don't have to think about it. And perhaps there is more that I can help you with." Their turn was coming up to shower, and they would be separated, sent by the guard under different showerheads. "We will talk more about this later. But count me in, Morgan."

They powwowed with Grushin out in the yard at dinnertime, going over the general outline of their escape. Morgan kept an eye on the guards, but mostly they just looked bored. They were just three prisoners talking, after all.

"I was thinking," said Badri. "We can lay down explosives to bring down the posts holding up the fence, about two hundred meters north of the gate. That way, we can drive the car right over the chain link."

"I think that'll work, if you can get the detonation right."

"There is something else," Badri said. "A car by itself won't get us far. They'll see us from a hundred miles away and come after us. They can send helicopters to smoke us out. It may take a few hours, maybe a day or two, but they will certainly find us if we are in any kind of vehicle."

"So what do you suggest?" demanded Grushin.

"I have people," he said. "Friends on the outside. They could bring in transportation. Maybe a small airplane. If they get it within a hundred kilometers or so of the prison, over by the mountains in the horizon, we can drive there and escape before they are able to catch us."

"How do we contact these people?" said Grushin. "It's not like we have cell phones. Not even the guards are allowed to have personal communication devices."

"But there is a communications tower," said Morgan. "And I know where we can get an Internet connection, if anywhere." He looked up at the window to Nevsky's office.

"No," Grushin said. "We can't."

"We must," said Badri. "There is no other way."

"You people are crazy."

"You said you didn't want to die here," said Morgan. "Well, it looks like this is our one way out. So. Are you in?"

"Of course I'm in."

Chapter Sixteen

"Mom, I'm *okay*."

Alex held the phone up to her ear with her shoulder as she looked through the viewfinder on the camera. A car pulled up to the mansion she was surveilling.

"I'm keeping safe. I put some professional people on the case. I'm really only overseeing their work."

"I know you, Alex. I gave you your middle name, and it's not 'safe.'"

Alex took a succession of pictures of the man who emerged, bald and tired-looking, until he disappeared into the house seconds later.

"I'm not putting myself in any kind of danger or anything." She hid her camera back inside her backpack. "Just hanging around Moscow. Taking some pictures to pass the time."

The mansion in question was a prerevolution urban manor that took up the whole block. The sun was getting low in the sky, and the shadow it cast reached Alex where she sat, in a park across the street.

The front door opened once again, and Alex took a

photograph of the person walking out—but it was a security guard, who surveyed the street and closed the door once again.

Alex hid the camera once more and leaned once again against the tree, pretending to be engrossed in a Russian language workbook, early intermediate level.

"How are you holding up, Mom?"

"I wish you were here," she said. "But I keep busy."

"How's Neika?"

"She's here. Dug up all my day lilies yesterday. I had to hose her down in the yard, which wasn't much of a punishment for her, let me tell you."

"Uh-huh."

A young woman had knocked at the service entrance of the mansion. Alex picked up the camera once more and photographed her as she turned around and lit a cigarette. She was young and pretty, blond, wearing heavy makeup and a black dress that, while not indecent, didn't leave much doubt about what kind of service she was there to perform.

"Well, I see you're otherwise busy, so I'll let you go."

The door opened, and the woman dropped her cigarette and ground it into the pavement.

"No, Mom, I—listen, I'll call you back, okay?"

"If you say so."

Alex hung up the phone and reviewed the photos. Two clear shots of her face.

The light was growing dim, and she was tired. Time to call it a day.

She packed up the book and the camera and walked away from the mansion, then six blocks south before hailing a cab and telling the driver to take her back to Dobrynin's.

Alex picked up a baked potato loaded with cheese and

mushrooms from a street vendor. She said hello to Agrafena at the counter, receiving a grumble in return, and ate alone in their tiny kitchen.

Dobrynin pushed his way inside as she was washing the dishes. To say that he was in a foul mood would imply that he was ever not in one.

"Anything today?"

She dried her hands and pulled the camera from the bag. He turned his attention to a wall where they had hung photographs Alex had taken on other days.

"Look, this man," he said, holding up the camera's viewer and pointing at a picture on the wall. "Same."

"Wish I knew who he was." Alex finished drying the dishes as he looked at the rest.

Over the course of the past week, it become obvious that Dobrynin never left the house, or indeed saw anyone. Agrafena, whose relationship with Dobrynin was never made clear—Alex figured wife or sister, but nothing between then suggested any definitive answer—did all the necessary shopping for groceries and other necessities, saw to all of the scant customers in the butcher shop, and also received the meat that arrived on Mondays, Wednesdays, and Fridays. Dobrynin, meanwhile, cut the meat in the reeking refrigerated room in the back.

"It's no use," Alex said as her host cycled through the picture. "Anyone who's at all important has tinted windows and brings their car in through the garage."

"Those people have no value to us," said Dobrynin. "Tell me, is it easy to get to Suvorov?"

"Um, duh. Otherwise what would have been the point of staking him out for fourteen hours a day?"

He belched, and a foul smell of alcohol reached her nostrils. "Do you think it will be any easier to get to someone important?"

"No, I guess not."

Dobrynin turned the camera's viewer for her to see. "This is weak spot. This is how we get him."

She was looking at a pretty girl, smoking, looking worriedly out into the street.

Chapter Seventeen

Morgan lay in bed that night with a sense of accomplishment. Things were lining up, and this escape plan seemed increasingly likely. He stared at the ceiling as the spotlight from the guard tower passed over the wall outside, shining in through the windows, casting a silhouette of the bars.

Men snored and shuffled in fitful dreams. Morgan closed his eyes and drifted off to sleep.

He was awakened by the opening of the cell door. His eyes opened in a flash.

Something was wrong. It was still dark, no wake-up siren, no nothing.

Other men who slept as lightly as he did also moved in their bunks, turning to see what was going on.

Several shadows came into the barracks. They made straight for Morgan's bunk. He tried to scramble off it and away from them, but in his sleepy state, he was slow and clumsy. They were on him in seconds.

He was pulled off his bunk and tossed on the floor, hitting it hard with his back.

By the light of the spotlight, Morgan saw Bortsov looming over him, flanked by four of his henchmen. Who had let him inside? Did he have that much pull with the guards?

Morgan moved to roll under the bed, but the goon was faster, and blocked his way. Together two of them held on to his arms. He tried to wrest himself free, kicking and twisting, but they held firm.

"This is your time to die."

"I'm protected," said Morgan.

"I don't see any protection," Bortsov said, making a show of looking right and left. "Do you?"

"Nevsky is going to get it from Suvorov, and then he's going to come after you."

"Eh, he will give me a few lashes, maybe. It will sting for two weeks. But you, you will be dead."

He was wrong, but Morgan stood no chance of convincing him. He had one chance to save his life now.

"Help!" Morgan screamed. *"Pomogite! Pomo—"*

They stuffed a piece of cloth in his mouth, muffling his voice. Others were awake now, but no one moved to help him. They were all too scared.

One of Bortsov's men handed him a rock almost the size of a basketball. Bortsov took it, his shoulders sagging under its weight. He raised it over his head. When he dropped it, it would come down and crush Morgan's skull.

"Now you die, Amerikanskyi."

Two guards burst into the barracks, shouting. They had heard his cries for help! An intense expression came over Bortsov's face, and he pushed the rock downward.

But the guards had distracted the men who were holding him, and Morgan twisted free, rolling out of the way as the rock hit the floor, breaking tile.

The guards drove Bortsov's men out first under blows from their nightsticks, then dragged off Bortsov himself. Then they told Morgan to stand and took him outside, across the yard to the place where they had shaved him on his first day there. After Morgan had been sitting for a few minutes under guard, the warden appeared. He was wearing a rumpled shirt and reeked of alcohol.

"You have made yourself very unpopular in your time here. A few weeks and already you have enemies." He emitted a resounding belch. "I would be happy to throw you to the dogs. Sometimes they even do it in interesting ways. It breaks up the monotony." He leaned over Morgan menacingly. His breath was heinous. "You see, most people here, nobody cares if they are killed. Me least of all. But General Suvorov has other plans for you. And then you will be regretting that B did not kill you."

Morgan didn't give him the satisfaction of a response.

"I would enjoy breaking you. I would also enjoy seeing what Bortsov's boys would have done. They can be very creative in their punishments. But you are too valuable to us to let die. That is left to General Suvorov." He turned and walked away, giving an order to the guard as he left.

They escorted Morgan out of the building and not into the barracks but somewhere else. And Morgan knew where.

It was a small building, one with only a handful of tiny cells in it, each with a heavy steel door with no openings but a slot low near the ground.

Solitary. He was going in the hole.

The guards opened the cell door and he got a peek inside. It was perhaps just big enough for him to lie down, and not comfortably. They shoved him inside and closed the creaky steel door, leaving him in pitch darkness.

Chapter Eighteen

The solitary cell was designed to make men crazy, this Morgan knew. He'd seen plenty in his day, and the concept was well familiar to him.

It doesn't seem like much, being put in a room by yourself. A naive observer might not even think it would rise to the level of punishment. But Morgan knew. Morgan had experienced it before, and had seen it happen to others. Isolation and sensory deprivation had their way of getting under even the hardest man's skin.

Silence makes you sensitive to every little noise, and total darkness makes you see shapes, lights and patterns that are not there. Soon you start to think you heard scraps of voices, people talking to you, sometimes even voices you recognize.

Morgan sat up and breathed, trying to hold back against the encroaching madness, trying to center his thoughts on his breathing, on feeling the ground under him, on the aches in his body, on resisting succumbing to the despair of his thirst and hunger. You do not know how fast time goes in the dark, when it's day and when it's night, and so time seems not to pass at all.

Thus, Morgan had no idea how much time had passed when the food slot opened and a partial face appeared and whispered, "Hello." Morgan could just make him out through the slot. He was blond and young, bony and angular, with wispy stubble on his cheek. "Come closer."

There was something conspiratorial about the way he spoke, not the barking orders he was used to. Morgan crawled toward him, every movement painful.

"I heard about what you did," he said. "In the mine. I do not know what you did to be in this place, but you do not deserve to be in here."

Morgan grunted in response.

"They beat Bortsov very bad. Nevsky is very angry." He pushed a bowl through the slot. "Here. Take it."

Morgan did. By the dim light he saw that it was filled with stew, not the prisoners' thin, rancid soup, but something borscht-like, filled with meat and potatoes turned pink from the fragrant paprika. Morgan was salivating at the smell.

"Don't let anyone see the bowl until I come back tomorrow."

"Wait," said Morgan. "Who are you?"

"My name is Filipov."

Chapter Nineteen

Alex Morgan had been searching through high-end escort service websites for—she checked the clock—seven hours now, and she found she'd become inured to the sleaze covered in a veneer of class that these establishments affected.

She scoured each website. Most had profiles for the girls, and Alex looked through each one, a parade of blondes and brunettes in suggestive poses, faces pancaked with makeup, fake tits in low-cut tops.

The Internet connection didn't help either. Dobrynin was not exactly what one might call an early adopter. He'd only switched out his rotary phone because the network stopped supporting it. So Alex used her father's money to buy a 3G modem, and it could take a full ten seconds to load a high-quality image—which didn't seem like a lot at first, but became an increasing pain as the photos Alex had to look through reached the hundreds.

She was now looking through a website designed in a black and gold theme, everything about it signaling luxury. She didn't even have to open the girl's profile. Alex recognized her from the thumbnail on the page.

She called herself Lara.

"Call them," Dobrynin said when she showed it to him. "Pretend to be secretary of American."

"What if they don't speak English?"

"They will."

Alex took her prepaid Russian cell phone and dialed the number on the website.

"*Zdrávstvujte.*" A woman's voice. Young.

"Hello, I need an English speaker, please? *Angliyskiy?*"

"Yes, hello, I can speak English. How may I help you?" Her voice was accented in Russian with a gentle inflection of Queen's English.

Alex put on her best secretarial voice. "I'm calling on behalf of my employer, Mr. Phillips. I'd like to engage one of your girls for the evening."

"Certainly, ma'am. Which girl would that be?"

"Lara? The fourteenth on the website here."

"I'm afraid Lara is not available for tonight."

"How about tomorrow?"

"Not for the rest of the week."

"Mr. Phillips is adamant that he wants this girl," Alex said. "He is willing to pay."

"Unfortunately, she is not working tonight," said the woman. "Mr. Phillips may perhaps be interested in—"

"Listen," Alex broke in, letting anxiety creep into her voice, "Mr. Phillips is not a very nice man, and when he sets his mind on something, he doesn't really take excuses, you know? Things could get *really* bad for me if I don't get her."

Alex heard dead air on the line. Then the woman said, "Listen, you can't tell anyone I did this, okay? She's taking some time off from us, but I know she does freelance. I can give you her phone number."

"Really? That would be wonderful."

Alex wrote down the number on her computer.

"Thank you so much," Alex said. "You really saved my life today."

Chapter Twenty

Alex dialed the number for the fifteenth time, and for the fifteenth time the call went straight to voicemail.

"This goddamn technology," Dobrynin said. "Stay. I will make a phone call."

He picked up the phone in the shop and dialed. "Let me speak to Sokoloff," he said in Russian, and she was surprised at the ease with which she understood. The studying was paying off.

Dobrynin tapped his foot and muttered under his breath while he was on hold. The next words out of his mouth were an insult, and then a deep laugh.

"How are you, you bastard?" Dobrynin continued. "I need some information. I have a phone number." He gave the man the digits. "Yes, that's right." He wrote something down on a piece of butcher paper and thanked the man.

"I got a name," Dobrynin said, now in English, holding out the piece of paper. "Maria Kapustin."

"Got an address?"

"What, I have to do everything for you?"

* * *

Alex had been waiting for hours outside the lumpen apartment building when Maria Kapustin walked out the front door, wearing sunglasses about two hours too late for them to be of any use.

Alex decided a head-on approach would be as good as any. Maria was walking fast, and Alex had to jog to catch up with her.

"Maria?" she said. The woman looked at her, and the sunglasses could not hide the panic in her eyes. "Don't worry," Alex said. "I don't want to hurt you."

From up close, Alex saw the edge of a black eye peeking out from under the glasses, and purple marks on Maria's neck not quite covered with makeup.

"Do you speak English?"

"*Da*. Yes." Maria did not lessen her pace.

"I'd really like to talk to you. Can I buy you dinner, or a drink?"

"I can buy my own, thank you."

Alex decided to take a chance. "It's about the man who did this to you."

Maria stopped walking and looked Alex straight in the eye. "What do you know about the man who did this?"

"I know he's a bad man," said Alex. "And I intend to hurt him back."

Maria resumed walking. "American girl comes to be a big hero to poor oppressed Russian women?"

Lying wasn't going to get her anywhere. "I have my own agenda," said Alex. "I'll admit that. This isn't about you. But you can get a bit of revenge."

Maria stopped and opened the door to a place Alex saw was a dive bar. She held the door open. "Well?" she said. "Are you going to buy me a drink or not?"

They settled into a corner table. The only other customers were the everyday drunks who'd probably already been there for hours. Maria ordered them a couple of beers before Alex could say anything. Then she removed her glasses, setting them on the table, and revealed a dark purple blotch under her left eye.

"Masha," the girl said. "That is what everyone calls me. Everyone who knows my real name, anyway. So what is your deal?"

Alex opted for full disclosure. "I'm looking for my father. I think Suvorov is the one who took him."

"If that is true, then I am sorry for your loss," Masha said.

"I'm not ready to believe that yet," Alex said. "What do you know about him?"

"I know he is a goddamn bastard," Masha said with bitterness. "And that all the girls are afraid of him. But when he calls, we cannot refuse. At least the money is good."

"He does this to all of them?" Alex asked.

Masha nodded. "We all know it. Go to see Suvorov, and you will not work again for two weeks until the bruises fade enough to cover up with makeup. It upsets the other clients, see." The waitress set down the pints of beer on the table and she downed half of it in the time it took Alex to take one sip.

"He likes us young and meek," Masha said. "His sick little games are more fun for him that way."

An idea was forming in Alex's mind. "Masha," she said, "do you think I could replace the next girl Suvorov calls?"

Chapter Twenty-one

The guard Filipov gave Morgan food whenever possible, and would sit outside his cell and talk to him whenever he was keeping watch by himself. It was Morgan's way of keeping time, his conversations with Filipov over rich, flavorful food, in between the long stretches of black nothingness, during which time he exercised as much as he could in the cramped cell to keep up his strength.

Filipov asked about American culture. He loved classic rock and Van Halen, *Mad Max,* and *Die Hard.* They even sang Elvis songs together quietly, Filipov with his heavy Russian accent.

By his reckoning, Morgan was in there for two weeks before he was jogged awake by harsh light cast on his face. He squinted, unaccustomed to the brightness.

A guard was standing at the door. "American. Out."

Morgan picked himself up off the floor. Thanks to the extra food and exercise, he felt better coming out than going in, but he made a show of bracing against the wall and of getting up on shaky legs.

The guard grunted with impatience. "Quickly."

Morgan emerged outside, feeling the harsh cold wind on his skin for the first time in weeks. The men were lining up for the evening count. Morgan found Grushin and stood next to him.

"So he emerges. Badri and I were beginning to think you were dead."

"Not dead. Just buried."

"What was it, two weeks?"

"You know better than I do," said Morgan.

"I was thrown in solitary once. I was talking to my toes on the second day." He looked Morgan up and down. "But you look hale and hearty, smell aside."

"It was all right. A little boring."

Morgan picked out the men who had attacked him in line. They were giving him stares that could melt steel.

"They are suspicious of you," said Grushin. "Because you have Nevsky's support. And people don't like that."

Morgan figured as much. Nevsky had bought him temporary safety, at the expense of putting him in greater danger in the long term.

"Badri and I have been talking. Working out the details of the plan. I think this is going to work."

"We need to put this plan in motion soon," said Morgan. "We can't wait any longer."

The chill set in as the count went on. Afterward, Grushin said, "Come with me. I want to show you something."

They walked together into the prisoners' barracks.

It was a grate that looked solidly in place but came loose after Grushin worked it for a few seconds.

"Through here, we can easily get outside," he said. "I

have left the barracks several times in the night to test it. Nobody knows about it. Nobody is watching. We need to get Badri in Nevsky's office. We can get outside, but I have no idea how to get into the building."

"I have an idea," Morgan said.

Chapter Twenty-two

Morgan lay in bed and waited for Grushin's signal, three taps on the bar to the outer doors. He got out of bed, careful not to wake anyone. Not that it would compromise the mission if he did—men got up to use the head in the middle of the night all the time.

He found Badri and Grushin already waiting for him at their arranged meeting spot. Grushin led the way to their secret passage out. They snuck under the grate, Morgan taking the lead and Grushin bringing up the rear.

Once they were outside, the wind chilled them to the bone. Morgan looked at the four guard towers, each housing a sniper and a spotlight that they shone over the camp in periodic cycles. The cover of the buildings meant that they never had to be in the line of sight of more than two towers, and often not more than one or none, so avoiding them was just a matter of watching out for the lights. Unless they were discovered, in which case it was a matter of luck whether they would survive the night. Then he searched for the dogs that patrolled the perimeter. Their attention wouldn't necessarily be called by their presence out in the yard, but if they caught their scent and decided to raise the alarm, it was all over.

They ran along the wall to the prisoners' barracks, keeping to the shadow. This was simple enough, with the light that would normally illuminate this spot burned out. Once they reached the end, they crossed the short distance to the building that housed the kitchen and laundry.

They heard footsteps coming from around the corner of the laundry building. Morgan held up his hand, then motioned for them to move backward.

They stood, backs glued to the building, as the guards walked past, chatting in Russian and laughing. They weren't expecting anyone out here. The patrol was a duty and nothing more.

They did not turn their heads, and didn't see them.

Morgan held his hand up as he waited for them to move away far enough, watching the lights from the towers as he did. Finding an opening, he motioned for Grushin and Badri to follow.

They ran across the gap at the far end of the laundry building. One more gap to cross to reach the door to the administration building, where Nevsky's office was located.

Behind them at the perimeter fence, a dog started barking.

Morgan had a choice to make. They could retreat to the prisoner barracks, where they could return with relative safety. Or they could press on, trying their luck at the risk of getting caught

Morgan opted to move forward. He took the lead, running full tilt toward their goal, the door two hundred feet away. He felt the two other men close behind him.

They crossed the distance to the sound of the barking dog. The spotlight from the nearest tower missed Badri's foot by inches, but left them shrouded in darkness.

Morgan tried the handle and found the door to the administration building unlocked, as Filipov had promised.

They closed the door and heard the sound of boots outside. Guards. This was the moment of truth. Had they been seen? Would the guards come in after them? Morgan held his breath, listening intently.

They passed, oblivious to the possibility that the two had gone inside. Morgan exhaled in relief.

He heard them talking, and Morgan caught the word *krolik*. Rabbit. Got the dogs barking wildly sometimes.

Morgan took the lead upstairs. He alone among them knew this building. He led them to the door to Nevsky's office—locked, as they had anticipated. He took out the improvised lock pick he'd taken from the garage and set to work opening the lock to Nevsky's door.

Within a couple of seconds, he turned it, hearing the *click* of the lock. Removing the pick and pulling the knob, he pushed the door open.

"After you."

The first thing Morgan did was to check that the curtains were closed, so that no one could see them from outside. Badri knelt and turned on the computer. Morgan looked through a crack in the curtains as the machine booted up. Everything outside was as quiet as they had left it.

"There is a password," said Badri.

Shit. How had Morgan not thought of this?

But someone else had. "I can do this," said Grushin. "You know those young Russian hackers you keep hearing about? Well, I was one of them when I was a teenager."

Grushin reclined in Nevsky's chair. "Oh my God, I have not sat in anything so comfortable in months. Seriously, you guys have to try this."

"Focus," Morgan said through gritted teeth.

"Cool your horses," Grushin said, and began typing. "This is going to be a breeze."

Morgan kept watch outside the door as Grushin did his thing. "Got it." He asked Badri, "How do you send your messages?"

Badri just shook his head and prodded Grushin off the chair. "I do this part." Badri typed at the computer, writing the message to his confederates for about two minutes. "Okay," he whispered. "It's done."

"Let me just wipe all records of us being here," said Grushin.

"Are you sure your people will come?" Morgan asked Badri as the Russian typed.

"They will come. It is only a matter of us being there to meet them."

Chapter Twenty-three

The call came two days later, when Alex was cooped up in Dobrynin's dark little kitchen, cramming Russian vocabulary.

"There is a girl," Masha told her over the phone. "Klara. She was called to Suvorov's house tonight. He has not met her before."

Alex checked her watch. It was still just after 3:00 P.M. "Then that's our opening."

"She still wants the money," Masha said. "But she is happy for you to take her place. She is black-haired. But we can resolve that. I will bring some hair dye."

"Oh, great." Alex ran her hand through her hair. Black was not going to suit her.

"And you need to be sexy."

"I can be sexy."

Masha giggled. Alex couldn't help feeling offended. "I will be around in a couple of hours," said Masha. "I will bring the dye and some clothes for you, and I will teach you. Crash course. Oh, and Klara says thank you."

Alex hung up and went into the refrigerated room to tell Dobrynin the news

"So you are doing this?" he said as he chopped up a hunk of meat with a cleaver.

"I have to," she said. "It's my only chance at this."

"Do not get caught," he said. "Do not let him know who you are. Get what information you can in his house—anything to trade for your father. That is your only chance. If you are found out, you will not come out of there alive."

"I know, we've been over this," she said with impatience.

"Insufferable girl. You want my help? This is my help." He brought the cleaver down hard against the cutting board, splitting a piece of pork loin into three parts. "Do not get yourself killed, okay?"

Alex knocked at the service entrance where she had first seen Masha days before.

Her hair was black, the smell of the dye still lingering despite her best efforts at washing it. She hoped no one would notice, but then again, Suvorov had not been promised natural hair.

She was wearing more makeup than she'd ever worn in her life, and her skin was exposed in all the wrong places. She liked slight outfits, shorts and tank tops, that gave her freedom of movement, which the dress Masha had lent her did not—not unless she wanted to flash the entire street.

A security guard opened the door and ordered her inside.

Alex had made great strides with her immersion in the language and Dobrynin's muttering instruction, and she made a particular effort to mimic the accent. She understood the basic orders relayed to her—come, stay, follow me—while keeping quiet and looking down took care of the rest.

She was searched and then moved out of the servants' area, and Alex realized she was in the most luxurious house she'd ever seen. Everything was marble and carved wood, walls hung with classical paintings with elaborate frames, thick oriental carpets draped on the floor.

She was shown to a room that wasn't a bedroom, but rather some kind of parlor appointed with several chaise longues and divans. There she was told to sit and wait.

She examined the room. The paintings on the wall Alex recognized as being nineteenth century by their style. On a side table was a statue of a faun, half man, half goat, made of bronze, and against an opposite wall was another of an angel, wings swept upward.

A set of double doors opened and a man walked in, wearing a suit. Suvorov. He was old, near sixty, although he was still strong and fit. He looked rather like a fish, with shallow eyes and a nose that jutted forward in his face. Alex felt a shiver of revulsion.

"Good evening," he said in Russian. Alex mumbled a response.

He crossed the room, closing the distance between them. "Speak louder."

She was afraid to. She was afraid he'd catch her accent, and that'd be the end of it. Masha had told her he liked them shy. So she'd be shy. She mumbled a "Good evening."

"Look at me. What is your name? Speak up."

She looked up at him and said, still mumbling, in her best Russian accent, "Alexandra."

"I said speak—" His open hand flew at her face. On instinct, she raised hers and stopped the blow.

Too fast. Too well-trained. She saw by the way that he was looking at her that she'd given herself away.

Suvorov moved to pin her down against the divan, and she rolled out of the way, onto her feet on the carpet. She brought both elbows down hard on Suvorov's back and twisted his arm, pulling it upward.

"Dan Morgan," she said. "Where is he?"

His eyes went wide with surprise. *Yeah, weren't expecting that, were you, asshole?*

"What is he to you?"

"Answer me. Where is he?"

"Far beyond your reach, you whore."

She pulled his arm harder, and he grunted in pain. "*Tell me.*"

Suvorov whipped his head back, catching her nose. Blood began to flow out. He freed his arm from her grip and he swung, his palm snapping against her cheek so hard it knocked her to her feet.

Stupid. You know how to take a blow better than that.

"Your interest in Morgan . . . I see a resemblance," he said, standing over her. He stepped on her hand and she cried out in pain. "Maybe it is the blood. What are you? His daughter?"

She gritted her teeth and fumed at him. From her vantage point, his face was wreathed with the clouds painted on the ceiling.

"He came here, you know," said Suvorov. "Called himself Bevelacqua. Said he wanted to buy guns from me. Got inside my house and tried to steal from me. Maybe deceit runs in the family." He ground his heel into her hand, and she yelled out in pain.

"What did you do with him?"

"We caught him, you know. When he broke in. He shot two of my security guards, broke the bones of three more. But we cornered him in the basement, finally." He leaned down and pushed a lock of black hair out of her eyes. "So pretty, too. And now mine. I'm going to have my fun with you, girl."

"Sorry, General, but I don't think fun is in the cards."

With her free hand, she punched him hard in the groin. He bent double in pain, and she pushed him off sideways. She stood and made a run for the door, but he ran after her. She ran for the far side of the room, then turned to face him. He was moving fast, bringing his superior weight to bear against her.

And she was going to use that.

She bodychecked him, which sent her flying backward, but was just enough to knock his path to the right—into the angel statue with the upswept wings, which were just sharp enough to pierce his belly.

Suvorov hollered in pain.

That was going to attract the guards.

The statue didn't do much damage, but it was enough for Alex to get back to her feet and run through the double doors he'd come from, into his private chambers—an office, and a bedroom beyond.

She heard the heavy footsteps of Suvorov's bodyguards, half a dozen at least, approaching from below. They were going to cut off all exits downstairs, so she had to do something they wouldn't expect.

She went up. She found a narrow staircase that led upstairs, to a long hallway of bedrooms, where the ceiling had the slant of the roof outside. She chose one two thirds down. The window would not open, so she grabbed a heavy brass lamp from the bedside table and shattered the glass, breaking the frames wide enough for her to pass.

Alex walked out onto the roof, bracing against the

window frame. She was barefoot, and her dress wafted in a cool breeze, not exactly ideal gear for the situation. But being barefoot was a hidden blessing on the rounded tiles. She walked over the ridge of the roof to the other side. No one outside seemed to be looking for her yet—they still thought she was inside. She looked over the edge, studying the pattern of the bricks. Yes, she could do it, even in a slutty dress. She sat on the eaves, hidden by darkness from anyone who might see her, and reached for a handhold, easing her way off to hang from the wall.

She climbed down the western wall, which was shrouded in darkness. She waited for the vehicle patrol to pass and jumped over the fence, dashing across the street and out into the night, as far away from Suvorov's house as her legs could take her.

Chapter Twenty-four

Morning count. Morgan, Grushin, and Badri got together to talk things over for a few minutes before the
guards forced them into the line.

"I asked them to signal from the west using lights
blinking Morse code," said Badri. "That's how we'll
know that they're there, and where they are."

"They'll get us away from here?" said Grushin. "Are
you sure?"

"They are loyal, and they have the resources inside
Russia. They will be there. They will get all three of us
out."

"If they actually manage to get here," said Grushin.

"We look to the west," he said.

"Because if they don't, then we are liable to be eaten
by—"

A siren sounded, the sign for them to line up for the
count. They prisoners shuffled into position, making a
wide semicircle in the yard. A murmur of activity propa-
gated from one end. Someone was approaching, and the

prisoners were turning to look. It was Nevsky, walking down the line.

Morgan's gut sank. Did he know? Was he coming to kill them?

He stopped in front of him.

"Prisoner Morgan," he said. "I am surprised at the people you have chosen to be your friends here. But you have my congratulations for managing to stay alive this long."

Nevsky kicked Morgan in the knees, and he fell on all fours. "Down like the animal you are. So you do not forget your place."

Morgan's face burned with rage, but he couldn't do anything about it without getting it worse. Nevsky was daring him to.

"General Suvorov is coming," Nevsky said. "He wishes to interrogate you personally. I just wanted to let you know. One more week. And then he will make you talk."

Chapter Twenty-five

Alex didn't dare take a taxi. Instead, she walked barefoot for three hours through the streets of Moscow until she arrived at Dobrynin's butcher shop. The shop was closed for the day, so she knocked, softly at first, but when she got no response, as the stress of the night caught up to her, she slammed her hand against the door harder and harder, as if it were to blame.

Dobrynin opened the door to admit her.

"Did anyone follow you?"

She pushed her way past him. "You aren't even going to say you're glad I'm alive?"

Dobrynin shrugged. "I guess I am glad you are alive. Were you followed?"

"No, I wasn't goddamn followed."

She grabbed a T-shirt, jeans, shoes and socks from her suitcase and changed out of the dress in the bathroom. When she came out, Dobrynin was waiting for him in the kitchen, a chair pulled out for her. "Sit. Tell me what happened."

She related to him what had transpired in Suvorov's

mansion and he listened, heavy lidded. When she was finished, he said, "You need to go home, girl. Your little adventure here is finished."

"I still haven't found my father. I think he might be alive."

"He knows your face, and soon, so will every policeman in Moscow, or worse. It is time for you to go."

"I won't go."

"Then you will go from my house," he said. "I will not have you endanger me and Agrafena with your presence."

"Fine," she said, getting up from the table. "I'll go somewhere else."

"You do that and you will be killed. And I will not be there to help you."

"Are you serious, Dobrynin? You haven't left this goddamn house. Not since I got here. Every moment I've been out there so far, I've been on my own."

"And do you know why I do not leave this house?"

"You're a shut-in," she said. "A coward."

"I am a dead man. I have been a dead man from the day your father came after me. To kill me."

She furrowed her brow. "Kill you?"

"Yes! Or do you not know he was an assassin? I was an agent of Russian intelligence. I gave information to the Americans because I was done with this piss pot of a country. They were supposed to get me out. Instead they sent a man to kill me."

"But he saved you," she said. "That's what happened, isn't it? Instead of killing you, he let you go and told you to disappear."

"He did. For me to live the rest of my life stuck inside, never going out in the sun. To live in this stinking house!"

Alex slammed her palm down on the table. "He saved your life!"

"Only from himself. I don't owe you nothing else. Get out. Get out!"

"Fine," she said, going into the tiny room she had been sleeping in and stuffing her things into her suitcase. "I'll go, and you can go back to being a miserable old man who isn't any good to anyone!"

"You are just a goddamn child!" he hollered. "I never asked for you! You came to *my* door!"

"Well, I won't make that mistake again."

She stormed out, slamming the door behind her with a ring of the bell that hung above it.

Chapter Twenty-six

Grushin helped Morgan up. They watched Nevsky walk away in his unsteady drunk's version of a military march, like a rooster surveying his chickens, as the guards resumed the prisoner count.

"He told me just to screw with me," Morgan told Grushin. "But you know what? It's not going to work. Because we're still going to get out of here."

"That's the spirit."

"Except we're going to need to do this in less than seven days."

"Wait, what?" said Grushin. "No. There's no way."

"No choice. After a week they'll move me to an interrogation cell. And I don't come out of that alive."

"Shit." Grushin rocked back and forth. "Shit. What do we do?"

"We have no choice," Badri said. "We do this with Morgan or we do not do this at all."

"Shit!" Grushin yelled. People turned and stared. Morgan hushed him. But it wasn't too suspicious. Not here. There was plenty to scream and curse about.

"We need to get word to my people," Badri said. "We need them to be ready in a week's time. That means—"

"We have to go back into Nevsky's office," Morgan said.

The hallway was dark.

They'd done this before, but there was a nervous energy now that hadn't been there before.

Morgan picked the lock once more and pushed open the door.

There was light inside the office, pale and dim. The computer was on. And at the desk, asleep, was Nevksy.

He was snoring like a drunkard, a snorting, gasping snore. He smelled of liquor.

Morgan looked at Grushin, who stared back in wide-eyed terror. Badri was calm. He was used to focusing under pressure. He was ready.

Morgan tiptoed to the desk and turned the monitor slowly around. He picked up the keyboard with his right hand, lifting it off the desk. As he carried it, he tipped over the pencil cup. His left hand shot out and grabbed it before its contents spilled all over the desk.

Nevsky stirred, snorting.

Morgan noticed that he was holding his breath, and started breathing again. He set the keyboard down on the desk for Badri to use.

Badri stood at the desk across from the sleeping Nevsky. Morgan kept his eyes on him, watching him for any twitch that might herald his return to consciousness. He was so vulnerable. It would be so easy to reach out and snuff out this bastard's life, and end all the evil he would ever do.

Except he couldn't. Not now. Morgan needed to let him live, so that they would have their chance to escape.

Badri hit *send* and closed the browser window. He then set the keyboard back where it belonged as Badri turned the monitor back around.

He nodded. *Done.* Time to get the hell out of there.

They slipped out of the room and Morgan locked the door behind them. The three issued a collective sigh of relief.

"It is sent," said Badri. "If everything goes to plan, they should be here in three days."

"If," said Morgan. "Let's hope they do. Or else it's my ass."

Chapter Twenty-seven

Morgan and Grushin met up at dinner after a day of nervous anticipation. The day's stew smelled pungently of spoiled potatoes. The wind seemed to have died down, and the weather seemed to be mild, if anything.

"Eat up," said Morgan. "We don't know when we'll have the chance to eat again."

This was the day.

"Are you both ready?" Badri asked.

"I got the dynamite," said Grushin. Morgan had already noticed the subtle bulge at his waist.

"The cars are ready," said Morgan. "I put metal shavings in the oil of all the cars except the newest jeep. If anyone tries to follow us, whatever car they use will run about as well as a brick within a few seconds."

"So we get past the fence and we're in the clear," said Grushin.

"Something like that. I also left the crowbar hidden in the grass outside the garage."

"Then we're ready," Grushin said. "All we have to do now is actually do it."

Morgan leaned back against the concrete wall of the prisoner barracks. "What are you going to do when you get out?"

"I'm going to a bar and I'm going to order myself a beer and a hamburger," Grushin said in a dreamy tone. "Then I'm going to find my girl. I don't care if she's moved on, if she's with someone else. The moment she sees me—that's all that's going to matter."

Morgan knew the story too well of what so often happened with the guys in the military who left their sweethearts behind. And this one had every reason to think he was dead.

But he needed something to cling to. And who knew? Maybe she was waiting for him after all.

"What about you?"

"I don't know," said Morgan. "I've been thinking about this a lot. And I don't know. My organization has a hell of a life insurance policy. My family's taken care of for life, moneywise. And there's something else. I'm marked. Suvorov knows who I am. He's going to leave them alone now that he has me, but if I escape . . . If I go back to them, I'm dooming them to a life on the run. Maybe they're just better off without me."

"You do what you have to do," said Grushin.

Morgan had to steady himself through evening count and the march into the barracks as adrenaline pumped through him in a constant buzz. He was ready. They were going to do this.

Morgan lay in the dark, excitement pounding in his head, until he heard Grushin's bird call. He met him and Badri outside. In his hands were two objects, long and thin. Two sticks of dynamite, which he handed Badri, who was already holding a length of rusty rebar. "Make it count."

"Just be ready to do your part."

They moved together as far as the laundry building. Badri broke away from them there, running toward the fence, where he would twist the rebar around the cable that tethered the dogs and then drive it into the ground. This would stop any of the dogs circling the perimeter from being able to approach him as he lay down the dynamite.

Morgan and Grushin, meanwhile, made their way across the yard to the garage. Grushin climbed through the unlocked window of the motor hangar and disappeared inside.

Leaving the Russian to do his part of the plan, Morgan made his way along the outer wall of the building. Around the corner was the large door through which the cars came out of the garage.

Morgan watched for the pattern as the spotlight shone around the grounds. He retreated from the corner as it passed, casting a long straight shadow on the ground.

He had to wait before breaking the padlock open with the crowbar. Once he opened the garage, they would have to move fast.

He stayed put and listened for the start of the engine that was the signal for him to spring into action.

Minutes passed, and the tundra wind howled. The light circled back, and then again. Morgan strained to hear, but there was no sign of the engine starting up.

This was taking too long. Badri was going to blow the gate and the truck would still be in the garage.

He couldn't wait anymore. He readied himself, tightening his grip on the crowbar. He waited until the light passed, then he ran, inserting the crowbar through the padlock and pulling down, using the leverage to break it open. It fell to the ground with a soft *thud*.

Morgan pulled the door open just enough for him to pass, revealing the dark garage inside, the black shapes of the trucks looming in the murk. He closed the door behind him.

"Grushin?"

The lights came on with a loud crack, and Morgan found himself staring down the muzzles of half a dozen submachine guns. Each was held by a uniformed prison guard.

In the middle was Nevsky, a diabolical smile plastered on his face. Grushin was standing stiffly next to him.

"Do you really think I didn't see the three of you scheming out in the yard? Do you think I don't know what goes on in my prison?"

Among the guards was Filipov, holding his rifle nervously, something apologetic in his expression. There was nothing he could do about this, he seemed to say.

"My men are bringing the Arab in as we speak. He, like you, is too valuable to dispose of summarily. I'm afraid I can't say as much about young Mr. Grushin."

Nevsky drew a knife and in an unhesitating movement pushed it deep into Grushin's throat. Grushin's face contorted in pain and surprise. Nevsky pulled it out with a spurt of blood.

He fell at Nevsky's feet.

"Oh, and before I forget." Nevsky drew his sidearm. Before anyone could react, he aimed at Filipov's head and fired. The guard crumpled to the ground on top of his submachine gun.

"See what happens to those who help you? See what happens to the people you rope into your plans?" He wiped his knife on a handkerchief. "I have orders to keep you alive until General Suvorov returns. But believe me.

Your end will be much less pleasant than your friend's here."

He punched Morgan in his side.

"You will be taken to solitary confinement. And there you will stay until the day you die. Don't worry. It won't be too long."

Chapter Twenty-eight

Alex returned to her cramped room at the Ustritsa Hotel from her morning run. The wallpaper was peeling, the air smelled of mildew, and something that looked like black mold was growing in the corner. But it was a place to sleep. And to plan.

She took a shower and sat down on the hard bed, setting the partial map of Suvorov's house she had drawn from memory on the bed.

The time was approaching to implement her plan.

She'd been studying the patterns of Suvorov's security. Two men sat in a car across the street from the mansion, all day, every day. But every night at around two a.m., the car moved out and new guards took their place. This would give her a narrow opening to move in on the house.

She'd wait across the street, hidden in shadows, until they were on the move. Then she'd move across the street, scale the fence, and then climb the wall of his house back to the roof and gain admittance from there. She knew she could do it going down. Going up wouldn't be any more difficult.

She'd go in through one of the windows that opened to the roof. From there, she traced the route through her map to Suvorov's private chambers. If she didn't find what she was looking for, she'd settle for killing him.

Alex got dressed and set out for another day of sur-veilling the mansion. She needed to make sure everything was according to plan.

She climbed down the stairs and moved out into the street, hailing an approaching taxi. It pulled up to the curb, and the driver stepped out to open the door for her.

Alex was too excited to be suspicious. As she put one leg into the car, she felt a prick in her neck and things started to swim before her eyes. She felt herself falling, and the driver held her, easing her into the seat, and closed the door. She tried to scream but her body was un-responsive. She heard the engine start, and the taxi started moving just as things turned black.

Chapter Twenty-nine

There was no food at all this time. There was nothing, just the blackness of solitary. Morgan had no idea how much time passed before the door opened again. He squinted at the hard light that shone into his cell, hungry, aching, and exhausted.

They yanked him to his feet and pushed him out into the hall. It was night, he saw. They led him down the hall and into a room in the same building that he had not been in before, but he knew it immediately. It was all white tiles. In the middle was a chair, around which the tiles were whiter than the surrounding ones, discolored by bleach. The grout was stained with brown dried blood.

Morgan had been in places like this before, on either side of the divide. He liked the other side better.

They sat him down on the chair and tied his hands around the back. Then they turned their backs and left him alone, locking the door behind them.

Morgan tested the cuffs. They were solid. But he had one last trump card.

He worked his tongue in his mouth until he got his improvised lock pick in between his lips.

Now came the hard part. He needed to get it into his hands, which were currently at his back. He turned his head over his right shoulder, adjusting the pick with his tongue to get the angle just right. He brought his hands as far to the right as he could manage.

He heard the door unlock. No time. He pushed the pick out with his tongue.

It bounced off his outstretched fingers and fell on the floor behind him.

He swore in his mind and turned his head as the door opened, and a man he recognized walked into the room. Alligator shoes, shined to a sheen. Green Russian military uniform, his chest festooned with honors and decorations. Eyes bulging like that of a fish, thick meaty lips, heavy eyebrows.

General Suvorov.

"I hear you have been giving Nevsky some trouble," he said as he rolled up his sleeves. "He will be glad to be rid of you, I think."

"I think we can agree on that."

Suvorov raised an eyebrow. He was a humorless man, grave and unfeeling. "Do you know what they call me in Ukraine?"

Morgan did. "The Barber of Lozhki."

"And do you understand why they call me that?"

He was known for scalping his victims and then slitting their throats.

"So you are aware of what is to happen to you?"

This Morgan did not answer. He tried to avoid picturing it with too much vividness. It wasn't good for his mental health.

"You can stop this," he said. "You can even save yourself. All you have to do is speak."

"Already? I wouldn't want to ruin the party. I'm sure you have a lot of exciting surprises in store for me."

Suvorov swung. He had a hell of a right hook, hitting Morgan in the temple.

"This will be very predictable. I will inflict increasing amounts of pain and mutilate you in increments until you speak."

"Here I thought the Barber of Lozhki would have a better sense of showmanship."

Suvorov swung again. This one was hard enough to tip the chair on its back legs.

This one hit him in the face, and he tasted blood in his mouth. "Come on," he said. "Is that the best you can do?"

"We are just getting started," said Suvorov, and followed up with an uppercut.

This time, Morgan pushed with his feet, and the chair fell backward. He grunted at the pain as it pinned his hands to the floor. He wriggled to give them some freedom of movement and felt for the lock pick.

"Oh, goodness, look what I've done." He lifted Morgan's chair by the back, set him right, and stepped back. "What I do not understand is why you insist on protecting the people who abandoned you. No one tried to find you, you know. No inquiries or requests to get you back from your government or any agency. Nothing."

No, he thought. *There is one thing.* Morgan held the lock pick between his fingers, already working the handcuffs. He had to keep Suvorov busy as he worked them open.

"Has it crossed your mind that maybe I just don't like you?"

Suvorov drew a military knife. It wasn't impressive, but it didn't have to be to cut into the flesh of a man tied to a chair. "Perhaps it's time to move on to mutilation." He touched the blade to Morgan's right shoulder and pushed it in, opening a gash that bled freely. Morgan bellowed in pain. "I find that cutting off parts is what really crosses a line for most people. When they see pieces of them removed, see their own bodies diminished . . ." He touched the edge of the blade to Morgan's earlobe. "Shall we start here?"

"How about we start here?" Morgan shook off the handcuffs and head-butted Suvorov. As he staggered back, Morgan picked the chair up off the floor and swung at him. He raised his hands in self-defense, dropping the knife in the process, and was knocked against the side wall by the blow.

This gave Morgan the opening to grab the knife. He then pushed Suvorov against the wall and held the blade to his neck.

"Tell the guard to open the door."

Morgan moved the blade to his eye. "If that door doesn't open in five seconds, you're going to be shopping for eye patches for next season."

Suvorov called out in Russian through the door. They exchanged some words. Suvorov barked exasperated commands.

Morgan heard the dead bolt being undone on the other side of the door, which opened to reveal the single guard keeping watch on the cell.

The guard was holding a nightstick, ready for action. He raised his eyebrows in shock when he saw that Morgan had Suvorov hostage.

"Drop it," he said. "Slide it over to me."

Suvorov translated for him. The guard let the nightstick

clatter to the ground and kicked it over. Morgan bent to pick it up.

"Inside," he said, motioning with his head.

The man walked inside the cell.

"Keys," he said, pointing. The man understood. He hesitated, looking to Suvorov for guidance. Morgan pushed the blade against Suvorov's neck, just enough to pierce the skin and draw a drop of blood.

The guard unhinged the key ring and tossed it to Morgan.

"Thank you very much. I'm going to be sticking around for a minute. If I hear a peep out of you, the general here loses an ear."

He pulled Suvorov out of the cell and closed the door, pulling the dead bolt shut.

That was one less to worry about.

He looked down either side of the hallway. No one there.

He looked at the row of other cells. Two of them were padlocked. Two cells containing prisoners.

He pulled Suvorov along with him and unlocked, one-handed, the nearest cell. He pushed the door open.

It wasn't Badri. Behind the door was Kolya the Cannibal. He stood as the door opened and looked at Morgan, his face expressionless as ever.

Suvorov twisted free of Morgan and slammed the door against him. Morgan was left dazed, which gave Suvorov the opening to twist his arm and wrest the knife away from him.

Regaining his grip, Morgan brought the nightstick hard against Suvorov's leg. The general screamed and fell on his back, inside the cell.

Morgan took a look at the general's leg. He had a compound open fracture where the nightstick had connected.

At a glance, Morgan could tell he wasn't getting up again, not without some serious surgery.

Suvorov held his knife defensively, wide-eyed with pain and fear. He could barely move from the pain. He couldn't defend himself, but Morgan didn't have time for this.

Kolya stared at Morgan. Blank. Empty. Then he looked down at Suvorov.

Morgan stepped out of the cell and closed the door, leaving Suvorov inside with Kolya, whose eyes were already hungry at the prospect of what was about to happen, the only sign of life Morgan had ever seen in them.

Chapter Thirty

Morgan ran to the remaining cells. As he undid the lock, he heard Suvorov screaming from Kolya's cell and tried not to think about what was happening. He pulled the dead bolt and opened the door.

Badri, haggard and exhausted, was sitting in a corner. He looked up at Morgan, goggle-eyed, blinking as the situation registered in his mind.

"Let's get out of here," Morgan said.

"How did you—"

"Let's go!" He looked up and down the hall for signs of any approaching guards. "I can tell you the story on the way out of this place."

Morgan didn't have to say it twice. Badri pushed himself up off the ground. "Where are we going?" he asked.

"We need a plan." Morgan rubbed his temples. "We're in a Russian gulag with no plan, no tools, and no weapons but a *stick*. Any minute now, we're going to be found."

Badri worked his muscles, cracking the joints in his neck and arms. "We seem to be at a disadvantage."

"I've been in worse," said Morgan. "Let's think."

"We need transportation out of here."

"Suvorov's jeep," Morgan said. "It's faster than any of the trucks in this place. That's our way out of here."

"They'll see us."

Morgan frowned. "Then we need to give them something bigger to distract them. We need something they can't ignore."

"You are talking about—"

"Dynamite."

Badri smiled. "I like how you think. Same plan?"

"No," said Morgan. "We take out the motor pool. The dynamite added to the gasoline tank . . ."

"Boom," said Badri. "Enough of a distraction for us to ram the gates."

"We need to get the dynamite," said Morgan.

"They still would not have taken the two sticks away from the prison," Badri said. "It is still on the grounds."

"And there's only one safe place to keep them on this camp. They'll be in the armory." Morgan held up the key ring. All were the same. He could bet they were all for the solitary cells. Armory access was not something given to any guard.

"Nevsky," said Badri. "He will have the keys."

"Then that's where we go. This way. Side door."

Having a plan, Morgan held the guard's billy club in his hand and took the lead down the hall, taking slow, measured steps. Suvorov's screaming stopped. Morgan wondered whether he was dead. Any alternative he could think of was worse.

As they neared the end of the hall, Morgan heard footsteps, heavy boots echoing around the corner. Morgan held his hand up for Badri to stop and then put his finger to his lips. Badri nodded.

As the first man rounded the corner, Morgan swung the stick.

He hit the closest guard square in the face. He bent double, clutching his nose, which was now squirting blood.

The second man came right behind. His hand went for his weapon, but Morgan swung again, bringing the club down on the man's leg. The guard stumbled, and Morgan brought his elbow down on the man's back. He collapsed face-first on the ground.

Badri, meanwhile, lunged at the other guy, bringing a fist to connect with his broken nose and throwing him down next to his companion.

Before either could stir to stand again, Morgan brought his foot down on each of the men's right legs in turn.

"They're not coming after us," he said, moving past them and leaving them screaming in pain.

Badri took the lead now, reaching the side door. Morgan unlocked it and opened it a crack. Badri looked up at the warden's window. "How do we get up there?"

Morgan looked at one of the watchtowers, which was within view. Waiting for his opening, he ran across the yard, hearing Badri's footsteps, muffled by the grass, close behind him.

They reached the administration building and went inside.

The place was deserted, all the doors in the central hallway closed. Morgan led the way, running up the stairs.

The double doors to Nevsky's office. No time to finesse this one. Morgan kicked the door. It caved on the second, swinging open.

"Look in the—"

"There will be no need, Mr. Morgan."

Nevsky was standing to his right. In his hand was a GSh-18 handgun. Standard Russian military issue. Aimed at Morgan's face.

Chapter Thirty-one

Nevsky kept the gun aimed at Morgan's head as he motioned for him to get inside the office. His hand was shaking. He had a drunk's unstable hands.

"How did you get out? Where is Suvorov?"

"He's about to die," said Morgan. "You can save him if you hurry. But you'll have to leave us here."

"Perhaps I can come up with a better idea." He aimed for Morgan's leg. Before he could shoot, Badri rushed him. Nevsky reacted, but not fast enough. Badri barreled into him. Morgan moved to help him, pinning Nevsky's arm and taking the gun.

He stepped back, with Nevsky at gunpoint. "Keys," Morgan said. "Your lighter, too."

Nevsky took a key ring and tossed it to Morgan, and then the lighter. "Here. I will enjoy your death from the vantage point of my office."

"You will not." Badri stabbed Nevsky in the gut with a letter opener from the desk. He pushed the blade in farther and twisted. By the angle, Badri got his kidney, maybe his liver as well.

Nevsky grunted and braced himself on his desk.

"Let us go," said Badri, pulling the cord from the intercom out of the wall. "He is done."

Morgan didn't make a habit of killing men in cold blood. But he had to admit that it was convenient.

They stepped out of the office and closed the door. Morgan took the armory key off the ring and tossed the remaining to Badri. "Get the doors to the prisoner barracks unlocked," he said. "The alarm is going up any second now. Let's kick up our distraction a notch."

Badri nodded.

They parted ways and Morgan made his way down to the underground armory. There was a light on down there. Morgan tiptoed his way downstairs. At the landing, he surveyed the room, hidden around the corner of the wall.

One guard, armed but distracted with a magazine, sat at a table in front of the locked armory cage.

Even one shot fired would attract the attention of every guard in the camp.

He was strategizing his approach when the prison's general alarm started blaring, deafening even here, underground.

Well. No use being coy now.

Morgan ran. The man saw him, drew his gun, and took aim. Morgan went low. The man fired and the bullet sailed above him. He took a running jump, holding on to the edge of the bed, and swinging his legs to kick the man in the chest. The guard fell backward.

This left him on the desk, sliding to the other side. The guard was reaching for the gun, but Morgan was already bringing the nightstick down to connect with the man's head. He was knocked out cold.

Morgan had seconds before guards would start streaming in.

He opened the lock to the gun cage.

He found a duffel bag under the shelves. He picked the dynamite sticks up carefully, putting them in the bag.

Since he was here . . .

He looked over the guns. Half a dozen Saiga 12-gauge shotguns, twenty Vityaz-SN submachine guns, two Dragunov SVD sniper rifles, and three racks of MP-443 pistols.

He loaded two of each of the SMGs, shotguns, and pistols into the bag, plus ammo. He slung it over his shoulder. He took an additional handgun.

He broke the key in the lock. No big guns for the guards. That should help even the odds for the prisoners.

He heard footsteps coming down the stairs. They would have handguns. Morgan drew a shotgun from his duffel and whispered to himself, "Time to make some noise."

Chapter Thirty-two

Morgan held on to the shotgun, a Saiga 12 with a twenty-round detachable magazine, and waited for the two men to come down.

The first wasn't expecting him, and didn't have time to react before Morgan fired, the gunshot reverberating in the cramped, windowless space. The second went for his gun. A second shell, and he was down.

Two more were at the landing above. If they consolidated their position, if enough guards amassed up there, Morgan would be trapped no matter how much firepower he could muster.

He cast down the shotgun and drew out a Vityaz SMG. Thirty-round box magazine. If he held down the trigger on automatic mode, he'd drain it within three seconds.

Morgan aimed blindly around the corner and fired off a burst upstairs. This gave him the opening to move up the stairs as the men took cover on either side. One of them made his move when Morgan was halfway up. Morgan loosed another burst, which caught him in the chest.

He slowed down as he approached the upper landing

and listened. What he heard was boots running away. The other man was beating a prudent retreat.

Morgan needed to get out of the building, fast. He ran in the opposite direction of the guard.

Outside, the siren alarm was blaring. The perimeter guard towers, the biggest danger at the moment, the only ones who would be armed, were flashing their lights wildly, looking for the source of trouble. Outside was a bad place to be. Too exposed.

Morgan saw Badri hiding in the shadows across the yard. Badri pointed to the car. Morgan signaled for him to go ahead, and then took off running at an angle. A light caught him, then moved to shine right on him. Shots fired, whizzing past him.

He pushed himself harder, staggering his pace to avoid sniper fire. He didn't stop until the garage was between him and the shooter.

He moved along the wall until he found the window in the northwest corner, the one Grushin had used to gain access. On the other side of this was the gasoline tank that fed the generator and the trucks.

This was going to make a splash.

He picked up a rock and hurled it through a window-pane. Glass shattered and clinked on the floor inside.

That's when he heard barking.

Dogs. Let loose and running toward him, fast.

If he ran now, he didn't have a chance in hell of getting away.

So he tried to concentrate. He balanced both sticks of dynamite on his left hand and drew out Nevsky's lighter with his right. He struck, and it did not light.

Two dogs were running toward him, heavy paws beating the pavement. He had seconds to get this done.

He struck the lighter again, and this time a flame

emerged. He held it under the fuses on the two sticks of dynamite, which hissed and sputtered as they caught fire.

He tossed the two sticks of dynamite inside through the pane and turned to run. The dogs were right behind him within a fraction of a second. And then he emerged out in the open yard, and a light was on him almost immediately. It was only a race now to see which would get him first, the sniper on the tower or the dogs snapping at his heels.

The explosion was more than he'd anticipated.

The corner of the concrete building shattered into rubble, and the fuel tank exploded in a ball of flame that rose upward, lighting the camp in bright orange before consuming itself.

It rocked the ground, knocking Morgan off his feet. Windows exploded in a rain of glass.

Morgan raised his head. The guards were no longer much preoccupied with him, and he found no sign of the dogs behind him. By the light of the fire—all electric lights had gone out with the destruction of the generator—he saw prisoners coming out of the barracks, taking their first tentative steps outside.

He heard the rumble of an engine, and then the bright white headlights. It was Badri with the jeep, speeding across the yard. He came to a skidding stop next to Morgan.

"Move over," Morgan said. Badri complied, and Morgan sat behind the wheel.

The windshield cracked. Sniper bullet. Morgan glanced at Badri, saw that he was unhurt, and gunned the accelerator. They were an easy target.

Morgan saw prisoners pouring out of the barracks now. He passed them in the jeep.

"How are we going to get through the gate?" Badri demanded.

A group of guards who had seen which way the wind was blowing had opened a pedestrian gate to the outside. It was too narrow for the jeep, but the gate was held up by thin, hollow steel poles, surrounded by chain link. Unlike the main gate, *this* he had a hope of ramming.

Morgan aligned the car with the gate. Guards scattered.

"Hold on to your butt."

They hit the gate full force. The windshield and driver's side window shattered, but the gate gave way, and with a terrible scraping sound the vehicle made it through.

The jeep skidded, and Morgan struggled until it steadied. He veered a sharp right, and within a few seconds they hit the road.

The wind blowing hard in their faces, Morgan and Badri looked at each other and laughed with the exhilaration of freedom. They took off into the night, toward their rendezvous point, as the prison behind them popped with gunfire.

Chapter Thirty-three

Morgan drove off the road after about an hour in the car. They were one hundred miles away, near the foot of the mountains. The terrain there became rocky and uneven. He had to move slowly. They might easily hit a rock and get stuck, and that might well be a death sentence for them out here.

"The light signal came from somewhere around here," Badri said.

Morgan looked back on the road behind them, lit by the predawn glow. The prison lay in the distance, a thin line of smoke rising from it. He wondered what the prisoners were burning.

He shuddered, trying not to think about the fate of the guards.

"Stop the car," Badri said.

Morgan parked, looking for a sign of what Badri might have seen. It took a few seconds for them to reveal themselves. Three men, Arabs with trim beards, swaddled in winter clothes. In their arms were Kalashnikov automatic rifles.

Morgan turned off the headlights and Badri opened the door to the jeep to show himself. The men lowered their weapons. Badri walked toward them like the prodigal son and embraced them one by one, kissing their cheeks.

Morgan emerged from the car. The three men got one look at him and pointed their rifles at him.

Morgan was getting really goddamn tired of staring down the barrels of guns.

One of them asked Badri a question in harsh Arabic.

Moment of truth. Either they would accept him or they would kill him.

"He is a friend," said Badri in English, for Morgan's benefit. "He helped me escape."

They did not lower their guns. "He is American," one said. "He is the enemy."

Morgan took a step away from the car, toward them. They tensed their grips on their weapons. "I have no more love for my country. They are murderers without honor."

They talked among themselves, and finally Badri yelled at them. The boss, laying down the law.

"Come on," said Badri. "They have an airplane hidden on the other side of the mountains. They're going to get us out of here."

Chapter Thirty-four

Alex woke up to a slap in the face. She opened her eyes, woozy, trying to get her bearings, and realized she was in the trunk of a car. It was open, and above her, silhouetted against the bright blue sky, stood a man. The taxi driver. A man some ten years older than her, green eyed, with black hair cropped short. He was a man she might have called handsome, in different circumstances.

She tried to get up out of the trunk and found she'd been tied up. She tried to wriggle free and her arm chafed against the scratchy felt interior.

"Who are you?" she demanded.

"No one important," he said. Russian, definitely, but his English was more than passable.

"You work for Suvorov?"

"You have other people in your life who would abduct you off the streets?"

"Real wise guy." She shifted her weight, trying to find a more comfortable position. She looked out, trying to get a feel for their surroundings. She could see trees, evergreens, but no buildings. "What happens now?"

"What happens is, I don't know," he said, throwing up his hands. "They tell me to take you, so I do, and then I find out Suvorov is dead—"

"He's dead?"

"—and now I have a girl in my trunk I have no use for."

"Then let me go!"

He smirked. "It's not that easy."

"I have money!"

"I took your money already. Come." He took her by the armpits and shifted her weight, getting a stable hold on her. "Don't move too much. The only reason I did not kill you right there in the trunk is that I hate moving dead weight. That and the blood. You know what blood smells when it stays in the trunk in the hot sun? I know. It is terrible."

He pulled her up and out of the trunk. She swung her feet, trying to hit him in the groin and missing. He released her, and she fell to the hard-packed dirt of the ground. She shook off her daze and took in her surroundings. She saw a barn some two hundred feet away that looked as if it hadn't been used in a long time. Back the way they came was a dirt road, overgrown grass intruding upon it from both sides. It was deserted for about a mile, where it bent out of sight.

"You had to make it hard, didn't you?" he said. "You could have had a little more time, it could have been pleasant. Maybe we have a little conversation, some last words for you. But no. You had to be a bitch."

Alex squirmed, trying to move into a position where she could see more than his feet.

"Now I have to kill you here and haul you all the way to *hurk*—"

A *thump* as the man's body hit the ground next to her. His face was inches from hers, a blank expression on his face. Blood was pooling around him, and sticking out of the back of his head was a massive meat cleaver. And she saw legs in leather boots, moving toward her and then behind her, and then a man's rough hands holding her wrists and the *scritch scritch* of a serrated knife, and her ties were loose.

With her arms free, she turned her body to look up and see Dobrynin unbinding her feet.

"Come on, girl," he said in his weary, guttural voice. "Let us get you home."

He drew out the meat cleaver, cursing as he shook off the blood, and then wiped it off with a handkerchief. He made a face and cast the handkerchief aside. Alex wondered whether he'd use the knife at the shop again. She felt certain the answer was yes.

Alex stood, rubbing her wrists to get rid of the soreness.

"Come," he said, motioning for her to follow him. "Car is down the road."

"How did you find me?" she asked as she caught up to him.

"I called friend, told him stupid girl was going to get in trouble. He watched you. He saw you taken and followed the car. And he called me. So I am here."

She moved ahead of him and stopped him with two hands. And then she gave him a tight hug, resting the side of her head against his bloody shirt. She knew he was mortified. But she didn't care.

"Thank you," she said.

"You want to thank me? Go home."

Chapter Thirty-five

They flew low until they cleared any reasonable search radius. The men ignored Morgan and spoke quietly to Badri. Morgan instead looked out the window on the Russian countryside, gaming out what his next steps would be.

With the riot at the camp, there would be chaos for a long time even after the Russian authorities managed to regain control from the prisoners. Hell, with weapons, they were practically in a fortress, and would be able to hold out for days, unless the Russians chose to bomb the place to oblivion, in which case they'd probably never be done sorting the body parts and would never find out there was anyone missing at all, except for a jeep, abandoned at the foot of a nearby mountain.

In any case, nobody would know to look for these two missing prisoners for a long while, which gave them plenty of time to get the hell out of Dodge.

They switched planes in an airfield a few hours out, then crossed the border to Kazakhstan in the back of a truck, squeezed in between bales of hay, daylight filtering through only in tiny pinpoints. And then Morgan slept.

When he woke up, to the sound of the truck's driver's side door opening, those pinpoints of light had grown dark. Morgan heard the tailgate being opened, and the bales of hay at the back were removed one by one.

They emerged into a dirt yard of a house surrounded by high walls on all sides. The sky was clear, and Morgan figured they must be in a small town, because he could see the stars with a clarity that's impossible near a city.

A man standing at the door embraced Badri and watched Morgan with suspicion. They exchanged some angry words, of which Badri had the last, and he called Morgan to come in.

In the small, sparse dining room, the rich smell of meat wafted through the air. They ate a meal of lamb and flat-bread, which, after weeks of almost nothing but spoiled potatoes and onions, seemed like the best thing he'd ever tasted. After they finished, Morgan wiping the last of the sauce off his plate and popping it into his mouth, a woman in a niqab served them black tea. Morgan said, "So what happens now?"

The Arab grimaced. "I don't know."

"I didn't really ever think we'd get this far. You dream of freedom for so long, of getting out, and now that I'm here, it's not . . . I don't have a life to go back to any-more, Badri. Even if I did go back, if they find out I helped you escape, or that you helped me—well, I can tell you they'll put me somewhere that's not any better than where we just got out of." He sat back in his chair. "Not that I'd want to. They abandoned me. Screwed me. So screw them."

"What about your family?"

"Better that they think I'm dead. They got a good payout from it." He drank tea from his cup, hot and bitter. "Won't do any good to anyone, my coming back."

"And your future? I could take you somewhere. Drop you off. We never have to see each other again. I may even be able to give you some money. You saved my life and won me my freedom. I owe you that much."

Morgan closed his eyes and took a deep breath. He found Badri looking at him expectantly. "What about if I help you?"

A heavy silence hung between them. Morgan studied Badri's face. He was looking off to the side, avoiding eye contact. "You are not even Muslim," he said. "Why—"

"—would I want to join the effort? I got screwed, Badri. I got no home, no family, nothing to live for. The only thing I got is this rage at the people who did this to me."

"I am sorry," said Badri. "I am grateful to you. But we cannot allow—"

"I can offer you something no one else can," Morgan said. "Information. Insight. On the inside, you told me you had something planned. Something big. I can help you with that. I know the vulnerabilities. I know how to cause damage."

"I don't know," said Badri.

"You don't trust me."

"I have put my life in your hands," said Badri. "In there. Out here, things are different. We are not joined by a common purpose."

"I'm telling you we are."

"No," said Badri. "Tomorrow, we have a long drive into Uzbekistan. But for tonight, we rest. It has been a long road."

Chapter Thirty-six

They arrived in Tashkent in Uzbekistan in the early morning, a driver taking the wheel and Morgan and Badri riding in the backseat. The car had no air-conditioning, and the ride under the Central Asian sun turned it into a hotbox.

Badri talked to Morgan like they were old friends, telling him about his childhood in Abu Dhabi, prosperous but not rich, and about his education in London. His family was made up of devout Muslims, but not radicals. His eyes were opened, he said, after he came back from college. It was not only the wars of imperialism, the meddling of the United States in the lives of Muslims, the deaths wreaked by bombs and soldiers and drones. He saw what Westernization was doing to his country, to all of the Arab world. Changing it, eroding its character.

Morgan listened in spite of the heat as Badri told him about getting married and the joy of having children. And he spoke about adopting the radical fundamentalist faith of the Wahhabists and its return to a true Islam.

"The entire world is becoming decadent," he said. "They need a wake-up call. And talk cannot bring the change that is needed. That is why I fight. That is why we must kill."

They entered the city of Tashkent in the middle of the afternoon. Like most ancient cities, it was marked by the juxtaposition of the old and the new. The city was sprinkled with old Soviet monuments, and many of the streets were lined with trees.

The driver pulled into a parking lot adjoining a large sky-blue dome. Chorsu Bazaar, their destination, was where they were to meet Badri's contact, who would send the terrorist along to his mission and arrange for Morgan to be transported where he wished.

"It's a pretty goddamn open space," said Morgan. "Lots of people, too."

"My contact insisted we meet here," Badri said. "He wanted a public place. He is wary of you."

Morgan and Badri walked together into the bazaar, a round area under the dome, arranged in concentric circles of wares. The butchers were along the outer rim in enclosed refrigerated shops. The floor held a wealth of foodstuffs, nuts and dried fruit and spices, pungent and rich, ranging from the vivid yellow of turmeric through the red of paprika to the black of pepper.

Morgan took in the space with trained eyes as they rounded the bazaar, Badri looking for his contact.

After they'd completed a full circle, Morgan leaned close to Badri. "We're being followed," he whispered.

Badri's eyes widened, but then returned to a neutral state. He was well practiced, Morgan saw, and knew how to keep his cool in a dangerous situation.

"Look, but use your peripheral vision. Pretend we're

looking for our contact. Guy over on the other aisle holding the briefcase. Guy looking at meats over at the butcher. Man leaning against the wall near the bathroom."

"We are surrounded," said Badri.

"It appears so."

"They do not look Uzbek. Nor Russian, I believe."

"Might be American," Morgan said. "Doesn't really matter."

"What does?"

"Getting out of here. Keep your eyes out and follow my lead."

They continued their way around, the men following them moving along to maintain a line of sight. The nearest one, now examining a table of nuts, began his approach.

"They're making their move," said Morgan. "Wait for my mark."

"What will that be?"

"You can't miss it."

The man was close now. He was wearing a baggy Hawaiian shirt, open over an undershirt, that covered a concealed-carry shoulder holster.

Morgan bided his time, waiting as the man approached from the side. When he was five feet away, Morgan turned and hit him with a head butt. As the man staggered back, Morgan reached into his shirt and drew out his gun. He turned to see the others closing in from the periphery of the domed market, three by his count.

Morgan aimed at the chest of the nearest one. A woman spotted his gun and screamed.

Morgan aimed down. He fired twice into a row of bags of spice.

A plume of red and yellow shot into the air. People

were coughing. The man covered his eyes, hollering in pain.

And people were running, panicked, away from the gunshot.

"Run!"

Keeping low, they ran under the cover of the spices and blended into the crowd. Morgan jumped over a stall, overturning a bucket of pistachios. Badri was at his heels. Morgan turned to look at their pursuers. At least one had spotted them, but the rest were running around trying to navigate the crowd.

There would be more waiting for them outside.

Morgan and Badri ran out into the hot sunlight along with the rest of the crowd. Morgan hid the gun in his waistband. Blending in might give them a few precious seconds.

He saw them—men dressed in various different guises as tourists, standing at the edges of the court that surrounded the bazaar, looking through the crowd.

No way out but through it.

He ran with the crowd as long as they were not spotted. And then the nearest agent looked into his eyes, and Morgan saw the expression of recognition.

He lowered his torso and hit the man full force, lifting him clear off the ground before sending him sailing on his back. He took off running with desperate speed, Badri behind him, as the other agents moved toward them. But they had broken the cordon, and now the agents were behind them.

Morgan and Badri were in the parking lot now. Morgan spotted a man getting into a Daewoo sedan. He pulled out the gun and pointed it at the driver.

"Out!"

The man stepped away from the car, his hands up,

holding his keys. Morgan grabbed them and jumped into the driver's seat.

"Get in!"

Badri got into the passenger seat and Morgan gunned the reverse before his door was closed. He cleared the parking space and put the car in first, accelerating, tires screeching, as their pursuers drew their weapons and readied to shoot. They accelerated away as gunshots hit the trunk. One bullet shattered the rear window.

Morgan turned at the end of the row and saw more trouble ahead. The exit to the parking lot was blocked by two cars. There were more agents there, guns already drawn and trained on their car.

He turned with squealing tires into the next row and gamed the situation out in his head. The exit was blocked, and the lot was separated from the street by a low wall that was probably too solid to ram.

That left one possibility.

He turned the car back toward the bazaar.

"What are you doing?" Badri yelled.

"Getting us out of here!"

He drove onto the pedestrian walkways toward the dome of the Chorsu Bazaar. The pedestrians had cleared it by now, and the door was wide, more than enough for the car to pass. Just one obstacle stood between them—a staircase, some twelve or fifteen short steps.

The car wasn't going to like it. But it would have to do. The Daewoo lurched as they hit the steps, and then climbed, heaving, until they were level with the bazaar.

Morgan felt the tires low, blown out by the impact. And then they crashed through the doors of the bazaar, sending glass flying in every direction. Morgan maneuvered around the space, deserted of people, sending up clouds of spices and rain of nuts and dried fruit.

They crashed through the door on the other side, bull-dozing through an aisle of the covered vegetable market. No one waiting for them there. No one thought they'd be crazy enough to make the maneuver. They came out amid a crowd of screaming people, who parted for them to pass. And then Morgan drove the car onto the street, with the two front wheels scraping the ground and the windshield cracked from end to end. But it was whole enough to carry them away from the bazaar, and from their pursuers.

Chapter Thirty-seven

"How did they find us?" said Badri in a fevered panic.

Morgan was driving the car away from the populated, tourist-thick area of the bazaar toward the outskirts of the city. They needed to ditch the car soon. They were attracting attention, with its front tires in rags and the grille and front bumber scratched and bent.

"They must have made your contact." Morgan's heart was still pounding, adrenaline still coursing through his veins, but he was calm. This was just another problem to be solved. "We need to get out of town. But we need a new car first. This car is going to get stopped as soon as a policeman sees us."

Morgan turned into a side street and parked the car. They got out on a street that bordered a series of office buildings, all concrete and reflective glass. Morgan took a tire iron from the trunk and led the way to the nearest parking lot. He checked that they were not being seen and shattered the driver's side window of a Chevy Cobalt. He motioned for Badri to get inside.

"We need somewhere to go," Morgan said as he pulled open the panel under the steering column and reached in for the wires.

"I have more people I can call. It is a greater risk. But it can be done."

Morgan touched the ignition wire to the power wire, and the engine came to life. He maneuvered the car out of its spot and drove through the parking lot and onto the street, wind blowing in through the broken window.

"They were American, weren't they?" said Badri.

"The agents? Yeah. I think so. Something about the way they carried themselves, the way they held their guns."

"You could have given me up, turned yourself over. They probably would've taken you back. You could've given them a story about using me to escape. Wouldn't even be too far from the truth. But instead you risked your life to escape with me."

"I told you," said Morgan. "I'm done with them. All of 'em."

"I think I didn't quite believe you until now." Badri looked out at the industrial suburbs of the city. "Okay," he said. "If you wish to join with us, I will stand by you."

Morgan turned to look at him to make sure he was serious. "You mean it?"

"Yes. I mean it. And I will tell you about this. I have something. We have had it since before I was captured. I will not tell you what, not yet, but I will tell you that it can kill thousands. *Tens* of thousands."

"I see. And this weapon—how will you get it into the United States?"

"It is already there," said Badri. "With some allies from my organization. But my people did not know how to deploy it effectively."

"But now that you're out, you can guide them."

"This can be a new 9/11," Badri said. His eyes shone with the fire of fanaticism.

Morgan's voice lowered to hardly more than a whisper. "You want to make this a new 9/11. I want to help you make this something greater. I can give you the means to cripple the US government in a way that they will not be able to recover from for decades."

Badri smiled. "Welcome to the cause."

Chapter Thirty-eight

Alex returned to an empty house in Andover, Massachusetts.

Night had fallen, too late for any kids to be out in the now silent streets. She got out of the cab and unlocked the front door, dropping her bag in the foyer and making straight for the kitchen. She opened the refrigerator, but there was no food, just a few condiments on the door, a half stick of butter and a little bit of cranberry juice in a container. Her mother was off on Martha's Vineyard consulting on the house of a client who was summering on the island. Alex figured she must've cleared out the fridge before she went.

So very practical, her mother.

She checked the freezer. In there Alex found a Tupperware of frozen ravioli with a note.

Welcome home, honey. Forty minutes in oven at 350 degrees. Sauce in the pantry.

Yes. Quite practical. Alex smirked in appreciation.

She set the ravioli in a porcelain dish and poured in half a jar of her mother's homemade tomato sauce, made and canned for an entire year at a time. Then she set the oven to 350, set a timer for fifty minutes, and put the dish in without preheating.

Leaving the oven to do its work, she went to the living room, flopped on the couch, and turned on the TV. This she hadn't done in a long time, but it was so easy to fall into old habits when she was at home. Especially when she was feeling as forlorn and defeated as she was then.

She clicked through the channels and settled on infomercials. She couldn't concentrate on anything anyway. The chipper chatter at least served as appropriate background noise for her wallowing.

She pulled out her phone and looked at the messages that had accumulated in her absence. Loads of junk email, a couple hellos from her friends Simon and Katie from her brief stint in college—Katie's more insistent and offended by her lack of response—and one from Karen O'Neal, some canned words of concern from a couple of weeks ago.

Alex checked the clock. Just past eleven at night. On impulse, Alex called her. The phone rang only once before she picked up.

"Alex?" She sounded awake, at least.

"Hi, Karen. I hope it's not too late to call."

"Please. Sleep doesn't even cross my mind before midnight. What's up? Are you okay?"

"I, uh, I've been out of town. I was wondering if there was any news about my father."

The question hung on the line. Crickets chirped in the hot night.

"I'm sorry," Karen said finally. "We haven't had any luck finding him."

"Right. Yeah."

"Do you want to grab coffee sometime this week?"

"Yeah. Sure. I'll text you."

She threw her phone across the living room to land on the couch and groaned. The absence of her father was a keen, stabbing pain. The past weeks had kept her busy, on track, doing something. Now that she stopped, all that she had left was the reality that he wasn't there and wasn't coming back.

What was life going to be without him? What was her life going to be at all? She felt like this changed everything.

She had done depression, and didn't care for a repeat. Would she go back to training? Follow in his footsteps? Would that bring her some sense of fulfillment, keep him alive in her somehow?

Then there was revenge. That might keep her going. But she'd read enough to know where that led. Death or disappointment.

But what else was there for her? How was she going to deal with life now?

The same way she'd dealt with the rigors of training, she told herself. One day at a time. One minute at a time, when necessary. Just the next push-up, the next ten feet of running, the next five minutes awake. This was just like that. Do what you have to do not to die right now.

So she wept, not caring how loud she was in the empty house, and buried her head in a pillow, screaming, and punching the couch cushions. She didn't know how long she was at it, but when the oven dinged, announcing that her ravioli was ready, she stopped, panting, drying her eyes, and stood up. One day at a time started right now.

Alex picked herself up off the couch. The smell of basil and tomato wafted to her nose, the comforting fragrance of her mother's cooking.

A warm meal at home. Seemed like a fine first step.

Chapter Thirty-nine

Morgan and Badri landed in Puerto Plata, Dominican Republic, in the late morning, bearing fake passports. The bored-looking immigration agent didn't give them a second glance as she entered their data on her computer.

They picked up a rental Kia hatchback at the airport that they had no intention of ever returning and drove west together, along the coastal highways under the noontime tropical sun. Morgan's hair, half an inch grown in, flowed like a field of wheat in the wind streaming in through the car window. On their right, the sea would sometimes peek through the dense jungle.

Once they had driven for two and a half hours, Morgan checked their position on the handheld GPS. He parked the Kia on the shoulder of the road and plunged into the woods, through the dense underbrush, slapping at the mosquitoes that harried them the whole way.

They trekked for hours under the shade of the green canopy, Morgan correcting their course using the GPS every few minutes.

"The jungle turns you around," he told Badri. "Stop paying attention for a minute and you're lost."

The sun was low in the horizon by the time they reached the shore, where the rickety wooden fishing boat was already waiting for them. On it was a weather-worn Dominican man, skin browned by the sun, shirtless and in ragged shorts, and a younger man in a wife-beater shirt and faded baseball cap. He tensed when he saw them at first, looking with especial wariness at Morgan, before Badri spoke.

"Señor Batista?"

"Sí," he said, nodding his head and grinning.

Batista waved them on board. Morgan took stock of the boat as he stepped onto the deck. The wood looked more deteriorated than Morgan liked for any boat going on the open sea, and everything from the hull to the cabin seemed cobbled together and patched over many times.

They set off without ceremony, leaving the island of Hispaniola behind and moving north. Morgan pulled on a Panama hat he'd bought at the airport to protect against the sun.

The two men stared at him openly as the boat chugged along, and Morgan understood very well why. He was not the kind of person they would normally carry across, not the kind of person who'd normally enter the country illegally. But an explanation was not forthcoming. Morgan was a paying customer, so he didn't have to explain a goddamn thing.

Morgan and Badri had brought along cereal bars to tide them through the passage, but the younger man, Diego, who Morgan learned was Batista's son, had caught some fish earlier that day. They grilled it on deck in a makeshift barbecue pit made out of a paint can and what might have been part of a dish rack. Morgan ate with relish, with his hands, the fish resting on a piece of banana leaf.

The hold was full of fuel canisters to get the boat through the long journey and back, so they had to sleep on deck, out in the open. Which suited Morgan fine enough—out there, they had at least a light breeze to combat the stifling heat.

They spoke little during the journey. Before, driving through Uzbekistan, Badri would talk freely about his family and his life outside the organization, and even a few stories of terrorism, of narrow escapes from the CIA, and his capture by the Russians. But now, the weight of their mission was bearing down on them, and they couldn't bring themselves to say anything about anything else. They did not even discuss the ultimate mission itself, instead focusing on the details of their passage, and then only so far as it was necessary. Mostly, Morgan looked out into the dark water as it disappeared far in the horizon, or in the dark of the night, lit by stars and a sliver of moon.

It took a day and two nights to come within sight of the shore, and then they spent a day of waiting because they couldn't approach in daylight. So they waited, the boat bobbing on the gentle sea, just far enough from the continent that they would not have to worry about the American Coast Guard finding them and either arresting them or escorting them back to their place of origin.

The boat started moving again at dusk, all lights off to avoid detection. They landed in the dead of night at a deserted bayou beach in Louisiana, where an ally of Badri's was waiting with an inconspicuous seven-year-old VW Jetta.

Chapter Forty

Morgan's confederate drove them into the night and past dawn, stopping only to refuel. The driver was a taciturn, grave man of few words, so they rode in silence almost the entire way, until they pulled into a country house in rural Virginia. There they were greeted by a soft-spoken young man with a shaved face. He introduced himself as Rasheed. Like everyone else along the way, he regarded Morgan with nothing short of total suspicion.

"He is an ally," Badri said.

He wanted to get them situated, but Badri was impatient. "Where are they?"

The young man, deferential, led the way down a solid old wooden staircase to the basement. Among the abandoned appliances, tools, and building materials, he walked to a working chest freezer and pulled it open. The top was layered with meats in grocery store trays and frozen vegetables. He removed them, setting them aside, to reveal a steel box underneath.

"Here they are," Rasheed said. He opened the box without removing it from the freezer to reveal six plain steel canisters, about as big as tennis-ball containers. Badri looked at them with ravenous eyes, filled with anticipation of the destruction that they would cause.

"Novichok," he said, his voice a whisper. "Russian nerve agent. The deadliest ever made. Not a gas, but a powder. Causes all muscles in the body to seize and contract. You cannot breathe, and your heart stops pumping blood. You die within minutes. Perhaps seconds."

He drew out a canister and held it out for Morgan to see. "Here is our instrument of destruction," he said. "Here is how we will bring America to its knees."

Chapter Forty-one

The farmhouse they occupied was old and two-storied, built of horizontal slats that were once whitewashed but now showed the faded gray of the wood underneath. The grounds were modest, but the house was shielded from view of its surroundings by trees. They were a few miles from Palmyra, the nearest one-horse town.

It was a spot well chosen for its isolation. You could spend months in here without anyone so much as sighting the house from the road.

Morgan heard the Chevy beater truck before he saw it coming up the driveway, carrying Rasheed. He got out of the car holding bags from the thrift store in one hand and Burger King in the other. Badri was out of the house, in the nearby woods, making a call to his associates in the organization.

Devout as he was, Rasheed was a slob. From the looks of it, he subsisted on mostly snack foods, and empty bags of chips and fast food were strewn about the living room, which held nothing but one ratty couch. It was some kind of warped jihadi version of a filthy bachelor pad.

Rasheed slammed the screen door open and set the bags down on the Formica table in the dining room. He greeted Morgan with undisguised disdain.

"Lunch," he said, tossing a paper-wrapped Whopper into Morgan's lap.

Not exactly his favorite—Morgan hadn't eaten fast food in years, at least not voluntarily—but he was famished. Even with Diego's fishing, food on the boat had been slim pickings. He unwrapped it and took a large bite out of it.

"I brought clothes," Rasheed said, dropping a thrift store bag at Morgan's feet. Eating the burger with one hand, Morgan sifted through the clothes with the other. Rasheed had an impeccable sense of style. Among the pickings were a shirt from a company barbecue so big that it wouldn't look out of place resting on a tent pole and a lime green button-down. But the clothes on Morgan's back were starting to get ripe, and this was what he had.

Morgan looked up from the bag to find Rasheed staring at him.

"I do not know what you did to fool Badri," he said. "But I do not believe you are here to help."

Morgan stood to confront him, chest out, hands balled into fists. "Badri believes me. And he's your boss. So I don't much care what you think."

"Infidel!" Rasheed spat on the floor.

"And what are you gonna do about it?"

Rasheed narrowed his eyes, and then drew a gun from his waistband. Magnum Big Frame revolver, .44 Magnum. Talking about stopping power would be damning with faint praise. At this range, it would be a question of how much of Morgan's face would remain afterward.

"Big man with a big gun," said Morgan. "Let's game

this out. You blow me away. Then what? What do you tell your boss?"

"It does not matter. You will be dead, and no longer willing to betray us."

Morgan's voice dropped an octave. "He trusts me. I've saved his life more than once, so maybe he trusts me more than he trusts you. And he wants what I have to offer. Kill me, and your punishment will come."

"Not as swiftly as yours," Rasheed said. But Morgan could tell he was shaken.

"Your plan will fail without me," Morgan said. "They'll catch you, and best-case scenario is that you die in the process. You won't have another 9/11 on your hands. You'll have another underwear bomber."

Rasheed gritted his teeth and grimaced. "You are lying."

"Then pay the price and kill me."

Rasheed cocked the gun. Morgan got ready to make a grab for it. Rasheed was brave but untrained. Morgan might be able to get the best of him.

"Rasheed!"

It was Badri, standing outside the screen door. He walked into the house speaking in harsh Arabic, and Rasheed, hissing, uncocked the gun and tucked it back into his waistband.

"What happened?" Badri demanded, in English.

"Friendly disagreement," said Morgan, turning away and heading for the stairs. "I'm going to take a shower. I have some clothes I can't wait to try on."

Chapter Forty-two

Morgan locked his door that night and braced the handle with an old wooden chair. He then set the moldy mattress on the floor against the wall. He wasn't going to risk Rasheed getting any ideas in the middle of the night.

He woke up with the cock's crow, but stayed in his room, stretching and doing his morning exercise. An hour later, he unblocked the door and walked out. The house was still, the other two still sleeping.

Morgan went downstairs and looked for something to eat for breakfast, but all he found were potato chips and packaged cake, so he settled for a glass of tap water instead.

Carrying the cup in his hand, Morgan walked to the basement door. He looked down, at the freezer, thinking of all the destructive power it contained. He felt chills as he considered it.

"See something you like, American?"

It was Rasheed, from the top of the stairs.

"Just thinking about the plan," said Morgan. "We're going to have to devise a strategy sometime soon."

"We will set them off in the White House," Rasheed said. "And we will kill the President of the United States."

Morgan chuckled at the notion. "You won't make it ten feet into the White House. You'll be shot down in the entrance hall. The best you can hope to achieve there is to kill a handful of tourists and security guards."

"Then you have a better idea?"

They were interrupted by the sound of Badri coming downstairs.

"Morning," said Morgan. "I was just about to tell Rasheed here that we need groceries and supplies. Proper food. Eating all this junk is expensive, too. We shouldn't be wasting the little money we have."

Rasheed leered at him, but Badri cut in. "What do you suggest?"

"Some beef, vegetables. The electric stove works, I checked, and there are a couple of iron pots we could use. No reason we have to live like animals here."

Rasheed opened his mouth to speak, but Badri cut in. "You are right. Make a list. Rasheed will get it for us."

"Don't you think it'd be better for me to go?" said Morgan. "I'm American. Nobody's going to think anything of my being there."

"Fine," said Badri.

"He will take our car and escape!" Rasheed bellowed. "He will send the police after us."

"He will not," Badri said with finality. Then he turned to Morgan. "I will get you the money."

Badri sent him out with twenty dollars. Morgan drove into Palmyra and parked outside the town's one modest grocery store. At the single register was a bored teen who didn't pry his eyes away from his phone for one second when Morgan came in.

He scoped the store, looking for the cameras. There

were none. He walked to the refrigerator and picked up a tray of beef and another of chicken thighs. He looked back at the teen, who spared him not so much as a glance, and then tucked them in his waistband, one in front and one in the back, well covered by his loose T-shirt. He winced as the cold came into contact with his skin.

He heard the door swing open, and turned to see a policeman walk inside. Morgan went stiff, then forced himself back to relaxation.

"Mornin'," said the cop. He wore a white Stetson, and had eyes that were constantly narrowed.

"Mornin'," Morgan said, picking up a head of broccoli and some potatoes.

"Sheriff Anderson," he said, lifting his hat.

"Dan. Dan Morgan."

"Just passing through?"

"That's right." Morgan took his groceries to the cashier, wondering whether the sheriff had noticed the bulges under his shirt.

But instead the sheriff looked outside. "Say, I've seen that car before." The sheriff pointed at the truck Morgan had driven in, parked outside the door. "You out there at the old Peterson place?"

"Four seventy-one," said the listless teen. Morgan dug into his pocket for the money, careful not to disturb the meat.

"I have no idea," Morgan said. "I'm staying with a friend."

"Young Middle Eastern fella?"

"The same," Morgan said. "Rasheed. A friend's nephew, actually. House-sitting for his uncle. He's worried about the boy, asked me to come down and have a look-see. Find out if he's all right. But I'm really just dropping in for a day or two."

"He looks a little perturbed," Sheriff Anderson said.

"He's got some issues. You know." He made a couple of circles with his index finger around his ear. "But he's a good kid. Harmless."

"Well. That's good to know."

"And he seems okay, all things considered. So I'm eager to tell his father that."

Sheriff Anderson frowned. "Wasn't it his uncle?"

Morgan cursed in his mind. "I know them both. His father is worried about him, too." Goddamn it. He was better than this.

"Well, you do that," Anderson said.

The cashier handed Morgan his change. "Here you go, sir."

Morgan walked out and started his truck. When he was out of sight of the store, he pulled the meat out from under his shirt and tossed it in the passenger seat.

He had one more stop to make.

He cruised the town until he found a mom-and-pop electronics store, Bob's TV and Radio. He went inside to find a balding middle-aged man he figured was Bob standing behind the counter. It was a small store, and it took him under a minute to find what he was looking for.

"I'll take one of these," said Morgan, setting the item on the counter.

"Prepaid cell phone?"

"Yeah. My phone got bricked. Need something to tide me over until I can get back home."

"I gotcha," said Bob. "That'll be nineteen ninety nine."

"All I got is fifteen," Morgan said, making a show of being flustered. "Fifteen dollars and . . . twenty-nine cents."

Bob raised a suspicious eyebrow. "Is that right?"

"Any chance I can get you to do a stranger a solid?" *Please.*

Bob rubbed his chin between his fingers. "Well, all right," he said. "Give me what you got. Still makes me a profit, if you can call that a profit. And I'm a good Christian man. I can help a brother out. Let's ring you up."

God bless you, Bob.

Morgan set the bills on the counter, and then dropped the coins. He walked to the truck on trembling legs, turning on the ignition and driving away. He waited until he was in the highway before turning the phone on and making a call.

"Hello?" A woman's voice.

"Bloch? It's me."

Chapter Forty-three

When Morgan arrived at the house, he hid the phone, still on, under a brick that was resting against the foundation. Then he went inside, grocery bags in hand.

"I brought a good haul," said Morgan, setting them on the table. "I'll whip us up some steaks on the iron skillet."

"We need to talk about our plan," said Badri. "We cannot stay here long. Every minute is a moment when we could be found out."

They sat down together around the table to discuss the plan. "Our target," Morgan said, "needs to be symbolic, and it needs to kill a lot of people. There's one day that's better than any other if you want to do this."

"What's that?" Badri asked.

"The Fourth of July. The most patriotic of holidays. The parades attract enormous crowds. You can kill thousands upon thousands on the day when Americans get together to celebrate this country. We're two weeks away, which means we can organize attacks on more than one city. New York, Chicago, Washington."

"I like what I hear," said Badri.

"Police won't be able to check everyone. They'll have bomb-sniffing dogs, but we won't need explosives. Those canisters have rapid-release mechanisms that can send up a cloud of the powder in something like a fifty-foot radius. Rasheed, do you have paper?"

They spent hours strategizing. Morgan drew the parade routes from memory as best he could, saying that they could check it online as soon as they had a connection, and marked likely spots, places that would cause the most deaths, the most panic, and how to set off a second device to target a wave of fleeing pedestrians.

It was late afternoon by the time they decided to break, and Morgan left Badri and Rashid to cook their dinner of steak and potatoes. He had long known that to impress people in the kitchen, you only need to do one or two things well, and this was his. The smell of searing meat filled the house. They ate together at the table. After the planning and the meal, even Rasheed seemed to be warming up to him.

After dinner, Morgan sat down on the couch and Badri pulled up a chair across from him. Rasheed went outside for a walk.

"I will be honest," said Badri, "I had my doubts about you, even until today. But your plan—I finally believe you are one of us, without reservation. We will do great things together, Morgan. You will be part of something here that will be remembered for generations, a definite blow to—"

Rasheed burst into the house, slamming the screen door open, gun drawn and pointed at Morgan. In his other hand was a cell phone.

"What is the meaning of this, Rasheed?" Badri demanded.

"When the American arrived, I saw him through the

window. I saw him bend down and hide something. So I went out to see what it was. I found this. A *phone,* Badri. Still on. He is a filthy traitor!" Rasheed tightened the grip on his pistol.

Badri raised his hand for Rasheed to stop. "Explain yourself, Morgan."

"I wanted to call my family," Morgan said. "I'm sorry. I know that I shouldn't have. But I couldn't resist. I bought this phone when I went into town. It's a burner. Untraceable. It won't compromise us. Please. I know how to be anonymous."

"He is lying," said Rasheed.

"I'm not," said Morgan. "Badri. I swear I'm not."

Badri struggled with this in his mind, and then his expression set, cool and stony. "I was deluded," he said. "I thought it could not be possible. But now I see that I was a fool to trust an American. Do not move! Rasheed, do not shoot him. We will find out what he knows."

Badri took one of the knives from the table, still wet with the juices from the steak.

"Badri, come on. After all we shared, you think I'd betray you?"

Rasheed laughed. "You will get what you deserve now, American."

Badri approached with the knife in hand. Morgan was seated, with a gun on him. Circumstances were not smiling on him.

But Badri was interrupted by a car, coming up the driveway.

"Who is it?" he demanded.

"Police!" Rasheed exclaimed. "I told you he was a traitor!"

"I promise, I did not tell anyone about you!" Morgan insisted. "He's probably just checking up on the house."

"He is alone," said Rasheed.

Badri frowned. He said to Rasheed, "Hide behind the front door. Morgan, you will stand there next to him. I will talk to the policeman. If you do anything to call his attention, Morgan, both of you die. Understand? Now come."

At gunpoint, Morgan moved to stand next to the front door, so that he would be hidden when it opened. Rasheed stood next to him, out of sight, gun pointed at his head.

"Keep your mouth shut," Rasheed growled.

They heard the boots on the porch steps, then there was a knock on the door. Badri opened.

"Good evening, officer. Can I help you?"

"Lots of people up in this old house, ain't there? I met a fella that drove this truck into town this morning, and I figured the young man would still be here."

"They are out," Badri said. "What can I do for you?"

"Just checking to see if you folks are all right," he said.

"Just fine," said Badri

"Now, you said they were gone, but I see three plates on the table," Anderson said. "Doesn't look like you've finished eating very long ago. And there's one road out of here, and I didn't see anyone driving past me."

"They are on an after-dinner walk. Now if there is nothing else—"

"I'd ask you for a glass of water, if it's acceptable to you. It's a hot day, and I'm parched."

Badri narrowed his eyes. "Of course. Please, come in."

Rasheed turned his gun to fire at Anderson as he walked in.

"No!" Morgan cried as he brought Rasheed down with a full-body tackle, sending the gun sliding across the floor. Sheriff Anderson went for his sidearm, but Badri swung the knife and buried it in the policeman's throat. Anderson fell on the floor, gasping. Badri took up his Colt revolver and pointed it at Morgan, who held up his hands. Rasheed stood and grabbed his own gun from the floor where it lay.

"We need to go," said Rasheed. "They will be looking for the policeman."

"Yes," said Badri, "we do."

"Then we need to take care of this filth right here," Rasheed said, meaning Morgan.

"Yes. We do. Please, Rasheed. Do the honors."

Rasheed grinned, triumphant. "Any last words?"

The sound of broken glass, and Rasheed's chest burst in a mist of blood.

Badri scarcely had time to react before a bullet hit him in the shoulder. He fell, dropping his gun with the force and shock of it. Then he looked at Morgan with anger.

"What did you do?" Badri demanded. "You traitor, what did you do?"

"What I had to do to protect my country." He heard the sound of men approaching, rustling in the foliage surrounding the house. "I want the end of this fight, Badri. I want my people to be safe."

"What about *my* people?"

"Do you think you're making them safer by attacking the US? By extending this goddamned war?"

"I do what I do for the righteousness of God."

Badri scrambled down the stairs to the basement. Morgan ran after him, but couldn't reach him before Badri had the freezer open and a canister in his hand, ready to release.

"You'll die," said Morgan.

"And maybe I will take you with me."

"You can still survive," Morgan said.

"And go to Guantanamo Bay for the rest of my life?"

"I really am sorry," Morgan said. "I wish we'd have met under other circumstances. I wish you weren't who you were. I wish you hadn't made yourself my enemy. But you can live. That's something. It's something I can offer you."

Badri pushed the button and the canister burst in a plume of fine white powder. Badri fell almost immediately, convulsing on the floor of the basement.

Holding his breath, Morgan ran upstairs, doing some mental math on the rate of dispersion. He reached the upper landing as the tactical team rammed the door, sending splinters flying into the foyer. They filed inside in formation, all wearing tactical gear and gas masks.

"Clear the area! Get as far from here as you can!"

He was feeling the weight in his chest as he ran out of the house. He stumbled within a few feet of the door, lightheaded, and then the world began growing dark. He hardly felt himself hitting the floor, and had the vague impression of someone slipping a gas mask over his face, and he saw someone else pull out a syringe with a gigantic hypodermic needle before he lost consciousness.

Chapter Forty-four

Alex Morgan walked into Diana Bloch's apartment with plodding steps. She had descended into a haze of gloom ever since returning home, crying herself to sleep every night. One day at a time worked, but it didn't make it any easier.

"Make yourself at home," Bloch said.

Alex collapsed on a white leather couch. "Did you make me chamomile tea again?"

Bloch sat cross-legged on a Barcelona chair, facing Alex. "I have something rather more potent. I'd like to tell you a story."

"Yippee."

Bloch cleared her throat. "Eight months ago, a cache of Novichok nerve agent was stolen as it was transported from a military research lab in Russia. This Novichok is really nasty stuff. It will destroy your lungs and make you drown on dry land.

"The group that took it was an al-Qaeda splinter group named Shining Jihad. But that's all we knew. We exhausted our resources trying to find the agent, or the group's leadership.

"Then, some five months ago, the Russians captured the group's mastermind, a man named Muhammad Badri. A clever and resourceful man, and certainly the one who planned the heist of the gas in the first place.

"The Russians knew he was a terrorist, but they didn't quite know what they had on their hands. So they sent him to a secret prison in Siberia, an old gulag camp where the Russian government keeps the people they want to forget.

"We knew it was a matter of time before Badri's people used the Novichok against us somehow. We needed to find the gas. And our only link was him. The Russian government was not forthcoming with aid, so we had to take it into our own hands. We had to send someone into the prison. And that meant letting someone get captured."

"Are you telling me—"

"The odds were always slim," Bloch said. "He had to escape from the prison with Badri, while gaining his trust enough to find out where the Novichok was. The mission rested on a razor's edge."

"Well?" Alex urged. "What happened?"

She heard footsteps coming from the inner hallway of the apartment. Heavy. A man's.

She knew him by his silhouette in the dim light even before his features resolved in her eyes.

"Dad!"

She leapt off the couch and at him, hugging him as hard as he could.

"I apologize," said Bloch. "I wish we could have told you. But it was imperative for his mission to remain in total secrecy."

"But I'm back." He squeezed her tight. "I'm back. That's what matters."

She released him, tears flowing from her eyes, and punched him in the chest. "How could you do that to me?" she demanded, in anger mixed with joy.

"I had to do it," he said. "My country needed me."

"Yeah. You had to go off and be a hero." She buried her face in his chest. "The world needs heroes like you. But Mom and I need you more." She raised her head. "We have to tell her! You don't know how sick she's been over this."

"I'd just like to remind you," said Bloch, "that all this is highly classified."

Alex wiped away her tears and looked at her father. He looked thin, haggard, and exhausted. "So did you have a nice vacation?"

"Oh, yeah," said Morgan. "Got some exercise, some cultural immersion, met all sorts of different kinds of people."

Alex couldn't contain herself and gave him another hug.

Bloch interrupted their reunion. "By the way, Alex, we know all about your little Russian adventure."

Alex blushed with shame. "I got captured, would've been killed if Valery hadn't been there to save me, and I didn't come close to finding you."

"How is old Valery?" Morgan asked.

"Miserable," said Alex.

"That's Valery all right."

"I'm so embarrassed," she said. "It was a complete failure."

"Funny," said Bloch. "That's not what I heard. I heard that a budding young operative was resourceful and quick-thinking. I heard she used her assets, faced danger head-on, and managed to infiltrate the house of a Russian general and escape with her life. What I read in my reports indicated that you show enough promise to surpass your father someday. And I expect you to report back for training Monday at oh-five hundred hours."

Alex's cheeks flushed, now with joy.

"And Morgan," said Bloch, "We're going to need an in-depth debrief from you."

"Later," Morgan said, holding his hand up. "Come on, Alex. Let's go home."

ACKNOWLEDGEMENTS

I must thank my immensely talented team at Kensington Publishing Corp., who work tirelessly to help make my novels the best they can be and are there whenever I have questions or concerns. Thank you to Steve Zacharius, owner of Kensington, who has made me part of the Kensington "family." There are just not enough words to convey how fortunate I am to have Michaela Hamilton as my editor. Her patience and guidance have been invaluable—she is a very special person.

I also want to express my appreciation to my literary agent, Doug Grad, as well as to Mayur Gudka, my webmaster and social media consultant. I also want to thank my partner in writing and creating my novels, Caio Camargo. I am so fortunate that you are members of my team and, more important, friends.

My wife, Lynn, continues to encourage me to pursue my writing career.

Lastly, I want to thank all of my very loyal fans whose support has helped grow the Dan Morgan series from one novel to six and still writing . . .

Don't miss the newest Dan Morgan
thriller adventure

DEEP COVER

Available from Lyrical Underground,
an imprint of Kensington Publishing
Corp.
Keep reading to enjoy a sample
excerpt...

Chapter 1

As soon as he stepped off the elevator, Dan Morgan knew that something was different in the hallway. His hand found the butt of his Walther PPK as his brain registered what it was: perfume.

He could smell a few distinctly different brands lingering in the air. That meant the women they had booked had arrived.

The models were necessary for their cover. American arms dealers operating in their particular corner of the business would have a parade of attractive women coming in and out of their suite.

Peter Conley had been making those arrangements with local modeling agencies. He had a knack for it, though the task was tougher in Turkey now than it had been in years past. It was a sign of the ways things were going in that country.

First they came for the swimsuit models, Morgan thought.

The smile died as it reached his lips when he heard the cries from inside the room. His Walther was in his hand and he was running down the hallway before the sound had fully registered.

As he got closer, he heard more cries and shouting. Though the sound was muffled by the door, he could definitely hear female voices. Something was going on in the suite.

Morgan's key card was in his free hand by the time he reached the door. There was no time for a stealthy entrance. As soon as the light on the lock turned green, he pushed the door open and threw himself inside.

What he saw stopped him cold. He'd run a dozen scenarios in his head as he'd raced to the room and he wasn't even close.

This is new, he thought.

Peter Conley was sitting at the small dining table that had been moved to the center of the living area of the suite. Four very attractive young women in cocktail dresses were sitting around him, laughing loudly.

There was a small pile of cash in the middle of the table and everyone there was holding playing cards.

All sound had ceased in the room and five pairs of eyes were now on him. Morgan holstered his gun and said, "Sorry, I heard some noise outside and thought there might be a problem in here."

"There is, these women are robbing me blind," Conley said.

The girls laughed as Morgan simply looked on, still baffled by what he was seeing. Peter Conley was in a room full of professional models and was playing cards...

"Sorry ladies, that is all of my money that you will get for today," Conley said. There were disappointed sighs from the women. "I'm afraid my partner and I have got to get to work. It will be time to go in a few minutes anyway; our clients will be arriving soon."

The women got up and headed to the other room to get themselves ready to leave.

As Morgan and Conley moved the table and chairs back against the wall, Morgan said, "Who are you and what have you done with my partner?"

"Run of bad luck. And one of those women is a graduate student in math. She was unstoppable. But give me another hour and I could have won it all back."

"Right," Morgan said.

Morgan hadn't been referring to the card game and Conley knew it. Something had been different about Conley since he'd met a former Chinese agent named Danhong Guo, or Dani—who was now part of Zeta. They'd had some sort of vacation romance and now there was something complicated going on between them.

And whatever was going on between them had stopped Conley from calling the three women he knew and occasionally saw in Istanbul. That was not only interesting, it was unprecedented.

If they'd had more time, Morgan would have ribbed his friend a bit more. But Conley was right, they did have a meeting.

They neatened the room, making sure that it wasn't *too* neat. After all, the penthouse "Sultan" suite, the beautiful women, and the expensive suits they were wearing were all designed to paint a picture—a picture that would attract the right kind of attention.

They had also spent money like rich idiots for the last two weeks in Istanbul. Their cover had been good enough to get them their first client meeting, which was now minutes away.

Right on time there was a call from the concierge, telling them that their guests had arrived. He added that the men appeared to be good businessmen. That was a code that meant they didn't appear dangerous.

That was as close to security as Morgan and Conley would get on this mission. No guards, no pat downs. The lax atmosphere would fit their cover as dilettante arms dealers.

The men arrived at the door and Morgan let them in. He recognized them from their photographs and ushered them into the suite.

The two Kurds wore Western suits. The senior partner was middle-aged and bald with a greying beard. He introduced himself as Barnas. He was with a thin, nervous young man named Hilmi.

"We spoke on the phone. I'm Dan and this is my partner Peter," Morgan said as they all exchanged handshakes.

"Can I offer you a drink?" Conley asked pleasantly.

Just then, the four women came bursting out of the other room. The two Kurds nearly jumped out of their skin and then looked in shock at the women.

"Excuse me," Conley said. "Ladies, thank you for coming. I regret that we have to do some business now."

Conley led them to the door and the women made a show of kissing him good-bye. Morgan saw two of them press slips of paper into Conley's hand.

That would be their private phone numbers, Morgan thought, shaking his head.

Whatever was going on with Dani, Conley had not lost his touch. Maintaining a cover was as much stagecraft as it was spycraft, and Peter Conley excelled at both.

He returned to the men and said, "Where were we? Can I get you a drink?"

The two men didn't respond, watching as the last of the women left the room.

"A drink?" Conley repeated.

"No thank you," Barnas said. "We would like to begin."

"Business first, that's fine," Conley said. "If you can come to the computer we'll show you—"

"With all due respect, we'd like to see the actual merchandise," Hilmi said.

"We can take you to our warehouse now. Will that be soon enough?" Morgan said.

"That would be ideal," Barnas said apologetically. "We have pressing concerns. We are from Diyarbakir, which is close to both Syria and Iraq. The new leadership in Ankara insists on intervening in Syria. We have no doubt this is a pretext for the new President to—"

"Let me stop you right there," Conley said. "We're sure your cause is just but please understand that this is just a business for us. And if you have cash, we can do business."

"So you would just as soon sell weapons to our enemies?" Barnas asked.

"The only thing you need to concern yourself with is that we are willing to sell you the weapons you need to defend yourselves, or fight for your cause, whatever it is," Morgan said.

Ten minutes later, the four men were in the hotel limousine. Morgan was not sorry to leave the hotel. It was expensive and depressing. When he had a choice, he always stayed in the Old City, much of which dated back to the Roman Empire.

Their hotel was in the aptly named New City section, and when you went outside it could have been any modern city in the world. Why anyone would come to this ancient place and stay there was beyond him.

They headed south for the town of Zeytinburnu, where they had rented a warehouse that was near the waterfront industrial section of the city. They were only a few blocks away from the hotel when Morgan saw that they were being followed. The tail car was a non-descript sedan. Though the vehicle was unmarked, Morgan recognized it as Turkish police issue.

Like most drivers in Istanbul, the hotel limo driver seemed to think the gas pedal had two options: off and to the floor. What made the driver good at his job was that he was even more aggressive than the drivers around him, who all seemed to view traffic rules as mere suggestions.

Remarkably, the police car managed to stay on their tail. After a few minutes Morgan turned to his partner.

"Do you see it?" Morgan asked.

"Yes, I admire their professionalism."

That was the problem with establishing yourselves as high-profile arms dealers. To attract customers you had to attract attention.

And not all of that attention was commercial.

Well, that was the job, Morgan thought. Behind them, he could now see that the driver and the passenger of the police car were wearing the distinctive blue uniforms and caps of the Turkish police.

"What is it?" Barnas asked.

"The good news is that we are making good time, the bad news is that we're being followed by the police," Morgan said evenly.

"*What?*" Hilmi said, nearly jumping out of his seat.

"Don't worry, I suspect they are primarily interested in us. And since we haven't done business yet, I don't think they will pay much attention to you, at least not right away. My partner and I will be getting off in a minute. Stay with the car. I will instruct the driver to take you back to the hotel. Then I recommend you leave Istanbul."

As instructed, the driver let them off at the next light.

They were six blocks from the warehouse and the two agents walked casually on the sidewalk. Morgan could smell the salt water from the strait of Bosporus that separated the two halves of the city—and the two continents of Europe and Asia. Up ahead he could see the Roman walls that had protected the Old City for a thousand years, before it fell to the Ottomans in the fifteenth century.

Morgan regretted that he wouldn't see the inside of the walls on this trip—not with the police car pacing them. They were getting braver and coming closer, and Morgan wondered if he and Conley would make it to their warehouse before being approached.

The agents passed an olive oil factory and were in front of the electronics warehouse next door to their building when they heard the unmarked car pull over behind them. Two doors slammed.

"Pardon, bakar mısınız?" Morgan heard behind them. Though, he knew almost no Turkish he knew that was the equivalent of *excuse me* in English.

Morgan and Conley ignored them and kept walking until they were in front of their own building.

Morgan would rather be inside. They were far too exposed on the street.

"Dur!" he heard one of the police shout behind them.

Before they could take another step, Morgan felt a hand grab his arm from behind.

Apparently they would have to do this outside, he thought as he turned around.

When they were facing the two stern police officers, he glanced over at Conley. His partner was smiling broadly.

"Is there a problem officers?" Conley asked, his tone friendly.

The policeman closest to him fired off a series of instructions in Turkish.

"I'm sorry, I didn't get that. Do you speak English?" Conley said, though Morgan had no doubt that his friend had understood every word.

"I'll handle this," Morgan said and then he said one of the few phrases he knew in Turkish. It was a phrase he had made a point of learning in a number of languages. *"Hoverkraftımın içi yılan balığı dolu,"* he said as pleasantly as he could. Or, in English, *my hovercraft is full of eels.*

He heard Conley chuckle as the phrase had the usual affect and the two policemen looked at him dumbfounded.

Before they could say anything in response, Morgan and Conley sprang into action. Morgan punched the policeman in front of him as hard as he could, square in the nose. Disoriented, the policeman raised his hands to his face. His vision would be compromised and blood was already flowing from his nose.

Morgan relieved the man of his handgun and then clocked him two more times until he fell to the ground, unconscious. At nearly the same moment, Conley's policeman collapsed next to his partner.

Morgan saw that though the street wasn't exactly crowded, they had attracted the attention of several people nearby.

"Let's get inside," Morgan said. As soon as he'd finished speaking, they heard the first siren.

And then the second.

By the time Morgan had the key card in the lock to their building's front door Morgan had lost count of the sirens.

Stepping inside, Morgan said, "I'm not impressed by your plan so far."

As Morgan slammed the door shut, he could see three marked police cars screech to a stop and heard even more pulling up.

"What do you mean?" Conley said. "It's working perfectly. They are taking us *very* seriously."

Photo by Kippy Goldfarb, Carolle Photography

ABOUT THE AUTHOR

LEO J. MALONEY is the author of the acclaimed thrillers *Termination Orders*, *Silent Assassin*, *Black Skies*, *Twelve Hours*, and *Arch Enemy*. He was born in Massachusetts, where he spent his childhood, and graduated from Northeastern University. He spent over thirty years in black ops, accepting highly secretive missions that would put him in the most dangerous hot spots in the world. Since leaving that career, he has had the opportunity to try his hand at acting in independent films and television commercials. He has ten movies to his credit, both as an actor and behind the camera as a producer, technical advisor, and assistant director. He lives in the Boston area and in Florida.

Visit him at www.leojmaloney.com or on Facebook or Twitter.

"An outstanding thriller that rings with authenticity."
—JOHN GILSTRAP
Patriot. Spy. Assassin . . .
TERMINATION
ORDERS
LEO J.
MALONEY

"THIS KIND OF AUTHENTICITY
CAN ONLY COME FROM AN INSIDER."
—John Gilstrap

SILENT
ASSASSIN

A DAN MORGAN THRILLER

FAST. EFFICIENT. LETHAL. . .

LEO J.
MALONEY

AUTHOR OF *TERMINATION ORDERS*

"A ripping story—rough, tough, and entertaining."
—MEG GARDINER

BLACK SKIES

LEO J. MALONEY

A DAN MORGAN THRILLER

The countdown has begun...
TWELVE HOURS
A DAN MORGAN THRILLER NOVELLA
LEO J. MALONEY
"A MUST!"—LEE CHILD

A DAN MORGAN THRILLER

ARCH ENEMY

LEO J. MALONEY

A Dan Morgan Thriller novella

For DUTY AND HONOR

LEO J. MALONEY

A DAN MORGAN THRILLER

ROGUE
COMMANDER

LEO J.
MALONEY

A DAN MORGAN THRILLER NOVELLA

DARK
TERRITORY

LEO J.
MALONEY

THREAT LEVEL
ALPHA

LEO J.
MALONEY

A DAN MORGAN THRILLER

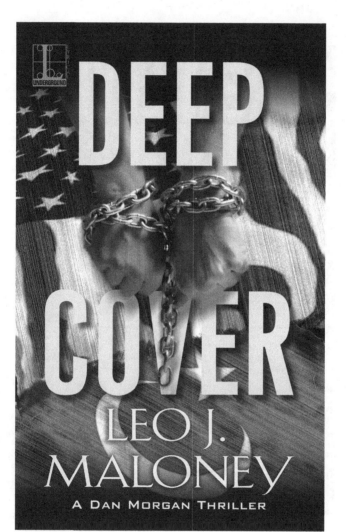

DEEP
COVER

LEO J. MALONEY

A DAN MORGAN THRILLER

Printed in the United States
by Baker & Taylor Publisher Services